IN REAL LIFE

ALSO BY JESSICA LOVE

Push Girl (with Chelsie Hill)

IN REAL LIFE

JESSICA LOVE

Thomas Dunne Books
St. Martin's Griffin
New York

THOMAS DUNNE BOOKS.
An imprint of St. Martin's Press.

IN REAL LIFE. Copyright © 2016 by Jessica Love. All rights reserved. Printed in the United States of America. For information, address St. Martin's Press, 175 Fifth Avenue, New York, N.Y. 10010.

www.thomasdunnebooks.com
www.stmartins.com

Designed by Omar Chapa

The Library of Congress Cataloging-in-Publication Data is available upon request.

ISBN 978-1-250-06471-4 (hardcover)
ISBN 978-1-4668-7099-4 (e-book)

Our books may be purchased in bulk for promotional, educational, or business use. Please contact your local bookseller or the Macmillan Corporate and Premium Sales Department at 1-800-221-7945, extension 5442, or by e-mail at Macmillan SpecialMarkets@macmillan.com.

First Edition: March 2016

10   9   8   7   6   5   4   3   2   1

For lagwgn101

ACKNOWLEDGMENTS

Hannah and Nick have been in my heart since I wrote the very first words of this story in 2012, and I learned so much about love, friendship, and being true to yourself as I wrote it and wrote it and rewrote it. Thank you so much for reading this book and becoming part of Hannah and Nick's journey!

This book would be nothing but some vague ideas in a disjointed e-mail if not for the brilliance of Elizabeth Briggs. Liz, thank you for being with me and this book from beginning to end.

Special love goes out to the people who turned this from a story into a book. Jill Corcoran, my agent, thank you for your patience as I dug to the core of this story and for your enthusiasm and support. Kat Brzozowski, editor of awesome, I am so lucky to work with you! I have loved, learned, and laughed through every step of this process, thanks to you. And to the entire fabulous team at St. Martin's, you are all amazing! I'm so lucky to have such a talented group of people on my side.

To all of the amazing writers and friends who helped me get to the heart of Hannah and Nick's story when I couldn't. Thank you for reading for me, laughing and crying with me, and answering all of my frantic e-mails. Jessica Cline, Dana Elmendorf, Melanie Jacobson, Emery Lord, Kelsey Macke, Ghenet Myrthil, Kristin Rae, Kathryn Rose, Robin Reul, Keiko Sanders, Rachel

Searles, Shana Silver, Katy Upperman, and Tameka Young, each one of you left your handprint on the heart of this book, and neither it, nor I, would be the same without you.

Thank you to the wonderful people at Spalding University's MFA program, specifically my Paris workshop group for helping me figure out where to begin. Edie Hemingway, for your support and cheerleading, and Susan Campbell Bartoletti for both your genius and your hatred of that one particular character that helped make this book a thousand times better.

To Steve Soboslai and Punchline/Blue of Colors, thank you for your music. If I had never heard "Universe," there would be no Hannah and Nick.

To Liz, Kat, Dana, Rachel, and Amaris, you are my people, and I would be lost without your support. It's always wine o'clock with you ladies. And to my NBC Writers, thank you for being with me and this book from the very beginning.

To all the people I have been to Vegas with, some of the things that happened there didn't necessarily stay there. Life tip: If you don't want your crazy Vegas story to end up in a novel, don't go to Vegas with a writer. (Hey, at least I didn't name names.) Erin, Claire, Tameka, Rachael, and Ashley, you will always be my favorite Vegas companions. I can't wait for our next trip.

To all of my students, past, present, and future, this one is for you. CHS class of 2014, I wrote this while I had you guys, so I will always think of you when I read it.

To my parents, thank you for always encouraging me to live a creative life, and to my grandma, thank you for being the most amazing woman I know.

And, finally, to my husband, who answered my random IM on AOL in 1998 and never stopped chatting, paging, calling, texting, and video messaging me. Thank you for being my best friend and not a catfish.

Why do you think I call you "Ghostie"?
Mostly because you're impossible to see.

—PUNCHLINE

IN REAL LIFE

CHAPTER 1

FRIDAY

My best friend and I have never met.

We talk every day, on the phone or online, and he knows more about me than anyone. Like, deep into my soul. But we've never actually seen each other in real life.

Sometimes, when I'm talking to Nick, I wonder how we managed to get ourselves into such a bizarre, complicated friendship. At first glance, our relationship probably doesn't seem all that odd. Like right now, it's the Friday afternoon that kicks off the spring break of my senior year. I'm lying out next to my pool with my feet dangling in the chilly water, my back flat on concrete, and I'm talking to him on the phone. This is how I spend pretty much every Friday from 3:30 to 4:25-ish, before he goes off to band practice and I have one of my various school or family obligations. Sounds pretty normal.

But the thing is, Nick lives in a different state, 274 miles away. Yes, I looked it up.

"Ghost," he says, because he never calls me Hannah, "you know I will do anything for my best friend, and this is no exception. I'll have this girl killed for you without a second thought. Just give me twenty-four hours."

I laugh as I swish my feet back and forth in the pool. "There's no need to resort to murder. It's just a stupid student government trip. I'll be over it by the end of the week."

As tempting as it is to plot Aditi Singh's violent end, the only reason she applied to go to the national leadership conference when it should have been a given that the senior class president (aka me) was going was because I got into UCLA and she didn't, so a big ol' middle finger to her. But she can't see my middle finger, because she's in Washington, D.C., for spring break and I'm at home with no plans like a big loser.

"Well, if you change your mind," Nick says, "just let me know. That's how much our friendship means to me. The code word is 'Platypus.' Just say it, and—poof!—I'll make her disappear."

I sit up and pull my feet from the pool, crossing them in front of me. "And how can you do that?"

"Hey, I live in Vegas. I have connections to the mob. Everyone here does."

"You're a senior in high school, and you live in a tract home in Henderson. You're not exactly Al Pacino."

"You don't know. Everything I've told you for the past four years could be a front. I need to have a cover. No one suspects the quiet, nondescript white boy."

"You're right. There is a lot I don't know about you. I mean, there are any number of huge secrets you could be keeping from me." I say it just because I'm playing along, but it's not true at all. I'm pretty sure I know everything there is to know about Nick Cooper.

I know when my sister met his brother at a concert four years ago and they told us we should start talking online, he thought I was one of his brother's friends playing a joke on him until I e-mailed him a picture. I know in the middle of junior year, he shaved his head when his favorite English teacher started chemo. I know the gravelly scratch of his voice when he wakes up in the middle of the night to answer one of my random "I'm bored, talk to me" phone calls. I know the hole in the sleeve seam of the lucky Rage Against the Machine T-shirt he inherited from his brother, Alex, since I've seen so many pictures of it. I know his middle name (Anthony), the date and time he was born (September 24 at 3:58 A.M.), and his favorite color (gray). And he knows more about me than absolutely anyone else, even the über-embarrassing stuff. We've IM'd, texted, sent a million pictures, mailed each other packages, video-chatted, and talked on the phone.

We've just never been in the same place at the same time.

I don't think it's strange to be so close to someone I've never met. Yeah, he's in Nevada and I'm in Southern California, but I talk to him more than to people I've been in classes with since kindergarten. I do wish we could go to the movies together or something normal like that, but we watch the same movies at the same time and mock them over video chat, which is pretty much the same thing.

On the other end of the phone, his laugh stops abruptly and his voice changes. "Secrets? What kind of secrets could I have?"

"Who knows!" I try to sound shocked and serious, but I can't keep a laugh from creeping in. "For all I know, you *do* have a secret mob life. Do you have some sort of gangster name I'm supposed to call you?"

His voice lightens again when he realizes I'm joking. "Oh yeah. Knuckles Nick. Or, no. Wait. Nick the Click."

"What does that even mean?"

"I don't know. It rhymed. Don't those names always rhyme?"

"I know nothing about mob names, Nick the Click. But rhyming names do make mobsters seem a bit less murder-y."

There's a shuffle, a thump, and a squeak on his end of the phone, and I imagine him collapsing backwards onto his twin bed. "I just hate that you're still bummed over missing out on the trip."

"It's not that I'm bummed, it's just . . . I followed all the rules, Nick. I did exactly what I was supposed to do. Serving four years as class president means I go on that trip, not Aditi Singh. Onetime vice-presidents don't get to go! It's supposed to be *my year.* She broke the rules, but she got picked. How do you break all the rules and get what you want like that? It isn't fair."

"Well, you know what they say. . . ."

"Life's not fair?"

"Well, that, too. But I was thinking rules are made to be broken."

Yeah, that *is* what people say, but it goes against my Good Korean Girl DNA. Rules are made to be followed—at least that's what my parents, who aren't Tiger Parents or anything but are still pretty serious, drilled into me starting the second I learned to crawl. And I've always followed every rule, done exactly what I've been told, and it always worked out to my benefit.

Until it didn't, and I found myself at home over spring break, trying to figure out how to make an Aditi Singh voodoo doll.

I hate rules.

A door slams somewhere in Vegas and echoes through my phone. "Oh, crap," Nick says. "I have to go, Ghost. The guys are here."

"Getting ready for the show tomorrow? Are you nervous?" Nick's band Automatic Friday landed a huge gig opening for a popular Vegas band by entering and winning a Battle of the Bands at UNLV back in February. I always knew they were awesome, aside from their dumb name that I tried all junior year to convince him to change, and I was stoked that other people would have a chance to fall in love with their music, too.

"Ummm, let's see. Instead of our usual backyard birthday party, Automatic Friday is opening for Moxie Patrol at the House of freaking Blues on the Strip. This will probably be the one and only chance to perform at a legit venue like a real band. I'd say 'nervous' doesn't quite capture the level of sheer terror going on over here."

"I'm coming to your show, by the way," I say. "I'll be in the front row. With an 'I Heart Nick' sign. Will you throw a guitar pick at me?"

"Even better," he says. "I'll throw the guitar at you."

"Hello? Concussion!" We both laugh. "I do wish I could see your one and only real show, though." He doesn't say anything, because we both know the odds of me ever seeing Automatic Friday play are right up there with me piercing some body part that's never meant to have a hole in it. "Okay, thinking about this *is* bumming me out. I'll let you go. Say hi to Oscar for me."

"I will. Did you get our package?"

"Oh yeah! I love the T-shirt. I wore it to school today." Yeah, after I slept in it last night. The black T-shirt with the band's name in the middle of a hot pink bass drum, the *A* and *F* made from drumsticks, is the best present he's sent me so far. I guess the box of cake balls I sent last week decorated to look like my cat, Bruce Lee, was a hit.

"Oscar designed the shirt. He wanted you to have it."

"Tell him thanks." I smile down at the T-shirt as I smooth the front of it. "Now I'll have to find something extra creative to send you back."

"I'll be waiting at the mailbox. Talk to you later, Ghost."

"Text me when you're done with rehearsal."

It never feels like our conversations are over when we say goodbye. I always think of a hundred other things I want to say after I hit End on my screen, but I save it all for later, because there's always a later with us.

I crawl back to the grass and flop down, letting the afternoon sun warm my face as I drift off into my typical Friday 4:26-to-4:45 post–phone-call daydreaming. After we hang up, I always zone out and imagine what hanging out with Nick in real life, knowing each other in-person instead of being only online friends and phone buddies, would be like. Today I'm actually picturing myself at one of their shows, cheering and dancing like a maniac in the crowd as he plays guitar, when—

"What are you dreaming about, weirdo? You have a huge grin on your face. It's creepy."

The sliding glass door slams shut, and I know my real-life BFF Lo will be standing over me in a matter of seconds. She's spending spring break at my house, along with my older sister, Grace, who is a senior at UCLA, while my parents celebrate their twenty-fifth wedding anniversary on a cruise down to Mexico. Mom and Dad said they wanted Grace to keep an eye on me and Lo, but knowing my sister, I'm pretty sure it's the other way around.

"Oh, you know," I say as I stand up, trying to shake the mental picture of Nick out of my head as I brush grass off my jeans. "Just thinking about hiring a mob boss to dispose of Aditi Singh for me. No big."

Lo has changed from her school look of jeans and hoodie into a short floral dress that covers her bikini, and she let her long, wavy black hair out of its usual ponytail. She looks me up and down and shakes her head. "You were talking to Nick, weren't you?"

I shrug. Being my real-life bestie, Lo knows all about Nick. Well, not *all* about him; I'm selfish when it comes to my friendship with him, and there's a lot I keep to myself. Even without knowing everything, though, Lo has insisted for years that I must be secretly in love with him. Lately she's been getting snippy when I bring him up, like she's jealous or something. Lo isn't the type who likes to come in second.

She drops her overnight bag on the grass, and she lowers herself to perch on top of it.

"Girl, you know what I'm going to say. It's high time you did something about this situation. Grace and I were literally just talking about this in the kitchen." She stretches back onto the grass and screams for my sister, who had been raiding the fridge when I walked outside to answer Nick's call. "Grace! Get out here! We need to powwow!"

I moan. "You really don't need to get Grace involved."

But it's too late. It's only a few seconds before my sister, Grace—clad in her usual uniform of black jeans, black T-shirt featuring some obscure punk band with a weird name, and wearing thick black eyeliner—is outside, too. She throws herself on one of the chaise longues next to the pool, a turkey sandwich hanging out of her mouth.

"What are we talking about?" she asks through bites of sandwich.

"We need to debrief about Hannah and Nick," Lo says. "Hannah, what is the deal here? Why haven't you guys met? You've been talking to this guy online for, what . . . four years? That's a long time. Are you sure he's legit?"

I shake my head, as if I could shake away this line of questioning. "He lives in Las Vegas, Lo. It's not like he just goes to a different school. And of course he's legit. I met him through Grace. Ask her."

Grace throws up her hands, sandwich flailing. "Oh no. Don't bring me into this. I met his brother one time at a show when I was in high school and talked to him for, like, a minute. I'm absolutely not vetting this dude."

"But you know Alex is real," I say. "And Nick and Alex look exactly the same, so you know he's not a troll or anything." I've shown Grace photos of Nick. She agrees that with his messy brown hair, thick-rimmed black glasses, and wide open smile, he's a dead ringer for his older brother, who caught Grace's attention at a concert all those years ago. The full-sleeve tattoo on Alex's right arm is the only visible way to tell the Cooper brothers apart at a quick glance.

Grace shrugs and goes back to mauling her sandwich. "Whatever."

I gather my hair and twist it into a bun. "I mean, Las Vegas is four hours away, across a state line. You know how Mom and Dad feel about this."

Lo stands and paces along the edge of the pool. "Here's the thing, Hannah. You're almost a legal adult. You have a car. I assume he drives. If you wanted to, you could make this happen. It's not an impossible distance."

"We tried once," I say. "It didn't work, and . . ."

"And what?" Grace has finished her sandwich now, and she picks the crumbs off her black jeans like she's hunting for treasure. "Yeah, that one time was a total disaster. And it was mostly my fault, which I still feel bad about, by the way. But why didn't you ever try again?"

Lo stops pacing when she reaches Grace, and she stands shoulder to shoulder with my sister. A united front. "That was years ago, girl. Things have changed."

That day is one of my huge regrets. Once I got over being half-relieved that our plans fell through, I used to wish there were a way to go back in time and have a redo. But Lo knows how my parents are. Mom said I wasn't allowed to drive out and meet Nick. And once Mom says no to something, I can't just go and do it. I mean, I'm not Grace. Far from it.

Grace and Lo keep staring. I never react well under pressure like this, with people in my face, trying to pry me out of my cozy comfort zone. The urge to run from their interrogation is strong, so instead of answering, I do the super-mature thing and roll my eyes. Then I do a nonchalant shuffle toward the house for a safe haven from their badgering. "I have to pee," I call back over my shoulder.

I don't have to pee, though, and I head upstairs to my bedroom instead of to the bathroom. I just need a break from Grace and Lo, so I flop down on my bed and click through my iPod until I find *Ghost in the Machine,* one of the playlists Nick made for me. It's a mix of Automatic Friday songs and other indie bands with the same mellow style. This particular playlist is my go-to because it has a lot of the angsty unrequited-love-type songs that have always been my favorite. I click Play and smile as the first familiar notes of the lead singer and songwriter's raspy voice fill my room.

I can't count how many times I have fallen asleep to these songs or driven around in my car with them blaring in my ear, taking over my thoughts. And there have been times, especially recently, where a lyric struck me in such a deep way that I wished it were Nick who had written it, and that he'd written it just for me. It was an unusual thought, because that's not how things are between us. Not at all. But there's something about the music that takes my head to strange places.

I asked Nick about the lead singer once, if the passion in Jordy MacDonald's songs was inspired by a girlfriend or some big lost love. Nick said Jordy's a total player, and I know he didn't mean of instruments. He said Jordy was with a new girl every weekend, and the other band members don't even bother to learn the girls' names anymore. I yelled at Nick about that because it made him sound like a total jerk, and he assured me he was just kidding, then proceeded to name the last twelve girls Jordy brought around, first and last names, told me what they all looked like, and added something degrading Jordy had said about each one the following day. I gave up on Jordy's sensitive side after that and stopped searching for a meaning behind the songs. But I didn't stop wishing.

Since Nick is on my mind, I pull out my phone and text him, even though I doubt he'll answer because he's at practice.

I HOPE YOU GUYS ARE PLANNING ON PLAYING MY FAVORITE SONGS AT YOUR BIG DEAL SHOW TOMORROW.

I always beg him to at least play the guitar parts of my favorite songs on our video chat sessions, but he's too embarrassed. I make do with imagining him playing my dream set list at his gigs.

My phone beeps his reply almost immediately. Odd.

WE PLAY THEM EVERY TIME, GHOST.

I look out my window and see Lo has stripped down to her bikini and jumped in the pool. She floats on my inflatable dolphin and talks to Grace, who made herself comfy on the lounge chair. From Grace's bobbing head, I assume they're rehashing Grace's recent breakup with her long-term live-in boyfriend, Gabe, for the millionth time, because it's all she seems to talk about these days. At least my sister isn't crying anymore. That's a happy development.

And *this* is my wild and crazy life, everyone. Spring break of my senior year, and I'm going to spend it sitting around the pool with Lo and Grace, swimming and hanging out, like we've done every weekend since Grace's breakup. My parents are out of town, college is around the corner, and I should be doing something exciting. But I'm staring down the barrel of the most boring, predictable spring break ever while Aditi Singh is on my student government trip and my best friend plays with his band at the House of freaking Blues in Las Vegas like a rock star.

Following the rules for the past seventeen years has gotten me absolutely nowhere.

I really need to do something about that.

CHAPTER 2

THE SUMMER AFTER TENTH GRADE

I'll never forget the day Nick and I almost met.

Our almost-meeting lived and died the summer after sophomore year. The inciting text came in while I lay sprawled out on my bed, trying, like the overachiever I am, to get ahead on my Honors English summer reading.

CALL ME WHEN YOU GET A CHANCE GHOST. I HAVE A WEIRD QUESTION FOR YOU.

I glanced at the clock. Grace was driving down from UCLA so we could go to lunch with Mom. But, as usual, she was late, because Grace Time had absolutely no connection to the actual clock. I punched Nick's speed dial icon.

"I thought you were at lunch with your sister?"

"I don't even get a hello?"

"Sorry. Hi, Ghost. I thought you were at lunch."

"Oh, you know Grace. She's not even here yet. And when she does show up, she's going to want to start her laundry. Lunch will turn into dinner at this rate." I laughed. "What's up?"

"Are you sitting down?"

"I am."

"I have a wild proposition."

"No, I will not rob a bank with you."

"It's not that wild. But close."

I bent down the corner of my page in *Slaughterhouse-Five* and reached around to adjust my pillow, pulling myself into an upright position. "I'm listening."

"Well, now that we both have our licenses, I think we should meet. Like, in person."

I jolted straight up. Meet in person? Me and Nick? What? We couldn't. That would be so weird. What would we say to each other? It would be awkward. And wrong. And the world might implode. And . . . no.

No.

"Um . . . Ghost? You there?"

"Oh, yeah, I'm just surprised. That's not what I was expecting you to say." Hello, understatement of the year.

"I have it all figured out. I can't expect you to drive all the way out here, and I don't know if my P.O.S. truck will make it all the way to you. But we can meet in Barstow. It's about halfway between us, and it's completely in the middle of nowhere, but it has a cool McDonald's on, like, an old train car. And there's a little outlet mall. And I'm sure there's a movie theater or something. We won't get bored. Not like we would get bored, though. Not if we're together."

He rattled off all these plans he had for us meeting in Barstow, but I was stuck on the fact he wanted us to meet at all. For two years we had talked—mostly online, but we'd just recently started texting and talking on the phone, too—but for whatever reason, I never considered him, like, a real person. Us meeting for real had never occurred to me, really.

And then there was the possibility we would meet in person and not even like each other. What if we didn't get along? What if our differences, which were fun and interesting on the phone, were too much to bridge in real life? Meeting meant risking our friendship the way it was, and I wasn't sure I could handle that.

"You're awfully quiet, Ghost. What do you think?" He was talking so fast, his voice higher than normal. "Let's do this."

"Yeah," I said, but with no conviction. This was one of those defining moments in a friendship, I thought, that could make or break it. I didn't want to break it, and I didn't want him to know how unsure I was and think my hesitation was because I questioned him or our friendship. I so didn't. I just had no idea how this virtual friendship would translate into real life.

"Yeah? Awesome." I could actually hear his smile. "We'll have to figure out a date and decide where to meet and stuff."

"I'll have to make sure it's okay with my parents if I drive that far." As soon as I said it, I realized if I decided I didn't want to do this, I could totally work the parent angle. Sometimes my parents were cool, way cooler than the parents of some of my other Asian friends, but most of the time they were pretty strict. But, for real, even non-strict parents would not be good with their sixteen-year-old daughter driving to the middle of nowhere to meet some strange Internet boy, right?

What kind of teenager was I, hoping my parents would say no to my outlandish request? Lo would smack me on the hand for this, for sure.

Well, if I told her.

"If they don't let you drive by yourself, bring Lo with you. I'd love to meet her."

Ack, that would be even worse. Lo knew Nick existed, but she didn't know much else. I had zero desire to explain this to her. I'd rather go alone and risk ax murder by Internet stranger so I could keep this all to myself.

"Well, I don't remember what you told me about the driving rules in Nevada, but California law says I'm not allowed to drive another minor in my car yet, and I'm not bringing Grace or my parents."

"Then it'll be just you and me, Ghost."

"If we meet in person, then you can't call me Ghost anymore. I won't be a ghost. I'll be real."

Nick had given me my nickname about a year before, during one late-night chat that turned from ripping apart the terrible movie we'd both happened to see the night before to an unusually serious discussion of our odd friendship. He admitted I seemed too good to be true, and he sometimes felt like there was no way I could be real. He asked me why I kept talking to him when we were so far away from each other, and I admitted he was different from anyone I knew in my real life, but in the best possible way, and that talking to him online was the absolute highlight of my day.

He agreed, and he said I was like something he could feel with him all day, even if he couldn't see me, like a ghost. I was so glad we were only talking online, because that description made me blush so hard, I thought my face was going to be red for the rest of my life.

Ghost was born that night, and he'd called me Ghost ever since.

I was never able to come up with an equally meaningful nickname for him.

"Nah," he said. "You'll always be Ghost, no matter what."

My relief surprised me. Maybe meeting in person wouldn't change things.

"I do have to tell you something, though. I know this is going to sound dumb, so don't laugh, okay?" He coughed, and I heard him shuffling around on the other side of the phone. "I'm sort of afraid you won't like me. I'm bad at real life, you know? Talking and stuff. I'm super awkward. I always say the wrong thing and mess things up."

I shook my head, even though I knew he couldn't see me. "I don't believe that at all. I talk to you almost every day, and you've never messed anything up."

He lowered his voice to almost a whisper. "Because I don't need to hide behind anything here. This isn't real, so you're the only person I can really talk to, Ghost. You're the only person I've ever really talked to."

I doubted he could be all that different in person, but I also knew it was much easier to be yourself when there was nothing, no older sibling or band or good-girl image, to hide behind. "Well, just be how you are right now, and I promise I won't think you're awkward."

We talked until Grace finally decided to show up, picking a meeting date and penciling in the following Thursday at lunch on the calendar. We'd meet at the train car McDonald's in Barstow and then play it by ear. We wouldn't bring anyone, and we would leave for home before it got dark. All we had left to do was check with our parents. Well, he didn't really. His dad, who had been in a cloud since Nick and Alex's mom died when Nick was eight, hardly noticed what he did. His brother, on the other hand, had been harassing him about meeting me since we were thirteen. In fact, I suspected that Alex constantly riding his ass about it was the catalyst for him suggesting this meeting.

There was no earthly way I could sell Mom on this plan, but I figured if I asked when Grace was around, there might be a better chance my sister would back me up with Mom. After all, it was Grace who'd introduced me to Nick in the first place, after she met Alex at a concert. Alex had driven four hours to see his favorite band, Strung Out, play some secret show near our house, and she talked to him online for a few weeks afterwards, until she got bored of him and moved on to something new and shiny. That was so Grace. She was the devil on my shoulder, always poking me with her pitchfork to be more adventurous.

At lunch, two hours later, I waited for the ideal time to broach the subject. Luckily, Grace gave me the perfect in.

"So, how's Nick?"

"Which one is Nick?" Mom sipped her coffee next to me in the booth and gave me a knowing look, as if I were hiding some juicy secret from her. I was about to tell her to settle down when Grace answered for me.

"You know, Hannah's online *boyfriend*."

I rolled my eyes.

"Oh yes, the one we can thank for the barrage of texts at all hours of the day. Thank God we don't have to pay for every single one of those texts like we did when Grace was your age."

"The good old days," Grace said, taking a huge bite of her meatball panini.

"Nick is *not* my boyfriend. Not even close. And he's fine," I said. "He started a band with his friends."

"Following in his brother's footsteps, I see." Grace wiped marinara from the sides of her mouth. "How long are you going to keep this online romance going? Are you going to pine away from afar for the rest of your life?"

"We're just friends," I snapped. "There is no romance. Absolutely no pining."

"A likely story," Grace said. "You talk to him twenty-four/seven. That's more than friendship. I don't think you talk to Lo that much."

"I see Lo every day at school. I talk to her ten times as much, but you don't see it." I kicked Grace's shin under the table. Even though I wasn't 100 percent sure about meeting Nick, I didn't want her to ruin the whole plan before Mom had a chance to shoot it down. "And it just so happens I was going to ask Mom about this." I shifted so I faced Mom. "I, uh. I was wondering if I could maybe go meet up with him. Next Thursday."

She pressed her lips together. "Where does he live?"

"Las Vegas," Grace said, her mouth now full of potato chips.

Mom's face twisted up into the biggest *hell no* scowl I have ever seen. I'd seen her pull it out on Grace frequently, but I think this might have been its first appearance while aimed at me. Why are moms so good at that look?

"But I don't want to drive all the way to Vegas," I said, kicking Grace again. "That would be ridiculous, right? We want to meet halfway. In Barstow."

Mom's face relaxed just enough to give me hope. She looked a lot more likely to keep listening since I was still talking about California. "Barstow is two hours away, Hannah. I don't think this is a good idea."

"I'll make sure the tires are filled and the oil is changed and everything I need is in the car. And I'll call every single hour to check in." I turned on the sweet and innocent face Grace taught me the summer before middle school that has served me well over the years. "Please, Mom? We've been talking forever. We're *friends.* We want to hang out."

Until this point I'd been waffling on this meeting, but as soon as I told Mom how much I wanted to meet Nick, I realized it was true.

I *did* want to meet him.

In real life.

Mom's forehead wrinkled. "This is not even an option unless you take someone with you. Can you bring Lo?"

"I'd love to, but I can't drive her in my car."

"I'll go with you," Grace said. I narrowed my eyes at her from across the table, and she shot me an evil grin in return. "Don't worry; I won't embarrass you or anything. I'll just make sure you're keeping it PG."

"Grace! I told you it's not like that. And don't you have class or something on Thursday?"

"Nope. Couldn't get into my summer school class, so I'm totally free. And I'm only messing with you. I'll be cool. Stop freaking out." She laughed. "Just think, this way you won't have to tell your friends about him. Your secret is safe with me."

"Why doesn't Lo know about this boy?" Mom leaned in toward me like I was about to share something illicit. Pssh. If it was *that* kind of story, I certainly wouldn't tell her the details.

"She knows who Nick is." I slouched down in the booth. "She just doesn't exactly know the specifics."

Mom tapped my shoulder to get me to straighten up. I did.

"You shouldn't keep secrets from your friends, Hannah." Grace was always able to mimic Mom's lecture voice perfectly. Mom and I both glared at her.

"Enough, Grace." Mom wrapped her hands around her coffee mug and turned back to me. "Now, I'll consider this on the condition that Grace drives you. But I'll have to talk to your father first."

I grinned. I was golden. Dad was a big-time lawyer, and super strict about my grades and extracurricular activities, but he softened to teddy bear status when it came to his wife and daughters. "Thanks, Mom." I rested my head on Mom's shoulder, and she patted my hair.

I could hardly sleep the night before Nick and I were supposed to meet. But as soon as I stepped out of bed, I knew everything was going to go wrong. I could feel it crackling in the air. Disaster. It was everywhere.

It started with Grace.

I popped out of bed without needing the alarm and went to the bathroom to get in the shower, but the bathroom was locked. And a nasty retching sound came from the other side of the door.

I pounded on the door. "What's going on, Grace? Are you alive in there?"

But she didn't need to answer. I knew what happened. She'd stayed with us the night before instead of at her place in L.A. so she could do laundry for free and eat a few non-fast-food meals before our trip to Barstow. She told Mom and Dad she was meeting up with her friend Priya for a movie. But she snuck out to see her ex, Patrick—the one Mom and Dad called He Who Must Not Be Named—which meant going to a party somewhere and getting drunk. That's what the retching was. Grace was really, really hungover.

"Just tell me you didn't drive," I said into the crack in the door.

"Patrick's friend drove the car home," she moaned.

Once I established that Grace wasn't dying and I didn't need to kill her myself for driving drunk, I needed to come up with Plan B: convincing Mom I could make the drive on my own.

But when I walked downstairs, holding our cat Bruce Lee in my arms as a buffer, I found Mom in the kitchen, drenched from head to toe with her clothes suctioned to her.

"What happened to you?"

If looks could kill, Mom could have launched a nuclear apocalypse. "Your sister," she said, "took my car out to meet Priya last night because hers didn't have gas. And she left the windows down."

"And it's raining?" I hadn't even looked outside, but now I could hear the rain pounding against the bay window in the kitchen and I groaned.

"Freak summer thunderstorm," Mom said, water dripping from her hair down to her face. "The inside of the car is completely soaked."

Stupid Patrick's stupid friend left the stupid windows down. Unbelievable. I opened my mouth even though I wasn't sure exactly what I was going to say, but Mom cut me off.

"Don't even think about going anywhere today."

"But, Mom—"

Bruce Lee, as averse to confrontation as I was, twisted out of my arms, drawing blood with his claws on the way down.

Traitor cat.

"Your sister has food poisoning and is vomiting her guts out right now. I'm not letting my barely sixteen-year-old daughter drive alone to the middle of the desert to meet a boy she knows only from the Internet."

"But—"

"Especially in pouring rain like this. You've had your license for only a few months, Hannah, and you don't have practice driving in this weather. You know everyone in California forgets how to drive when it rains. I'm sorry, but there's absolutely no way this is going to happen. Please don't ask me again."

Tears stung my eyes. Mom was still all drippy, but she came close and tried to pull me into a hug. I didn't let her get near me, though; I turned my back on her, stomped off to my room, and plopped on my computer chair, staring at my laptop and wondering how I was going to tell Nick.

If our meeting spot had been closer, or if it hadn't been raining, or if Grace had just gone to the movies like she was supposed to, or if someone would have rolled up the stupid windows, or if a hundred other things, I might have been able to talk Mom into it. But it was like the universe was determined to screw me over.

Twisting back and forth in my chair, I briefly considered sneaking out. Telling Mom I was going somewhere with Lo and driving the car to Barstow anyway, soaking wet seats and all. It sent a thrill through me, the idea of breaking the rules and going against a direct order. But as soon as I entertained the thought, the what-ifs marched in. I could get a flat. I could get lost. Nick could turn out to be a kidnapper-murderer-rapist, and no one would know where to find my chopped-up body.

I picked up the flattened souvenir penny Nick had sent in the mail the month before—the first present he ever gave me. It was from the Circus Circus Hotel and Casino, and it had arrived in my mailbox taped to the back of a "Vegas Strip at Night" postcard. I'd responded in turn with a penny I'd gotten at Disneyland a few years earlier, pressed with a picture of the three hitchhiking ghosts from the Haunted Mansion.

I ran my fingers over the impression of the clown face on the penny. It was silly to think I might be able to break the rules. That was Grace's area of expertise, not mine.

And why was I even doing this anyway? What was the point? Nick was my friend, but he was just my friend. We didn't need to meet in person.

I couldn't explain why, but I felt somewhat relieved all this crap happened. Maybe everything went wrong for a reason.

Hannah: Bad news.
Nick: nooooo no bad news
Hannah: It's raining here.
Hannah: Pouring, actually. Out of the blue.
Nick: noooooooooooo
Hannah: And Grace is sick. She got drunk last night and she's barfing it all up.
Nick: noooooooooooooooooooooooooooooooo
Hannah: And she ruined the car.
Hannah: It's like the world decided to crap all over me today.
Nick: so you're not coming?
Hannah: I can't.
Hannah: I'm sorry.
Hannah: Are you there?
Nick: yeah
Nick: i'm just bummed
Nick: i was really looking forward to this
Nick: we'll plan it for another time, right?
Nick: right?

CHAPTER 3

FRIDAY

Maybe it's Automatic Friday's new song playing on repeat, the moody one where Jordy's scratchy vocals are so raw, it sounds like he's right here on my pink polka-dot comforter singing to me. Maybe it's the thought of them playing a real show at a real venue tomorrow and me not being there. Maybe it's my memory of that doomed day Nick and I were supposed to meet and the strange mix of regret and relief over how everything went wrong that still haunts me, almost two years later. Maybe it's residual bitterness toward Aditi Singh and the smug look on her puckered-up face when Mrs. Marx told her she'd be the first senior class vice-president in the history of our school to go on the Washington, D.C., trip. Or maybe it's seeing the Circus Circus penny sitting on my dresser, a little dusty.

I don't know what it is, but some combination of these things prompts me into action, and before I even realize my legs are moving, I pick up the penny and run downstairs and out to my backyard, where Lo is still floating and Grace, who must never eat when she's away at school, is now working her way through a can of Pringles.

"What if we went to Vegas?" I blurt the second I close the sliding glass door behind me.

"Whaa?" Grace spits out a few of the Pringles bits.

"Ew, Grace."

"Sorry," she says, wiping chip crumbs off her face with her sleeve. "I think I must be in the wrong yard. What did you say?"

I take a deep breath and let it out slowly, thinking about each and every word before I say it. "The three of us. Spring break. Let's drive to Vegas tomorrow and go see Nick's show. The show is a big deal, and I want to be there."

Grace processes what I'm saying, and I think I actually see the wheels in her head turning. Grace, who spent her teen years sneaking out her window to go to punk rock shows on school nights. Grace, who came home from a show once, talked to a hot guy she'd met there online for a few days, and said, "He has a brother your age, you guys should talk," before ditching the hot guy and moving on to the next dude. Grace, who constantly tries to get me to do something, anything, outside of what is expected of me. To break any rule, no matter how small.

Her smile almost overtakes her entire face.

"Are you saying what I think you're saying?" Lo hops out of the pool, grabs a towel from the end of Grace's lounge chair, and whips it around herself, all within what seems like half a second. She stands toe-to-toe with me, her long hair dripping on my feet. "Are you, Hannah Cho—perfect student, daughter, and citizen—for real suggesting that we secretly drive to Las Vegas, Sin *freaking* City, to see this dude you've never met in person without telling our parents where we are?"

I stick the penny into my back pocket. "Screw them," I say, but I wince as soon as the words escape. "No, I don't mean that. I love Mom and Dad. I mean, screw the rules. Screw people telling me what I can and can't do." I feel energized. Alive. "It's just one night. Drive out tomorrow, go to the show, stay the night in a hotel, drive home the next day. They'll never even know we aren't here."

Grace's excitement practically explodes off her face as she rushes from the lounge chair and gathers me into a tight hug. "I knew it! I knew you had it in you! There were times I wondered if there was any way we were actually related, but I knew you'd do something completely illegal and make me proud one of these days."

Lo joins in the hug, too, but she's still drippy from the pool, so we both shake her off. That does nothing to deter her excitement, though. "I've always wanted to go to Vegas," she says, hopping from one foot to the other. "And I've always wanted to witness you breaking through the chains of your good-girl shackles and letting Crazy Hannah out to play. It's going to be Girls Gone Wild up in here!"

"Don't get it twisted," I say. "I have a cardigan collection. I'm not exactly the Girls Gone Wild type."

"Oh no," Grace says. "If we're doing this, we're doing it right. We'll raid Lo's closet for you. She has all that hoochie wear—"

"Hey, now," Lo breaks in.

"And we'll get you looking so hot, you won't even recognize yourself. Oh, and Nick . . . damn, he's going to die when he sees you."

"Settle down, you guys." Hands in the air, I back away from Lo and Grace, who both look at me like I'm some kind of arts and crafts project. "It's not like that between us."

Grace breaks into a loud, hearty laugh. She's so caught up in it, she falls back onto the lounge chair.

"What's so funny?" I ask.

"Of course it's like that between you two," she says as she tries to pull herself together.

I look to Lo to help me out, since she knows Nick and I are nothing more than friends. She doesn't know about all the feelings that have started to surface when I listen to his playlists, but she knows I've had a long string of boyfriends over the past few years, so it's not like I'm that girl pining away for her guy best friend. In fact, the past month or so is the first time I'd been single in a long time. It's taken some time to get over the Josh Ahmed disaster, since I thought he was going to be *the* boyfriend. I mean, I don't want to get involved with someone before I leave for college. It's not like I have feelings for Nick, or he has feelings for me. No.

So, yeah, I expect Lo to defend me to Grace, who's been at

UCLA and playing house with her ex and probably doesn't realize how non-Nick-centric my life actually is. But instead, Lo walks up to Grace, slips a wet arm through my sister's, and says, "Oh yeah, Hannah. You've got it bad."

The reality of what I have just committed to do sets in after Lo runs home to gather her hoochie wear and I'm left alone in the living room with a very excited Grace. My sister bounces on the couch, poking at her cell phone, while I wear a trail of trauma into the carpet with my pacing.

"Where are we going to stay? How are we going to get a hotel without Mom and Dad knowing? The only money I can use is that 'for emergencies only' credit card, and I seriously doubt this is up there with car problems, fire, or bodily harm."

Grace looks up from her phone. "Hey, you deciding to do something crazy is a five-alarm emergency in my book. We need to jump on it before you change your mind."

I shoot her a dirty look, but she waves it off.

"I'm texting Nick." I reach over to the coffee table to pull my phone off the charger. "Maybe he knows where we can stay."

"No!" Grace stretches across the couch and grabs my phone before I can reach it. "No texting. This should be a surprise."

"Why?"

"Because it's more fun this way. Imagine the look on his face when you show up at his show. He's going to flip."

I feel wrongness down to my gut when I think about doing something this big, this game changing, and not cluing Nick in. My stomach tightens like a fist at the thought of keeping this secret, even if it's only for twenty-four hours and even if it's a fun secret. I tell Nick everything. Well, almost everything. But I tell him more than I tell anyone else. Even Lo.

But then I let myself picture this scene Grace has set up: Nick at House of Blues with the band. Onstage, playing guitar. Seeing me in the crowd. The instant of recognition. The smile. The hug. The excitement.

This is the moment that launched a thousand daydreams,

the moment I thought I gave up forever once I decided meeting Nick was never going to happen and gave the relief power over the regret.

I can keep a secret for one night if it means getting that experience.

"Okay. Fine. Surprise." I pull my hair out of its bun, shake it loose, and then wrap it up again. "But that doesn't solve the hotel problem."

Grace hops up from the couch, hands me my phone, and slaps me on the butt. "Oh, I have that handled. Thanks to *Rocker*."

"*Rocker*? How?" I have no idea how Grace's internship at *Rocker* magazine equals hotel, but I'm all ears.

"Well, this internship was an issue between me and Gabe, as you know—"

"One of many, yes."

Grace rolls her eyes. "Anyway, since we broke up, I've totally thrown myself into things there. I've been trying to pitch some story ideas," she says. "I figured since they're full of experts on L.A. music there, I could do some research on the Las Vegas scene or something. Local Vegas bands. My editor loves that kind of stuff." She looks so pleased with herself, and it's comforting to see a look of confidence on her face again. This breakup almost broke Grace; I thought Gabe had taken that confidence when he left.

"You're an intern, though," I say. "You make coffee and copies, you don't pitch story ideas."

She digs around in her distressed leather purse and pulls out some memo or something. She yanks a hot pink sticky note off it and shoves it in my face. "Check this out."

Scribbled across the sticky note is *Great story idea, Grace! I'd love to see more like this from you.*

I shake my head and toss the sticky note back at her. "So?"

"So, I just texted my editor and told her I was heading to Vegas. Apparently she's some kind of high roller at Planet Hollywood, and when I told her I wanted to do research for a story idea while I was there, she complimented my ambition and offered up her discounted rate. Can you believe that?"

"Well, a discount is great, Grace, but what about the rest of the cost?"

"Girl, I know you hoard your allowance. Don't act like you're all poor. And Mom and Dad left me grocery money for the week. I think this is a much better cause."

"Better than food? You'll starve without a bottomless supply of Cheez-Its."

"This is worth it." Grace elbows me. "Don't say I never did anything for you, little sister."

I collapse back onto the couch. This whole thing, my whole stupid idea, had just seemed like talk until now. But now that we have a hotel room . . . are we really going to Vegas?

"I don't know," I say. "I know I never say this, but I think I'm wrong. We're going to get in trouble. Mom and Dad'll find out. Nick won't want me there. I'll find out he's some old pervert or something. This is a terrible idea. Let's just stay home and Netflix it up instead."

"Hannah," Grace says, grabbing my hand. Her eyes are serious and sad. "I need this. I need to get out of here. I haven't felt like myself since . . ." She doesn't finish her sentence, but she doesn't need to. Even though Grace doesn't live with us anymore, and hasn't since she left for college, she still spends a ton of time at home, and I saw firsthand how devastating her breakup with Gabe had been. Gabe was a crappy boyfriend, controlling and stubborn, and my strong-willed sister bent to his demands and became a different person. When he left her, he left her crushed. Little pieces of Old Grace are emerging from the rubble, but it's taking longer than any of us expected for her to put herself back together.

"I know."

"I just . . . I know this is for you, but it's for me, too." She lets go of my hand and absently tugs at the silver Tiffany key necklace around her neck, a gift from the A-hole himself. I wish she'd stop wearing it. "I want to go to Vegas so I can do something besides sit around and think about him, you know?" Her voice gets quiet. Distant. Then, just as quickly as her funk came on, she snaps herself out of it and lets the necklace fall against her chest. "Look, you know what I'm talking about. You just had a breakup, too."

Yeah, Josh Ahmed, my most recent perfect-on-paper boyfriend, and I had called it quits back before Christmas. But Grace and I both knew my breakup was amateur hour compared to hers.

"Fine. We're going."

"Fabulous," she says, her face lighting up. "I am so excited for you to finally make out with this guy tomorrow night."

"Grace, you need to get over this idea. I'm so not making out with him." I shove her hard on the shoulder. "I told you, it's not like that with Nick."

But it's not like I've never thought about it.

CHAPTER 4

FOUR MONTHS AGO

Truth bomb: I actually thought about Nick like that a lot.

Like, all the time, really. But I made myself pretend I didn't, and somehow I believed my own lies, which doesn't even make any sense when you think about it.

It all started when I broke up with Josh Ahmed.

"Hey, Ghost," Nick said after picking up the phone on the first ring. I don't remember how or when it happened, but at some point, he'd gone from being someone I chatted with online now and then to someone I texted occasionally to the first person I called when I needed to talk.

"Are you busy?"

"What's wrong?"

I knew I sounded desperate. I was desperate. I had just run out of my boyfriend's house. Shaken up and on the verge of tears, I was trying as hard as I could to hang on to my sanity and my dignity and my self-esteem. They were all slipping from my shaky grip, but now I had Nick. He would help me feel better. He always did.

I panted into the phone, trying to catch my breath.

"Talk to me, Ghost. Are you all right? What's going on?" I could tell Nick was scared for me. His voice sounded hesitant. Gentle.

He had no idea if I was being attacked or set on fire or abducted by aliens.

"Hold on, okay? Talk to me for a minute. Tell me what you're doing while I walk home." It was dark, and the streets were empty. Josh had picked me up earlier, and when I dashed out of his house so quickly, I forgot I didn't have a way to get back home—easily thirty minutes on foot—without him. But a long walk would be good for me. I could pull myself together on the way home.

"Um. I went out to dinner with Alex and his new girlfriend," he said. "She had a friend in town, so he wanted to show off and take them to this ridiculous restaurant at Caesars Palace. So overpriced—and of course, he made me pay for myself *and* the friend. She loved it, though. I guess that's good, even though I was a total weirdo, as usual."

"What's her name?" I was surprised by the flash of jealousy I felt when he mentioned this random girl. But I was also thankful for the twinge, because it slowed my breathing, held back the crying for now.

"The friend? Kate."

"Was she cute?"

"I don't know. She couldn't stay off her phone. I'm pretty sure she wanted to make me disappear."

That calmed me even more. "What did you order?"

I kicked a rock down the sidewalk as he described his chicken tacos in great detail, glad for the distraction and the company on my strange walk of shame.

"That sounds good," I mumbled.

"It was." He coughed. "Are you okay now?"

"I just broke up with Josh."

"Oh, Ghost. I'm sorry. What happened?"

"Can I ask you something personal?" He knew almost everything about me, but it was an unspoken thing that the *real* personal stuff was off-limits between us. He mentioned his girlfriends, but never in detail. He knew I'd had boyfriends, but I didn't divulge too much about them. But he was the only person I could talk to right

now, so I needed to cross that line. I wasn't ready to talk to Grace
or Lo or anyone who knew Josh in real life.

"You can ask me anything. You know that."

"I know, but I mean *personal* personal. Like, stuff we don't
usually talk about."

"Oh." He coughed. One of those forced coughs you do when you
need to fill an empty space. "Hold on." I heard the creak of the door
closing and then the squeak of him sitting on his bed. "All right.
What do you want to ask?"

"This might be weird. I know we don't usually talk about this
stuff. But, are you . . . I mean, have you . . ."

"No," he answered before I could finish. "I haven't."

"Not even with Christine?" His last girlfriend. They'd been
pretty serious. I thought they had been, anyway. But he didn't tell
me anything about her until after they broke up. "Why not?" Even
though he swore he was awkward, Nick was a good-looking guy
who seemed to have lots of girls after him. I couldn't imagine a guy
like him at my school still being a virgin. Even the dorks at my
school were getting laid.

"I don't know. I don't let a lot of people in, Ghost. And with her,
it . . . it wasn't right." His voice was so quiet, like it wasn't even on
the other end of my phone, but just a thought in my head.

"Yeah. I know what you mean." I let out a long sigh. "I almost . . .
um, you know, with Josh right now. We'd been talking about it for
weeks. And I thought it was the time and he was the guy and I
thought I was ready to go. But there we were—" I stopped before
I gave too many details. I didn't want to paint a vivid picture for
him or anything. "—there we were, and instead of feeling sexy,
I felt like I was going to throw up."

Nick laughed.

"Don't laugh at me."

"I'm not laughing at *you*. It's like your eighth-grade boyfriend."

"What?"

"Remember? When we first started talking? What was his
name? Jeremy Martinez. You said he was trying to kiss you or

something and it made you feel sick. You called your mom and had her pick you up from school."

"You remember that?" I was shocked. I hardly remembered that.

"I remember everything you've ever told me, Ghost." His voice was serious, and I think the tone took us both by surprise, so he laughed, probably to ease the tension just a bit. "I'm like an elephant. And anyway, I'm—I get it."

"You do?"

"I've felt like that, too. Like it's getting all hot and heavy—"

"You did not just say 'hot and heavy'—"

"And I know I'm supposed to be all into it, and I am, but I'm also . . . I don't know, not. Like I'm somewhere else."

"Yes!" I couldn't believe he'd felt the same way. It made me feel so much less alone to hear that.

"I've asked some of my friends about it, and Alex."

"What did they say?" I stopped, sat on the curb, and leaned my head against a streetlight post.

"That it's not normal."

"Oh."

"So, I guess we're both freaks. According to Alex, anyway. But he thinks I'm a freak regardless."

I drew circles on the leg of my jeans with my finger. "Do you think we were just nervous? Like, stage fright? Do you get like this when you go onstage with the band?"

He did that coughing thing again. "Uh, I don't get stage fright. But I do get a little nervous before presentations and stuff in school. This didn't feel the same."

"Yeah. It never felt like normal nervous to me either." Then without thinking, I said, "I wonder if it would be like that with—"

"With who?" He jumped in so quickly, cutting me off, and I was flooded with relief that I didn't have to finish my thought.

I stood and started walking again, like a change of location would change the subject. "Um. Someone else."

I'd been about to say "*with you*." I was wondering whether I would have the same nervous feeling with Nick, someone I've known so well for so long. But the two of us never, ever talked about things like that. Things like being real people to each other. We were ghosts. Ghosts didn't exist in real life. You couldn't touch a ghost.

But I took a second, only a second, to let the thought fill my head anyway: the same nervous fumble I'd just gone through with Josh, but with Nick instead. I was pretty sure Nick was taller than Josh, and slightly skinnier, if his photos told the truth. I let the scene flash through my mind, me fitting perfectly against Nick's chest. Nick's arms around me.

More than one second went by, I know. A few seconds, at least. I wasn't saying anything, because I got caught up in imagining and forgot Nick was on the phone and not here with me. I let myself think thoughts I had never thought before. I let myself think of Nick "that way," which I'd promised I would never, ever do. I lost myself in it.

"Ghost."

His voice on the phone snapped me out of my thoughts. I hadn't even realized I'd stopped walking and was standing still in the middle of the sidewalk. What had I done? Had I just fantasized about Nick? My cheeks burned, and I was so glad we weren't video chatting, because he totally would have caught me.

"Sorry." I was so flustered. "I was . . ." Picturing myself alone with you. Wondering what your skin smells like. Imagining your arms around me.

"Where did you go just now?" His voice took on a softness I had never heard before, and I could tell he knew what I'd been thinking. I don't know how he knew it, but he did, and he sounded almost . . . hopeful? No. "Were you thinking about—?"

"Thinking about Josh," I said quickly. I needed to change the subject. I couldn't let Nick know it had been him in my thoughts, that I'd let my mind wander to the off-limits territory of us, together.

Admitting that could ruin our friendship. And our friendship was one thing I wasn't willing to risk.

"Oh, got it," he said with a nervous laugh. "I thought maybe . . . never mind."

We spent the next hour, long after I'd made it home safely, talking about trivial things, my mind traveling far from Josh. But I couldn't get the image I'd conjured of Nick out of my brain. That was the first time I'd thought about him in that way.

But it wasn't the last.

CHAPTER 5

SATURDAY

I'd say I was jolted awake by the sound of a commotion in the bathroom, but the truth is, I don't know if I ever actually fell asleep. My mind spun in anxious circles all night, playing through scenario after scenario of how this trip to Vegas could end up being a trip to hell, each vision more ridiculous than the last. I mean, I know there won't be an avalanche as we drive through the high desert, pinning us in Grace's SUV and forcing us to figure out which one of us to eat for survival, but try telling my crazy mind that right now.

Then, every time I thought I might drift off, Lo—who'd come back with pizza and two bags of hoochie attire, then passed out early on my floor—started snoring so loudly, I think Nick could probably hear her in Vegas.

Maybe it's the commotion that wakes me up, or maybe I'm already half-awake, my mind halfway on the road to Vegas, but something about that loud thump and subsequent gurgling sound in the bathroom strikes fear in my heart, and I'm out of bed and on my feet immediately. Lo is still sawing logs on the floor, so that means the clamor in the bathroom must be Grace.

Oh no. Not again.

I run down the hall, hopping over Bruce Lee, and bang on the bathroom door.

"What's going on in there, Grace? Don't even tell me you went out last night and got wasted, because, I swear to God, I will run you over with the car if you did that to me again."

But once I stop banging, I realize that the gurgling sound isn't puking—it's just the bathtub draining.

The door swings open. "Sorry," Grace says. "I knocked the lotion into the trash can." She stands there in the doorway with the hair dryer in one hand, a brush in the other, and her soaking wet hair, newly dyed red, falling over her shoulders.

She didn't bleach it first, so it's not like the color is a huge difference from her natural black. The red is more of a highlight. An enhancement. But there's something about the subtle change that makes her look like the Old Grace. The pre-breakup, pre-Gabe Grace.

And there is also a light in her eye. A crazy, looking-for-trouble, devil-on-my-shoulder glint. I haven't seen it in a long time.

"Go wake up Lo," she says. "Let's get this party started."

In less than two hours, the three of us are showered, packed, and loaded up in Grace's SUV. As we pull onto the freeway, I follow Grace's advice and send a preemptive e-mail to Mom and Dad, who are checking in daily via the pricey Internet café on their cruise ship. I let them know the three of us are spending a very boring day seeing as many movies as possible at the theater, and that I will check in later.

"Service may be spotty as we drive through the desert," Grace says as she merges into traffic. "A good rule breaker always thinks of things that could go wrong and addresses them beforehand. Be proactive."

"You need to use these powers for good and not evil," Lo says, shoving Grace on the shoulder. She's one to talk.

E-mail sent, I lean back in my seat, absently rubbing my thumb over the clown penny as I watch the mass of cars on either side of us and go through our plan. The drive from Orange County to Las Vegas should take only about three-and-a-half to four hours, depending on how many stops we make and how NASCAR-like Grace drives, but this traffic is going to put us so behind schedule. I can't miss the show because of stupid OC traffic. I can't miss Nick.

Luckily, traffic eases up as soon as we get to the 15 freeway and head into the desert. But we're on the 15 for only a few miles before Grace drives the car across the lanes to an exit. "Pit stop," she says.

I do a double take at the sign. "We're in Fontana. What could we possibly find in Fontana that we need in Vegas? It smells like a cow pooped out a diesel engine here."

"Exactly." Lo sounds downright sinister.

I turn around and narrow my eyes at her. "What are you up to, crazy girl?" When Lo gets that tone in her voice, I know she has some insane scheme planned. She's notorious around school for her "great ideas." Challenging Siraj and Manny to jump from the roof into the pool at Seth White's party last summer ended in at least three broken bones for those poor guys. Organizing a faux Hunger Games with the freshman soccer players was hilarious until their coach found out what they were planning on using their cleats for. My personal favorite is the time she showed up for the home-coming football game as a queen nominee, already wearing a huge crown. I try my hardest to keep my distance from her antics and maintain a 100 percent positive reputation in the guidance office, but as her best friend, it isn't easy. Fortunately, all her past she-nanigans have managed to bypass me. Until now, when I'm stuck in a car with her and my out-of-control sister. And if I know Lo, she's going to be activating those crazy-plan powers.

"I'm turning on the GPS." Grace's smile is as evil as Lo's voice. I hate when they gang up on me.

Grace's navigation, with its snobby English accent, directs us down one sketchy Fontana street after another, until we end up in the parking lot of a grocery store, a Laundromat, and a check-cashing place. "Are you selling me into sex slavery for gambling money?" I ask. This parking lot is the textbook definition of "shady." Broken glass is scattered across the asphalt, and crooked-looking characters wander aimlessly past the storefronts. This is exactly the kind of place you see on news stories about teen girls who go out for a night of fun and are never heard from again.

"You got it," Lo says, typing into her phone again. "You hot Koreans get top dollar. Between the two of you, Mama's going to get a new pair of shoes tonight."

"Who are you texting?" The whole sex-slavery thing is a joke, obviously, but when a homeless guy starts screaming at a boarded-up window, I realize I'm a little—okay, a lot—apprehensive about what we're doing here.

"His name is Max," Lo says.

My face wrinkles up in confusion. "The homeless guy?"

"No, silly." She undoes her seat belt and leans toward me. "Now, promise you won't freak out."

I groan. Typical Lo. That phrase always precedes a freak-out-worthy plan.

"You'll be fine, Hannah." Grace pats my arm. "Calm down and listen to Lo."

"Lo has almost gotten me arrested before!"

"That was an accident," she says, making Grace laugh.

"I have to hear this story," Grace says.

"Can we please get back to why we are in this random parking lot?"

Lo smiles. "So, this guy Max is friends with my cousin Carlos. Remember Carlos? From my Fourth of July party a few years ago?"

"The one who went in the pool in his jorts?"

"Yeah, that's the one. He has this friend, Max, and Carlos said Max would hook us up."

"Hook us up with what? Lo, you know I don't want to do drugs or anything. If you do, then—"

"No, no. No drugs. I promise." Before she can explain further, a full-sized van peels into the parking lot and screeches to a stop right next to us. There's a picture airbrushed on the side of the van—an artist's rendering of that exact van being chased by two cop cars and a helicopter. I know it is that exact van because the van in the painting has a picture of a tiny van and mini–cop cars on the side.

"Wow," I say.

"That's Max." Lo hops out of the SUV, and she pounds on our

front windshield for me to follow suit. I take a deep breath, unfasten my seat belt, and slowly open the door.

"I'll stay in here," Grace says. "Don't worry, scaredy-cat. I'll call 911 if he tries to get rapey."

Max doesn't get out of the van. Once Lo approaches the driverside window, he looks us up and down. "Hey, Paloma." Lo's family members are the only people who get to call her by her full name. Sketchy-as-hell family friends do, too, apparently.

He slides two envelopes through the window to Lo, and a lovely pot smoke odor comes along with them. "This is the best I could come up with based on what Carlos sent me." He looks us up and down again. "I think they'll do just fine."

My pulse races, and I shoot a desperate look at Lo. I wish she'd tell me what was going on here and why we're standing in a creepy parking lot in Fontana with a strange guy who has a picture of a high-speed chase painted on the side of his van.

I don't do well with surprises, and I'm fighting the urge to run.

Lo elbows me in the ribs and hands me one of the envelopes, jerking her chin at me. "Check it out."

Inside the envelope, I find six California driver's licenses, all belonging to Asian girls. I look over at Lo and see she's holding the same thing, but all with Hispanic-looking girls. "What—?"

"Pick out the one you think is the best," Max says. "Then it's thirty bucks each. That's a special deal, since Carlos is like familia."

"We're getting fake IDs?" I hiss into Lo's ear.

"Isn't it awesome?" she whispers back.

No, it isn't awesome. It's really, really illegal.

I have a promise with myself, and with my parents: keep my eyes on the prize during high school. Boyfriends are fine, as long as they don't negatively impact my grades. No drugs, no drinking, no partying. No rule breaking. Then after high school, I can do what I want, as long as what I want involves a four-year university. I'd kept that promise and gotten into UCLA, my first-choice school, like my sister. Since that's set, I feel justified in going on this secret weekend romp to Las Vegas and getting a little wild.

But not "fake ID" wild. Not "illicit parking lot purchase from a creeper in a van" wild.

But then I look back to the car and see Grace grinning at me like I'm opening a Christmas gift she picked out special for me, the red in her hair glinting in the sunlight.

I sigh.

"It's time to let loose a little, Hannah," Lo says. "College is right around the corner. Stop being such a control freak, and let's get some party practice in." I don't like her calling me a control freak like it's a bad thing, so I kick her in the shin. She doesn't care, though. She knows she'll eventually get me to do what she wants.

"Can you guys hurry up?" Max crinkles his eyebrows at us. "I'm missing *Ellen*. It's a makeover special today."

"Fine," I say to Lo, "I'll get a fake ID. But I don't have to use it. Just getting one is breaking enough laws for me right now."

Lo pats my shoulder. "Good girl. Now, pick."

I shuffle through the IDs in my hand. None of them look all that much like me. "How do I choose?"

"Check out the height," Max grumbles. "That never changes. You don't want one that says you are five-seven when you are clearly five-two." He obviously knows the ins and outs of this business.

"Where did you even get these?" I ask him.

He narrows his eyes. "Don't ask questions. Hurry up."

I look again at my options:

Tran Nguyen isn't even Korean, and she's five feet tall and looks like a man, so she's out.

Kristy Chang is way prettier than me, but she has a round face like I do and even has my dimples. And we're the same height and weight. Perfect.

I hold Kristy's ID up next to my face. "Do I look like Kristy Chang from Riverside? Can I pass for twenty-three?"

"You look beautiful, dah-ling." Lo has chosen Sarah Kingston, a Pisces whose address is not too far from our school.

"That chick isn't even Mexican."

"I know, but she looks way more like me than these other girls. Look at this one's eyebrows. Like I would ever."

"You girls all set?" Max asks, clearly annoyed with our indecision.

Lo hands back the envelopes. "We're ready for Vegas, baby!"

He stares at us.

"What is he staring at?" I whisper to Lo. In those few seconds, I imagine Max, who seems nice enough despite the pot smell and the whole van situation, turning all Mr. Hyde and pulling us into his van, speeding off, and leaving Grace screaming and shaking her fist at the heavens in the parking lot.

"My money," he says, snapping me back to reality. "This ain't free, you know."

"Oh yeah." Lo digs around in her purse and pulls out an envelope of cash. "My treat, Hannah. As long as you promise to use it. I don't want my investment to go to waste."

"Yeah, I promise." I have zero intention of using it, but I'm also not going to tell Lo she'd be better off taking her money, walking up to the roulette table, and slamming it down on red. I'll go along with this, but I don't drink and we'd agreed on no clubs. Plus, Grace triple-checked that the show at House of Blues tonight is all-ages.

"I would've given you my old ID to use," Grace says once we're back in the car. "But since we're going out together, I couldn't exactly have you using mine while I was using it, too. We couldn't both be the same Grace Cho walking into the same place."

And just like that, we are out of Fontana and back on the long road to Vegas.

"We're almost there," Grace says.

I don't know how she can tell. We took a bathroom break in Barstow at the infamous train-car McDonald's, and since then, it has been all desert, all the time. The landscape has looked exactly the same since we left Baker, home of—no joke—the World's Tallest Thermometer. These are the kinds of thrilling attractions you have to look forward to when you're driving through the desert: dirt, piles of dirt, an abandoned water park, a place that sells something called Alien Jerky, a freeway exit called Zzyzx Road, and a ridiculously large temperature device.

The initial thrill I'd felt about this trip slowly died during the course of the long and boring drive through the middle of nowhere. I tried texting with a few friends, but most of them were off with real spring break plans, so I mostly passed the time by telling Grace and Lo stories about Nick from the past four years. Even that got old after a while, though, and Lo pretty much begged me to shut up after the tenth word-for-word reading of one of Nick's inside-joke-riddled text conversations with me.

"The California state line is coming up here in a bit." Grace fumbles around in the center console for her water bottle, but she drank the last sip about forty miles ago and doesn't seem to remember, so I hand her mine. "Then we'll officially be in Nevada, and Vegas is not far from the state line at all."

"Is that it?" Lo points ahead at a small cluster of color. As we get closer, I notice it's casinos we're approaching—right in the middle of desert, desert, and more desert.

"They get you in a casino the minute it's legal, don't they?" I say. "Who comes here? Why don't people keep on driving to Vegas if we're so close?"

"Desperate to gamble? Hiding out from the mob?" Lo suggests. "Who knows, but I'm glad this isn't our stop. It looks like the place hope goes to die."

We all cheer as we cross out of California and into Primm, Nevada, and I peer out the window at what's waiting for us in this new state. Outlet mall, those three hotel casinos that look semi-impressive—because they're out in the middle of nowhere and are surrounded by tumbleweeds—but probably pale in comparison to what is waiting for us in Vegas, and—

"Oh my God," says Lo. "Look at that huge roller coaster."

The second casino on our right side—named Buffalo Bill's, according to the large neon sign with a buffalo wearing a feather headdress—has an enormous yellow roller coaster track wrapping its way around the entire property.

Grace laughs. "Should I stop so you can ride the roller coaster, Hannah?"

"You want to torture me?"

Grace jerks the steering wheel and the car to the right. "You know you're dying to."

"It doesn't even look like it's running." We all watch the track, but we don't see a single car zoom by. "It's probably broken. Or condemned because it is a total death trap. This random roller coaster in the middle of the desert has probably killed innocent kids, and someone's on their way right now to tear it down for the good of Primm."

"Settle down, settle down." Lo leans forward and pats my shoulder. "No one's making you ride the roller coaster. Look, it's behind us."

I hate that she talks to me like I'm a baby she's dropping off at day care, but Lo has been with me on a couple of ill-fated Disneyland trips, so she knows firsthand how much even the idea of roller coasters sends me into a panic spiral.

Truth be told, I've never actually been on one, but I have no desire to even try. It's the out-of-control feeling, the free-falling. I know some people love it. But some people also jump out of planes for grins and giggles. Some people are insane.

With the death trap safely behind us, we drive on the final stretch of the 15 freeway to Vegas. I'm relieved this is the last leg of the trip. We've been in the car since McDonald's, and that stop was almost two hours ago. My legs feel tight, my shoulders beg for a good stretch, and I'm about five minutes from making Grace pull over so I can pee behind some rocks. I hate to be the annoying little sister, but I feel like I can hardly sit still any longer.

Nick is so close.

"How much longer?"

"Wait a few minutes," Grace says. "I'll show you something cool."

My knee bounces up and down and my fingers drum on my thigh as we continue through the desert. I can't imagine what she could possibly have to show us, and I am in no mood for a pit stop in some ghost town or run-down casino.

"Here we are." Grace lifts a hand from the steering wheel and points ahead.

"It's mountains," Lo says. "That's all we've been looking at for four hours now. What's the big deal?"

But the words are barely out of Lo's mouth when we round a small corner and the hills on either side of us open up. Now, instead of mountains, in front of us is this unbelievable view. It's not even dark out, but I can still see the sparkling lights of the casinos and the hotels and the buildings that make up what I assume is the Las Vegas Strip.

"Wow," I say. It's like straight out of a movie or a postcard or something. I can't believe all those lights are real.

It definitely looks like the sort of place where amazing things happen. I can see why it's a place people go with their dreams. And how fitting that I'm coming here, to this home of big dreams, to meet my best friend at last. Dusty, boring Barstow and that weird McDonald's wouldn't have been the place for us. Our friendship needs lights and sparkles and music and surprises. This is our place. I can feel it.

The lights come closer, and I'm mesmerized by them, until a noise from the center console catches my attention. My text alert.

DON'T KNOW IF WE ARE READY FOR THIS SHOW TONIGHT. YOU SHOULD SEE OSCAR'S HAIR. OMG. I THINK HE TOOK A TIME WARP TO 1983.

"You're smiling," Grace says. "That must be Nick. What'd he say?"

"Nothing."

I reply:

I WISH I COULD SEE THAT.

About thirty seconds go by before I get his answer.

ME TOO, GHOST. I WISH YOU COULD SEE IT ALL.

CHAPTER 6

Las Vegas Boulevard is even more of an assault on the senses than I imagined. Enormous hotel casinos line the Strip, lights sparkling and signs flashing. POKER TOURNAMENT! PRIME RIB SPECIAL! And, ew, LOOSEST SLOTS! The sidewalks are crowded with tourists of every age, shape, and style; cars and cabs pack the streets; and the three of us press our faces to the windows as we drive, trying to make sense of all the dazzling chaos.

It doesn't take long to find the massive Planet Hollywood hotel. The huge white building, plain except for the red sign on the top of the rows upon rows of windows and the waves of shiny silver bubbles at the street level, is toward the south end of the Strip, so we don't have to drive too far. Grace pulls into the parking garage and we walk through the attached mall with our bags, window-shopping as we find our way to the sparkly check-in area.

"It's like the DMV in here," Lo says. "I swear, I've seen every single walk of life."

Every walk of life includes, but is not limited to, an overweight couple sporting matching Mickey Mouse T-shirts and slushie drinks in giant plastic Eiffel Towers, three bikini-clad girls in sky-high stilettos with only sheer caftans covering them, and a busload's-worth of tourists taking endless photos of the gift store across from the check-in desk. Three kids chase each other in circles, and I pray someone is actually in charge of them. But not the bikini girls, God willing.

Then there's us: two Asians and a Mexican. Seventeen, eighteen, and twenty-one. Grace in all black with a beanie, Lo with wavy brown hair pulled high in a topknot and wearing a floral sundress with motorcycle boots, and me, with my skinny jeans, black cami, and stick-straight hair, looking like the most plain and boring person in this entire city.

The check-in line is long, and as we wait, my mind runs through every way this too-good-to-be-true hotel thing is going to crash and burn. But the room is waiting for us, just like Grace's editor said, and as the three of us ride the elevator up to our floor, I can't help but hope the name-dropping of *Rocker* earned us some ridiculous *Hangover* suite or something.

But it's a normal room. No suite, just two beds, a chair, a small table, and a killer view of the Strip.

"What's *Empire Records*?" Lo asks. Every room at Planet Hollywood is decorated with memorabilia from some movie or another, I guess. We got some film I'd never heard of.

"It's a classic from the '90s. I've never seen it. But here's some shirt some guy wore in it." Grace points to the wall where a red T-shirt hangs behind a panel of Plexiglas.

"Like someone would want to steal some old, sweaty T-shirt," Lo says. "I wish we would have gotten a cool room, like *Pitch Perfect* or something. Do you think we can call down and have them switch us to the *Pitch Perfect* room?"

"Shut it, Lo." Grace tosses her bag on the bed closest to the window. "You have a free room and you're going to like it. Even if it is decorated with sweaty T-shirts from a movie no one has ever seen."

I sit on the edge of the chair in the corner and study my phone. It's four o'clock; three hours until Nick's show. I need to change and do my makeup and get some food and figure out how to get over to House of Blues and mentally prepare for life as I know it to be completely altered. Three hours should be enough time for all that. My knee jiggles up and down as I chew on the inside of my cheek.

Grace plops herself down on the bed and bounces while she studies me. "Okay, Hannah. I can see you panic-attacking over there. What's on your mind?"

"Well, House of Blues is at Mandalay Bay, and we figured out that's probably too far to walk, right? So we need to change and either drive or get a cab over there and we need to have dinner at some point because that McDonald's isn't going to hold me for much longer."

"They have a bunch of great restaurants at Mandalay Bay," Lo says, scrolling around on her phone. "It looks like there's a pizza place. How does that sound?"

"Perfect," Grace says. "We get spruced up, we taxi over to Mandalay Bay—I don't even want to deal with driving—and we eat at this pizza place." She leans over and pats me on the knee. "Then we go to the show."

"We go to the show," I say as I pull my knees up and wrap my arms around them. "We go to the show and we meet Nick."

Grace had been pushing me about this since I let the crazy idea slip from my lips yesterday, but now she gets up from the bed and crouches in front of me, placing a comforting hand on my leg. "You okay?" she asks. "You sure you can do this?"

I don't know. Can I? Do I want to? I don't answer, and I stare at the window. I can't see the Strip from where I'm sitting, but I can see the Paris Las Vegas hotel next door. The Eiffel Tower, where the couple in reception likely got their huge drinks, pokes up into the sky. I'm in Las Vegas. I crossed a state line. I can't turn back now, can I? Does it matter at this point if I can't do this? I pull the clown penny out of my pocket and flip it around in my fingers.

Lo leans on the arm of the chair. "Can I say something you don't want to hear?"

I side-eye her, which she seems to take as encouragement to word vomit.

"I know I said this before, but I need you to listen. I know for sure you have some serious feelings for this guy. Like, more than just best-friend feelings." She pokes at my penny, and I let it fall flat in my palm.

I don't say anything. I let this sink in.

She goes on. "I don't think you're ever going to have a boyfriend longer than a few months until you explore what those feelings are."

Grace clears her throat.

"What?" I snap at her.

"I totally called it," she says, all smug. "Nick is the reason you and Josh broke up."

I roll my eyes. "No, that's not why." I sound irritated, but the thing is—deep down, I feel like she may be right.

God, they're both right.

"So, what do you think?" Lo says. "Do you think you might have 'more than friendly' feelings for Nick?"

"Like, 'kiss his face with your face' feelings?" Grace grins.

I stick my tongue out at her, then turn to Lo and ask her, my voice serious, "But I haven't met him. How can I know if I have those feelings?" The truth is, I always have feelings when I think about Nick. My stomach flutters when I hear his ringtone. His familiar voice makes me happy, no matter what mood I'm in. And I scroll through his pictures so much, I'm sure the images are going to burn onto my phone screen.

But it's impossible to know if that will translate into reality. And I've spent all these years telling myself I don't want it to be reality.

"Well," Lo says, "from the stories you've told me, I get the feeling he for sure has those feelings for you."

"Really?" I stare down at the flattened copper clown face in my hand and think about the postcard it was once attached to, which now hangs on my bulletin board. *To my favorite ghost, I thought hauntings were supposed to be scary, but you make it fun. Love, Nick.* That was the first time I'd considered that Nick might think of me as more than a friend, and it wasn't the last, but I always push the possibility down deep. Because it isn't practical, Nick's having feelings for someone he's never met. Or my having feelings for someone who lives in another state.

I have no use for things that aren't practical.

"Well, then." Lo gives me two quick pats on my shoulder; then she stands up and starts pacing the room. "We are going to make this work. This isn't going to be a friend meeting a friend for the first time. Oh no, this is going to be love at first in-real-life sight. We're going to make you look so hot, he won't be able to look away from you, and if all goes according to plan, he won't even be able to play guitar or whatever he does in this band, because he's going to have his hands all over you."

Lo and Grace, spurred into action by a project, dig through my bag, dump out their makeup, and start putting into motion whatever crazy things they have come up with to make me look less like myself and more like some combination of the two of them.

Normally I would protest, but I'm distracted from the ridiculous pile of brushes and eye shadows scattered across the white comforter by this idea Lo left floating around the room. Could it be I do have feelings for Nick? Is it possible he has feelings for me?

I guess we'll see what happens.

And after four years of waiting, something is going to happen tonight.

CHAPTER 7

Mandalay Bay Resort and Casino is at the very south end of the Strip, a quick taxi ride from Planet Hollywood. Tall and golden, it's the first big hotel in the long, long line of lights and buildings, and House of Blues is inside. At the pizza place, I wolf down three slices and a third of a chocolate cake slice the server brings after Grace and Lo tell him it's my birthday while I'm in the bathroom. I'd never eat like such a pig under normal circumstances, but I don't even realize how many carbs I'm chowing down, because I'm so focused on Nick. Nothing else matters.

After dinner, we walk out to the casino and practically run right into the club. I know I'm going to have to do this now.

Legs shaking, I trail behind Lo to the box office. In front, Grace asks for three tickets to the show and shoves one in my unsteady hand.

"Ew," she says. "Your hand feels like it was licked by a Saint Bernard."

"Sorry." I stuff the ticket in my back pocket and wipe my hands on the front of my new jeans. When we were getting ready, the girls deemed even Lo's hoochie attire unacceptable, and we ran down to the mall inside Planet Hollywood to get me an entirely new outfit. The low-cut sparkly tank top and tight jeans look amazing, but I don't feel like myself. It's like I'm walking around in someone else's body. But at least that body had the wherewithal to veto the sky-high heels Lo was trying to push in favor of sassy-yet-comfortable wedges. "I don't do this sort of thing every day. It's freaking scary." "Scary" is an understatement. I wasn't even this shaky and unsure of myself before the SAT, and my entire future had depended on that test.

"I thought chocolate cake was supposed to calm me down," I say to Lo. "I can't stop shaking right now."

"Don't stress," she says. She grabs my hand and we follow Grace to a roped-off line where a bouncer in a black polo shirt checks IDs. "Get out your ID," she whispers to me through clenched teeth, pushing me in front of her. "Your new one."

We rearranged our wallets on the drive in, hiding our real licenses behind library cards, school IDs, and Starbucks gift cards and putting our newly acquired identities in the clear plastic sleeves in the front.

I take a deep breath as Grace gets her ID checked by the bouncer and breezes through the line. I quickly consider pulling my real license out from its hiding spot and showing the bouncer that one. What will it hurt? The show is all-ages, so it's not like I won't be able to get in. The only benefit is the access to alcohol, and I'm not planning on drinking anyway.

But I remember Lo and Grace making fun of me for most of the drive from Fontana to Barstow when I said I had no fake-ID plans for this trip, and I decide to live a little and use it, even if it's making my heart beat so loudly, I swear the bouncer can hear it over the clamor of the casino. I promised them I'd let my hair down and have fun. And I think about all the crazy things I'd passed over during the last four years. Following the rules had been safe, but safe was boring. I pull that new ID out of my wallet, hold my breath, and hand it to the bouncer, trying with everything in me to keep my nervous hand steady.

He holds a flashlight up to the back of the card, then looks closely at the picture, up at me, then down at the picture again. He flicks the side of the card with his thumb, runs it through a little scanner, and says, "Riverside, huh? I have a cousin who lives out there."

Panic floods me. He's going to ask me questions about Riverside, and I won't know the answers. I've never even been there. What's my fake name again? I'm going to get found out and arrested and hauled off to Vegas jail. The cops will call my parents and my school, and I won't be able to go to UCLA. Damn you, Lo and Grace and Aditi Singh! Damn you all for ruining my life.

I force a smile, but I'm sure it looks more like some creepy jack-o'-lantern face. *Improvise,* I think. *Fake it. Do something.* "Oh, yeah. I just moved out there a couple of years ago. Um, after high school."

"Aww, too bad," he says. "I was gonna ask if you went to school with her. Mercy Jordan?"

I shrug. "Nope. Sorry."

He hands the license back to me and smiles as he wraps a paper wristband around my arm. "Oh well. Have a good time." Then he turns to face Lo, who is right behind me, and he takes her ID.

Oh my God. I can't believe that worked. I used a fake ID at a casino in Las Vegas on spring break and got away with it. Who *am* I right now?

I snake through the ropes and linger around the still-empty merch table outside the door to the House of Blues with Grace, waiting for Lo. I try to update Grace on my success, but she elbows me. "Keep cool until we get inside."

The bouncer guy seems to be staring hard at Lo's ID and asking her questions. Oh crap. I've been so worried about getting caught myself, I didn't even think about her and her stupid non-Mexican photo. I chew on my lip and try to look nonchalant, like a perfectly legal girl waiting for her perfectly legal friend, but inside, my stomach is doing a gymnastics routine and I'm imagining Lo being carried through the casino and tossed out the front doors.

"What year did you graduate?" the bouncer guy asks. Thankfully, Grace made us practice this sort of question in the car. He frowns at her answers, but his eyes flick up at the line of people growing behind her. He scowls at the line, scowls at Lo's ID, scowls at Lo—but then he hands her card back, slaps a wristband on her, and waves her through.

"What happened?" I grip tightly to Lo's arm, flooded with relief that she made it through the gauntlet to stand next to me.

"Did you see that?" she asks, keeping her voice low. "I thought I was busted for sure. He was sketching on my ID so hard."

"I told you you should have picked a girl who was actually Mexican."

"But this girl looks more like me than the Mexican girls!"

"Whatever. It worked. Did you hear him asking me if I knew his cousin?"

"I'm proud of you for coming up with that story about moving there after high school," Grace says. "That ability to lie under pressure is a super-marketable Bad Girl skill. Now, let's go!"

The three of us walk into House of Blues, and I stop in my tracks as I'm assaulted by all the colors and sounds in the restaurant area. "Wow," I say. "Look at this place!" The walls are covered with kitschy signs and sculptures and decorations that look like something you would use in a voodoo ritual. Loud pop-punk music blares from the speakers as people eat dinner and drink. We make a left to walk down the stairs under bright lights that spell out SAY YEAH, and I grip the railing, white knuckled, because my legs are shaking even harder now than they were outside. The downstairs space—stage against the back wall, bars lining the other three—is already starting to fill up with people sipping drinks and chatting with each other in groups in front of the stage area, even though Nick's band is the opening act and he told me he didn't expect anyone to show up for them. Moxie Patrol, the headlining band, isn't on for a few more hours, and Nick said they're the ones people care about.

But I don't care about Moxie Patrol. I only care that I'm inside the same room as Nick Cooper. I'm going to see Nick in person before the night is over.

There had been a merch table outside the doors, but it was just loaded up with boxes that contained T-shirts and CDs from tonight's bands. I didn't see Nick there, or anyone I recognized from his pictures online, so now my eyes dart from crowd to stage in search of him or someone who looks familiar from the many photos he's sent me. My heart pounds and my face heats up like it's on fire. I'm not sure if it's better if I see them or not. Either prospect is completely terrifying.

"I don't know if I can do this," I say into Lo's ear. "I'm freaking out over here. What if I don't recognize him?"

"Hannah, you have a million pictures of him on your phone. You've video-chatted with him. Don't be ridiculous. You're going to recognize him."

She's right—I know she is. But I need to look at a picture of him, just in case. My hand shakes at the thought of real-life Nick, though, and I have a hard time controlling my phone. I somehow manage to sort through my saved pictures until I find one of my favorites. He texted it to me a couple of months ago, when Alex found a stray dog wandering around the skate park and they brought him home. In the picture, Nick holds the dog they named Bobo—a schnauzer mix with a majestic mustache—close to his face as he licks Nick's cheek. The picture catches Nick's surprised laughter, and I can imagine the sound of his laugh in my ear—full and loud and sudden—when I look at it. His laugh always sounds like he's having a much better time than anyone else in the room, and it makes me want to join in as soon as I hear it. In this picture, his light brown hair is spiked up in a faux hawk and his black glasses are sort of slipping down his nose, his eyes are crinkled on the side just enough, and he has this huge, genuine smile on his face. He's absolutely beaming. I love this picture because it's totally natural. I know this is how Nick looks when no one is watching.

Lo peeks over my shoulder at the image on my phone, then looks at me, her mouth hanging slightly open.

"How have you not driven to Vegas and jumped his bones before now?"

"I don't know, okay? It's seriously not like that with us."

"Let me see more pictures," she says. "You know, so I can help you spot him." I hand her my phone so she can scroll through the pictures herself. "Not that we'll have any problem finding the hottest guy in the room. Jeez, Hannah. I don't know why you don't go for guys like this at home. Your usual guys are so boring."

"Fine. I get it. I'm stupid."

"I'm not saying you're stupid. I'm saying you better not mess this up tonight." She hands back my phone. "Let's find a place to strategize. It looks like we have about thirty minutes until the show starts."

We push our way through the small groups of people gathered so far. Grace always says most people don't care about the opening bands, and these kinds of things don't get packed until closer to when the opening act starts. I wonder if these people here are friends of Nick's and of his band. It's a bit dark for me to recognize anyone from the pictures I've seen, but I search the faces anyway.

"Is he here?" Lo asks as we move through the tiny crowd.

"I don't see him." I try to play it cool, but the thought of seeing Nick for the first time, *really* seeing him, has me so undone, I don't think I can actually get words out. I wipe my sweaty hands on my jeans again and turn to face her.

Clearly my nerves are written all over my face, because Lo grabs my shoulders and pulls me close. "You can do this," she says. "It's obvious how he feels about you. Seeing you here will absolutely make his life. You know that."

Somewhere in the back of my head, I do know that. In the place where I keep our whispered late-night phone conversations; all the secrets he's shared with me, like the constant tensions with his brother; and the softness in his voice when he calls me Ghost. I try to hold on to these things I know, but the part of my brain that wants to tell me what a mess I am won't shut up. *You are wrong, Hannah,* it says. *He's going to be embarrassed. You are ruining everything. Leave now before you eff things up.*

I try to smile at Lo.

"You look like you're in pain," Grace says as she squeezes up behind Lo, drink in her hand. "Nick's not going to want to make out with you if you look like you're about to throw up on his shoes." She jerks her head down to the stage area, where there's an empty space off to the side.

The three of us maneuver through the small crowd and gather in a circle.

"Okay," Grace says. "We need a plan of action."

"I think it's important you see him before he sees you," Lo says. "That way you won't be taken by surprise."

I nod, still unable to talk.

"That's why this spot is perfect." Grace sucks up a long sip of her drink. "We're sort of in the corner, so we can see everyone. Ideal for spying."

"And we have a good view of all the hot messes," Lo says. "Look at that guy over there. I hate when guys think basketball shorts are acceptable attire for going out in public. Dude, you look like you're in pajamas. Put on some real pants, por favor."

I tune out their color commentary as I scan the stage and the crowd. Guys wander across the stage to set up the equipment for the first band, which has to be Automatic Friday. I don't recognize any of them at first, but then a dark-haired guy walks out with a guitar, and I know right away who he is. I would know even without the horrible '80s hair.

"That guy!" I whisper-yell, and point to the stage. "That's Oscar. He's Nick's best friend."

"Which one?" Lo asks at the same time Grace says, "The one in the Volcom shirt?"

"Yup. Oscar Patel. He plays bass. He speaks three languages. He has a cat named Mando. He's terrified of heights." I could rattle off the other random Oscar trivia I've acquired through Nick over the years, but I'm overcome by the large stone in my belly again. Oscar is here, right in front of me. That means Nick is in this room. Somewhere. I try to take a deep breath, but I choke on it and end up coughing for several seconds before I can breathe again.

Lo smacks her open palm on my back. "You're a mess."

"So if Oscar is here, then Nick is here somewhere. He has to be." Grace takes another big drink and shares it with Lo as I keep searching the crowd. Will he be wearing a hat? Will he be wearing his lucky vintage Rage Against the Machine T-shirt? Will he have his glasses on tonight? Will he look the same in person as he does in all the pictures he's sent me?

"I think that's him!" Lo squeals, and I follow her finger across the room. Now on the stage, behind the drum kit, is Nick. Rage T-shirt with a hoodie and a leather jacket layered over it. Brown hair messy and sticking up everywhere, exactly like in his pictures. Glasses. Look of concentration as he works hard to set up something or other on the drum kit.

It's him. In real life.

The world around me screeches to a halt, and my mouth falls open. I tried to prepare myself, and even hoped a little, for the possibility he might not be as cute in person as he is in his pictures. But the thing is, it's the opposite. He's even better, completely gorgeous with his mouth twisted up as he screws the cymbal thing onto its stand.

Nick. Right here. Four years of friendship and online chats and late-night phone calls, and here he is, across the room from me, more real than he's ever been.

"Stop staring and go say something to him," Lo says.

"There's a barricade in front of the stage," I say. "I can't—"

Grace leans over and pushes me on the shoulder. "It's not a brick wall. He can still see you. Go," she says. "Go now, before the show starts."

I don't know if I can make my legs move, because that negative voice in my head is back and louder than ever. What if he doesn't care? What if he's mad I'm here? But I have to see him. I have to talk to him. After all this time, at the very least, I need to stop being a ghost.

"Here we go," I mumble, and start toward the stage. I figure I'll go up to the barricade and call his name and then . . . see what happens. Maybe he'll pick me up and twirl me around. Maybe he'll even kiss me right then and there. I can't keep a smile off my face at the thought of it.

Lo and Grace shout out encouragement, and I will one foot in front of the other until I'm almost there, and then— . . .

And then a girl walks out from backstage. A tiny girl with red hair. Not ginger red, but red like a crayon, dyed herself, probably, in some sink or bathtub like Grace this morning. Tight jeans, a loose T-shirt—but not so loose that you can't see her huge boobs— she looks the part of hipster or groupie or *oh, I'm with the band* girl. And this ridiculously cool-looking tiny girl with her red hair, she walks up behind Nick and she wraps her arms around his waist. Then she leans forward and kisses him on the neck. And right as she does this, he smiles, probably at the weight of her leaning on his back and the brush of her lips on his skin. And as he smiles, he looks up, straight into the crowd. Right at me, standing there at the edge of the barricade like an idiot, mouth open in horror as I realize that Nick has a girlfriend.

CHAPTER
8

Eyes locked, Nick and I stare at each other for several seconds or hours or eternities before either of us makes a move.

Actually, it's the girlfriend who breaks the gaping silence.

"Oh my God, is that Hannah?" She untangles her arms from Nick's waist and scurries to the edge of the stage, where she bends down and gets right in my face. "Hannah! You're here! I've heard so much about you!" She hops off the stage and pulls me into a tight hug over the barricade. "It's awesome to meet you. I'm so excited!"

I stand there and let this tiny girl who knows my name hug me because I don't know what else to do, but my arms dangle limply by my side and I'm still staring at Nick, who looks as shocked and confused as I feel.

The girlfriend pulls away, but she doesn't stop talking. "I am so sorry. How rude am I? I'm Frankie, Nick's girlfriend."

I fight the urge to throw up in my mouth when she says it out loud. If there had been any doubt about my feelings for Nick, the fact that meeting his girlfriend is making me want to empty the contents of my stomach pretty much cements that.

"Nick didn't tell me you were going to be here." She looks back at Nick, and I guess she sees the shock on his face that matches mine, so she finally catches on. "Oh snap, was this a surprise? Yay!

I love surprises!" She pulls me in a hug again—freaking A—and jumps up and down. I still don't hug back. This time I swivel my head toward Lo and Grace, and I find them staring at us, mouths agape. There's hardly a closed mouth in this place.

"This is killer," Frankie cheers. "I'm so happy you're here."

I'm trying to make sense of what is happening, but the inside of my mind is like a bounce house, thoughts flying everywhere. Who? What? By this point, Nick has walked to the edge of the stage, but he's still silent, his eyes open wide in shock and his mouth opening and closing like a caught fish thrown on the deck of a boat.

Finally, Frankie gives me back my personal space. "Nick, I can finish setting up the drums. You two need to talk!" She holds her hand up to him and he pulls her back onstage, where she jumpy-claps, kisses him on the cheek, and walks back to the drum kit to keep doing whatever it was Nick had been in the middle of.

That leaves me and Nick alone, still gaping at each other. He's up on the stage, towering over me, so he jumps down so we're facing each other.

He's right here. Right in front of me. After all this time.

And he has a girlfriend.

"Ghost," he says, his voice sounding so very much the same, like it always has in my ear during our long conversations. But so different, too, without the phone or computer humming between us. I consider digging in my pocket and showing him the penny, just to do something, to say something. But before I have a chance to make a move, he hops the barricade, pulls me into him, and wraps his arms around me.

I'm fighting anger and disappointment and denial and a deep, aching sadness, but as soon as Nick touches me for the first time, all those feelings disappear somewhere and I'm left with how ridiculously perfect he looks and how seeing him in real life is the answer to so many questions I never realized I'd been asking myself. I lean my head into his shoulder and wrap my hands tightly around his back, feeling him for the first time. The leather of his jacket is soft under my fingers, and he smells like hair product and some clean-guy smell. He is real. A real person in my arms, and not just a voice on the phone or a name on the screen. "Hi," I say into his jacket.

I want to stay here in his arms all day, and from the firmness of his hands on my back, pulling me close, I get the impression he wouldn't mind that one bit. I'm surprised when he pulls away, and he shifts around uncomfortably when I tilt my head up at him again.

"What are you doing here?" He sounds incredulous and his voice is low, but it's not like anyone is around us, and even if they are, they wouldn't be able to hear over the loud music pumping through the room.

I shrug, and I bullshit. "Grace got this opportunity to come out here for her internship." Lies come out even easier now than they did with the bouncer outside. "It was a last-minute thing, and . . ." Without thinking, I reach out for his hand to squeeze it, but the second we make contact, we both pull away quickly. I look at my hand. I'm not used to having this kind of contact with him while we talk, and I can't handle it. He's too real. So real, it hurts. ". . . I thought I'd surprise you."

Nick's face twists up, and he runs his hand through the side of his hair, messing it up even more. The air between us shifts, and the warmth and comfort are replaced by a chilly polar vortex. Weird. While just a minute ago, hugging him and reaching for his hand felt like the most natural thing in the world, like breathing or talking, now there's something cold between us, making that breathing a struggle or that talking muffled and difficult. What changed?

"Um." I start blabbering in hopes of getting us back to where we'd been a minute ago. "I'm excited to see the band." I smile, but that makes him grimace for some reason, and the weirdness becomes blocks of ice stacking up like a frozen wall. "And, uh, Frankie seems nice." "Nice" is one word for her. "Insane" is another. "Huge freaking unwelcome surprise" is also a solid choice. "How long have you, uh—?"

"About three months," he mumbles. He shoves his hands in his pockets and looks at the ground.

Three months. For three months, he has had this girlfriend and he never mentioned her. Three months, he's kept this secret. He's lied. I told him about Josh the night we made it official. I told him about every boyfriend I've ever had. I can't even imagine keeping a secret like this from him.

"Wow. Three—"

I need more information, but he turns to the stage—where Frankie is still busy setting up the drum kit—cutting me off. "She's great."

"I, uh . . ." I don't know what to say. Of everything I'd been expecting when we met, I never thought we'd have trouble talking. Talking is the thing we do best, the thing we can't stop ourselves from doing. Somewhere in the back of my head, I thought maybe our meeting in real life would be uncomfortable, but I never, never imagined not being able to talk to him.

The startling distance stings in a dark place deep inside me. I catch him looking at the stage again. Frankie. This is her fault. This stupid girlfriend.

I decide to hate her.

"Well, I guess I'll let you get ready for your show." Leaving isn't what I want to do, but I have to get away. This isn't how it's supposed to be, not at all, and I'm irritated with both of us. "I'm over there." I wave my hand toward our corner, where I know Grace and Lo are watching all this go down like it's some trashy reality show. "If you want to talk afterwards or have anything else you want to tell me."

As soon as I turn around to walk back to them, I feel my face crumple. I want to go back to five minutes ago and do this over. Or go back to six minutes ago and not walk up to the stage. Back to yesterday and never make this awful decision to ruin our friendship—or three months ago and take back what I said to Nick that time he drunk-dialed me.

Damn you, time travel. Why can't you be possible?

"What's he doing?" I say as soon as I get back to them.

"What the hell happened?" Grace asks.

"What is he doing?" I hiss through my teeth.

"He was staring at you with his mouth open when you walked over here," Lo says. "Then he went back on the stage, and now he's talking to that Oscar guy. Oooh. It looks like they're fighting or something."

"What—the hell—happened?" Grace asks again. "Who is that girl?"

I let out a long, pained sigh and cover my face with my hands. "That's his girlfriend. The chick with the red hair and the huge boobs. Her name is Frankie and they've been together for three months and she's like an Easter Peep on speed and she's his girlfriend."

"Oh shit," Grace says. She's on her second drink, and she sucks it down like she's on a deserted island and it's the thing standing between life and death. "That's unexpected."

"It's awful." I uncover my face to look at them. "It was so good for a minute. He hugged me and it was amazing. But then it got all weird and neither one of us knew what to say and he probably doesn't even want me here so I freaked out and left and now he's probably never going to talk to me and I ruined everything."

Grace frowns. "First of all, you ruined nothing. You're not the one with the secret girlfriend, so don't blame yourself. Second— here. You need this." Grace hands me her drink.

I consider waving it off, but I change my mind and take a big sip. Drinking wasn't on the to-do list today, but neither was Nick's having a girlfriend, and Grace is always telling me I need to be more flexible. The taste of lemon-lime soda mixed with rubbing alcohol fills my mouth, and my whole body shakes as I force it down.

Fake IDs and booze in one night. I don't even recognize myself right now.

"I don't feel better yet," I say as I hand the glass back to her.

"Okay, don't turn around," Lo says. I turn my head back toward the stage, but Lo grabs my arm and yanks me forward. "I said don't turn around. Jeez, follow directions."

"What's happening?" I can't keep the panic out of my voice as I imagine every worst-case scenario—which, apparently, had all been lurking in the shadows of the sunshiny best-case scenarios I daydreamed for the past few years. "Is the band packing up and running away before I notice? Or is he kissing that girl right there onstage?"

"No." She leans into us, like there's some chance Nick and the people onstage might hear her. "He's still arguing with that Oscar guy. And Oscar was totally looking over here and pointing." She chews the side of her mouth. "Oscar is super hot, by the way."

"Can I turn around now?" I look at the stage without waiting for an answer. Nick's back is to me as he waves his arms around; his posture and body language scream upset or annoyed or wanting to be anywhere but here. Oscar laughs. My heart sinks to the basement of House of Blues.

"Look, he's trying to figure out how to get rid of me." I turn back to the girls. "Should we go? God, I've made such an ass of myself already, it's obvious he doesn't want me here."

"No way, man," Grace says. "We came all the way out here. We listened to you go on and on about this guy for four hours in the car. And, hell, we've been hearing about him for years now. We are staying for this show."

"But—"

"No buts, Hannah. So things didn't go the way you expected. Deal with it. You aren't throwing away four years of friendship because of one uncomfortable conversation."

"And a girlfriend," I say.

"So he has a girlfriend," Lo says, patting my shoulder. "Whatever. I'm sure he's had other girlfriends since eighth grade, right?"

He has had several girlfriends, like I've had several boyfriends. But those girlfriends of his never bothered me. Partly because he never told me much about them until after it was over, so the focus was on why they didn't work out, and partly because I didn't think of Nick that way. They were just girls; they weren't competition.

But this girl? I don't know anything about Frankie yet. He's never mentioned her, not even once, so I have no idea if they're serious. If she's actually competition.

And he was mine first.

"Yeah, but—"

"Good," Grace says. "You dealt with it then and you're going to deal with it now. Put on your big-girl panties, watch this show, cheer for your friend, and talk to him again when they're done playing. I bet things will be a lot better then, and you can figure out WTF he's doing with a girlfriend then."

I hate when my wild sister is the voice of reason. But she's right—I can't leave. Not like this.

"You know you want to hear him play those songs," Lo says.

And that's what keeps me here. I do, more than anything. I want to see if he looks at me when he plays. I know Jordy is the one who writes the songs, and sings them, but I feel such a connection to the lyrics, I do need to hear them live, just to settle something in my soul.

"Fine," I say, covering my face with my hands again. "One song."

CHAPTER 9

THREE MONTHS AGO

There's a Nick story I didn't share with Grace or Lo. I've kept it to myself because I've never been sure what it meant, and I know I'll never share it with them because I realize, after Frankie, after the weirdness, that it doesn't matter.

About three months ago, I was in the middle of a dream about going to Berkeley, but Berkeley was on a tropical island and I went to all my classes in a coconut bra that kept slipping down, when something jolted me back to reality.

My phone.

Nick's ringtone.

I shot up in bed and felt around my bedside table until my fingers landed on my phone. I didn't know what time it was, but I had been well into my dream and it was still pitch-black outside, so it must have been the middle of the night.

"Nick? What's wrong? Are you okay?" I figured the only reason he would be calling so late was because he was dead on the side of the road or something.

Loud noises blasted through the phone. "Ghost!" he yelled over the din. "I'm going outside so I can hear you. Hold on." Shuffle, shuffle, loud bang, and then the background noise faded away.

"Where are you? What's going on?"

"I'm at a party. I'm at Jeff's party."

"Are you okay?"

"Yeah, I'm fine. I'm fine." His voice sounded all mushy. Drunk. "I texted you before. I texted you. Did you see my text?"

I looked at my phone and saw a notification for three new texts in the corner of my screen. "I must've slept through them," I said, yawning. "What did you want?"

"I just wanted to talk to you," he said. "Let me sit down, hold on." More shuffling on his end, then a loud thump. "I dropped you! I dropped you in the grass!" His voice was distant. "I can't find you. Say something so I can find you!"

"Nick," I said as loudly as I could. My parents aren't the deepest sleepers, and explaining this middle-of-the-night phone call would not be fun. "Nick, I fell in the grass. Pick me up!"

"I'm coming," he said, sounding closer. "Here you are! I got you!" His voice was clear in my ear again. "Why are you trying to run away from me, Ghost?"

"You know how clumsy I am. Can't take me anywhere."

He was silent for a few seconds, so I tried again. "Is everything okay, Nick? Do you need something? Do you have a ride? I don't want you driving home like this."

"I'm not driving. The band played at the party. Alex is here. He's driving me home. He's not drinking. But he's, uh, busy right now. Busy with some girl. I don't know. They're in Jeff's bedroom. Jeff is pissed. You know how Jeff gets."

"Not really. I don't know Jeff." I was annoyed to have been woken up, but not enough to hang up on him. Drunk Nick was entertaining.

"No, you don't, Ghost. You don't know my friends. Because you are a ghost. Why are you a ghost? Why aren't you here? Why are you so far away from me?"

I rolled over on my side, pressing the phone closer to my ear. "Because that's how it is. You live in Vegas and I live in Orange County and there's nothing we can do about that."

"It's not that far, Ghost. It's not that far."

"It's four hours in the car. It's across a state line. That's a long way."

"I would do it right now, you know? I'd get in a car and drive four hours to see you. I want to see you so bad, Ghost. I would drive there right now."

Something inside me tingled, and the hairs on my arms stood straight up. He'd never said anything like this before. When our Barstow meeting fell through, we never spoke of it again, understanding it was a distance we couldn't logistically deal with. We both agreed anything more than virtual friendship simply wasn't meant to be.

"You're not driving anywhere right now. How much did you drink?" Subject change, *stat*. This conversation was heading into dangerous territory, and there was no way I'd be able to maneuver around these land mines at dark o'clock in the morning.

"I had some beers. There's a keg here, but it's done now. The keg is done. And Alex made me take a shot or two of something because he said maybe if I'm wasted, I'll act like a normal person and stop being so freaking awkward all the time, or something. Something Alex-y like that. I don't know."

"Asshole," I mumbled. "Are you feeling okay?"

"Yeah, I'm fine." He let out a sigh. "You always take such good care of me, Ghost. Even on the phone, you always look out for me. You didn't get my texts? I texted you."

"I see them on my phone. Do you want me to read them right now? Or do you want to tell me what they said?"

"Read them later. I don't want you to hang up on me. Stay on the phone with me. Alex, he's trying to make some other girl jealous by hooking up with this girl. The other girl doesn't care, though. It's dumb. He's dumb." He laughed. "You're the only person I can talk to. Stay with me until Alex comes out of Jeff's room to take me home."

"Of course," I said even though I had no idea how long that was going to be. I fluffed my pillow and curled into a ball, propping the phone up so I didn't have to hold it. He launched into a rundown of the events of Jeff's party—who was hooking up, who was having drama, and who was a hot mess. Alex and the girl he was trying to make jealous. He always talked to me like I knew all these people personally, and by the end, I felt like I was there at the party.

"You should have been here, though, Ghost. You should be here right now."

"Mmmm." I was getting very sleepy now, but I forced myself to stay awake because I'd promised I would stay on the phone with him. My eyes fluttered closed, but I gave my head a small shake to force them open again. "Mmm."

"You should be with me, Ghost. We should be together, don't you think?"

My fluttering eyelids flew open. "Wait. Nick . . ."

"What?" He sounded genuinely confused about my reaction, as if he'd already forgotten what he just said. But I couldn't forget it.

And I didn't want him to say it again.

"Stop it."

Nick lowered his voice to a whisper that was almost conspiratorial, like he was about to fill me in on his top-secret plan for world domination and he wanted me to help execute it. "Don't tell me you've never thought about it, Ghost. Us. You know you have."

"No. I haven't." I shook my head even though I knew he couldn't see me. In fact, knowing he couldn't see me made me shake it harder, like my head shake in Orange County might butterfly-effect itself into a hurricane of "no" in Vegas. "I don't think of you that way, Nick. I never have. There's just absolutely no way."

It wasn't true. In fact, it was such a ridiculous lie. I'd been thinking of him that way more and more. But the lie was the first thing that came to my mind and my lips, and once it was out, I couldn't take it back. And that lie was an easier way to live, anyway. It made way more sense than the truth. I could never be with Nick. He lived hundreds of miles away, and it's not like I wanted some long-distance, online boyfriend. The way things were between us, friendship, *just* friendship, online, on the phone, video-chat friendship, was the only logical thing.

So I just kept word-vomiting out the lie. It's like I couldn't stop.

"I mean, I couldn't have more platonic feelings for you. You're hardly a dude to me. You might as well be Lo."

Nick let out a long sigh. "I get it. You don't have to keep saying it over and over." His voice was still mushy with beer, but it was resigned now. Defeated.

My emphatic insistence that there would never be anything between us was such a knee-jerk reaction, I didn't stop to think of how he would take my flat-out rejection of him. And when I heard that sadness in his voice, and understood it was my fault—well, for a second I considered taking it all back. Apologizing and saying, *Never mind. I lied. I'm sorry.* Because if a lie was making him sad, why not fix that with the truth?

But there was a commotion from his end of the phone, and the opportunity passed.

"Alex is done," he said. "I mean, he's here. He's going to take me home. I have to go now."

With everything hanging between us, I didn't know what to say. So I said, "Okay."

"Can we just—?"

But I didn't let him ask me if we could pretend it never happened. Things were already uncomfortable enough between us.

"Text me when you get home, okay? Let me know you got home all right."

"Nick! Hurry up!" Alex's yelling was so loud, I could hear it clearly on my end of the phone.

"I will. Um. Bye, Hannah." And before I could say anything back—tell him good night, give him crap for using my real name, make a dumb joke in a halfhearted effort to cut the weirdness between us—he hung up.

I sat up straight on my bed, blinking into the darkness and trying to process the conversation we'd just had. He was drunk—he was so drunk. His words were slurred, and he had no idea what he was talking about. Me and him together. There was no possible way he'd really meant it. Shooting that idea down right away was the only logical thing to do, the best way to avoid tomorrow's inevitable awkward conversation.

Right?

I looked at the time on my phone: 2:15 A.M. This was not the time normal people made phone calls to express their feelings. This was the booty call hour. It must have been the booze talking.

I clicked on my incoming texts. Three, and all of them from Nick at various points in the night.

At 11:57: YOU AWAKE, GHOST? THIS PARTY SUCKS. I WISH YOU WERE HERE.

At 1:03: WHY DO YOU HAVE TO BE SO FAR? THIS COUCH NEXT TO ME WOULD BE A MUCH BETTER PLACE FOR YOU TO LIVE.

Then, at 1:41: ME AND YOU. WHAT DO YOU THINK? ASKING FOR A FRIEND.

I stared at the screen of my phone, trying to make sense of any of this. Drunk texts should never be taken seriously. I learned that from being friends with Lo. I had to physically restrain her from texting at parties sometimes, because I knew she'd be telling all her exes nonsense she didn't mean at all.

That meant this, all of this, was nothing I should take seriously. And if it was nothing to take seriously, I shouldn't feel bad about lying to him.

Right?

Sleep was impossible after that. He texted me about fifteen minutes later to tell me he was home, but for the first time in four years, I didn't know what I was supposed to say to him. I replied with a thumbs-up emoji, like I usually did, and I tried to close my eyes, but my mind replayed his texts and our conversation and my reply on an endless loop.

My reply? Who was I kidding. My lie.

It took at least an hour before my mind calmed down enough to get sleepy again. I didn't get a restful sleep, though. I tossed and turned and half-listened for my phone, thinking he might call or text back with something more.

Thinking I might get a chance to take it all back.

The next morning, I knew I needed to say something to him, but I didn't know what. After hours of thinking about it and not

being able to concentrate on my homework at all, I decided to go
for it and text him.

HOW ARE YOU FEELING THIS MORNING?

There. Totally innocent, but opens a conversation.

I turned my phone over in my hand until he replied about a
minute later.

NEVER DRINKING AGAIN, BUT I'M ALIVE.
GOOD. I WAS WORRIED ABOUT YOU.
SORRY FOR CALLING SO LATE.
NO WORRIES. YOU KNOW I DON'T MIND.
THAT'S WHY YOU ARE THE BEST, GHOST.

I frowned at the phone. How was I supposed to respond? Did he
want me to say something about what he said? It would be best
to get it out of the way, move beyond it, get things back to normal
ASAP.

Before I could think about it too much, I typed

I KNOW YOU WERE DRUNK LAST NIGHT AND DIDN'T MEAN WHAT
YOU SAID, SO WE CAN FORGET IT HAPPENED, OK?

and hit Send.

Whew.

He didn't reply right away, which was odd because I got his
earlier texts almost immediately after sending mine. It took about
five minutes before my phone buzzed with a response.

OK was all he said back.

After that, just like Barstow, it was like it had never happened.

And just like that, I started living a lie.

CHAPTER 10

It takes about twenty more minutes, two more drinks for Grace, and three panic attacks for me before it's time for Automatic Friday to take the stage. I wrap my hair up into a bun and then shake it back out about seventy-five times, and I practically chew off my thumbnail. Lo and Grace, in an attempt to distract me, make up dirty stories about almost everyone in the place, and I try with every ounce of self-control I have not to look at the stage, run out the door, or cry about all the ways my most treasured friendship is now ruined.

It's damn near impossible.

My main focus is getting myself out of this situation. I'll watch the band play one song, then I'll tell Grace and Lo I drank too much or ate too much or whatever, and I'll cab it back to our hotel. I don't need to have this girlfriend conversation with Nick in person. And certainly not with her standing right next to us, big boobs all in my face.

Nick and I do everything else online or on our phones. This can happen there, too.

I'm trying to craft the perfect exit strategy when the lights dim and the cheesy pop-punk music shuts off mid-song. The crowd whoops halfheartedly and my phone vibrates in my back pocket.

I look at my text as the band takes the stage. It's from Nick.

I AM SO SORRY GHOST.

Sorry for what? For the weirdness? For Frankie? For keeping her a secret? I shove my phone back into my pocket in disgust, annoyed with the sight of his name on the screen for the first time ever.

My fingers drum my thigh as the lights go up onstage, and I feel a rush of excitement despite myself. Yes, I'm mad at Nick, but this music has been the soundtrack of my life for the past few years, and a thrill rushes through me at the thought of seeing the band perform live. Jordy the Player at the front; I recognize him right away from his tagged pictures on Nick's profile and the band's YouTube videos. He's wearing a T-shirt with the sleeves cut off to showcase the tattoos all over his arms, and a grin spreads over his face as he licks his lips and scans the crowd. He's loving this. There's Oscar with his bass draped over his shoulders, toe tapping the pedal at the end of the stage, '80s hair pointing everywhere. Nick was so right about that. On drums is their new guy, Drew: short, chubby, and not in with the rest of the guys quite yet. Then, on guitar—

"That's Alex." Grace grips down on my arm so tightly, I think she touches bone. "You didn't tell me Alex was in this band."

Sure enough, the guy plucking on the guitar isn't Nick. It's Alex, his older brother.

If I hadn't seen Nick already, if I had walked into House of Blues right as the band took the stage, I probably would've thought Alex was Nick. Same build, same height, same brown hair, and he's wearing a trucker hat pulled down low over his forehead, hiding the details of his face in the semi-dark, and a leather motorcycle-style jacket, similar to the one Nick is wearing, hiding the tattoos on his right arm.

But it isn't Nick playing the guitar. It's his brother.

The band launches into one of their faster-paced songs. Despite all the tats and ripped T-shirts onstage, their music is surprisingly mellow. They sound great live, and Jordy's gravelly voice totally pops in this small club. They've slightly changed the arrangement of the song "In My Head," one of my favorites, just enough to make it different from the recorded version I play in my room on repeat when I'm alone.

But what happened to Nick? Why is Alex onstage in his place?

"They sound killer, don't they?"

Somehow Frankie sidles up next to me. She holds a small tablet in her hand and a huge camera dangles from her neck. She's not looking in my direction, her focus is totally on the tablet as she taps on the screen, but I know she's talking to me because she's pretty much screaming in my ear.

"Yeah." I shake Grace's hand off my arm and shoot a look to her and Lo, both of whom are staring, confused, at the stage, exactly as I had been a second ago. "So, uh. Where's Nick?"

She places the tablet between her knees and squeezes them tight while she holds up the camera, snapping photos of the band in action. "Oh, he's out doing merch. The usual." She drops the camera so it hangs from its strap and picks up the tablet again. "Do you mind if I hang out here for a sec? You have a rad view of the stage, and I have so much crap with me tonight." She scoots in toward the girls. "Hey, I'm Frankie."

"Uh, this is my sister, Grace, and my best friend Lo." We're still screaming at each other over the music from the stage.

"Wait. Nick always does merch?" Grace asks Frankie.

But I don't even need to hear her confirmation to know it's true. I think some small, hidden part of me must have known all along.

Nick doesn't play the guitar in Automatic Friday.

Nick sells the T-shirts and sets up the drum kit.

That's what his "sorry" text was for. Not for Frankie or the awkwardness but for another lie. For telling me he was in this band when his brother is the one on the stage.

Without even thinking, I bolt from Frankie and the girls and weave through the people watching the band. Automatic Friday has now moved on to their second song after a loud "How you doing tonight, Vegas?!" from Jordy and an apathetic mumble from the crowd. I push through the people who are paying no attention to Jordy's earnest vocals, and I apologize for knocking into their drinks. I rush up the stairs, through the door, and out to the front of House of Blues, where Nick sits on a folding chair behind the merch booth, a pile of Automatic Friday CDs and Moxie Patrol T-shirts arranged on the table in front of him and a crumpled piece of paper that says TIPS APPRECIATED! THINK OF US AS BARTENDERS WHO GET YOU SHIRTS INSTEAD OF DRINKS! taped to the wall behind him.

He stands up when he sees me, but his face falls as soon as we make eye contact. "Ghost."

"Don't call me that."

He flinches like I slapped him. "Hannah, please."

I know I told him not to call me Ghost, but my real name sounds so foreign coming from his mouth. Hearing him call me Hannah hurts almost as much as the lying.

For the first time since he coined my nickname, I don't want him to use it. But I don't want him to use my real name, either. I don't want him to call me anything.

All I want is answers, and then I want to leave Las Vegas and never look back.

CHAPTER 11

"Were you *ever* in the band?" I point to the door that leads down to the stage, where "Free Fall," another one of my favorite Automatic Friday songs, is blasting, Jordy singing my favorite lyrics. But knowing Nick has nothing to do with any of this music makes it seem so far away, like a bad cover version. "Was it always Alex?"

"I am so sorry." His hands cover his glasses and run their way up to his sloppy hair. "I suck at guitar," he says. "I'm really terrible. At bass and drums and singing, too. And life."

"So why did you tell me you were in this band?" I struggle to keep my voice under control, but I can hear it wavering.

"Well, I never *really* told you. I said one time I was going to band practice and you sort of assumed."

"That's not my fault, Nick. You should have told me."

"No, it's not your fault. I didn't mean that." His voice shakes in a way I've never heard before. "I know I should have told you. I'm sorry. I just didn't know what to say."

"Say, 'Hey, Hannah, my brother is in a band, not me.' Say, 'I sell their T-shirts' not 'I play the guitar.' It's not that difficult. God, no wonder you would never play the guitar for me. Did you laugh at me every time we talked about this? Did you think I was that stupid?"

"Oh my God, no. It's not like that at all. I'm so sorry." He leans forward, flattening his hands on the merch table "Actually, there's something I've been meaning to—"

I shake my head and put up my hand to stop him. "You know what? No. I don't want to hear whatever it is you have to say right now. Just . . . don't."

"Please, I need to—" He must see something in my face that changes his mind, because he gives up mid-sentence and simply says, "There's no good explanation. I'm sorry."

"Stop saying that."

My heart aches with regret over every choice I've made in the past twenty-four hours as I stare down at the T-shirts on the merch table, including the one Nick sent me that I'd been wearing yesterday. I'm sick over every single choice that led me here, every rule broken, but most of all, I regret letting myself think there could be something between me and Nick if I came here. I'd kept my feelings for him so under control, so locked away, for the past four years. But I have this one moment of weakness, I give up control this one time, and this is what happens.

Disaster.

"And Frankie," I say, still focused on the T-shirts. "Three months? Why didn't you—?"

"I didn't know what to say," he says, his shaking voice barely audible over the music coming from inside. "I didn't think you would care."

"Why wouldn't I care? You're my friend. You've told me about your girlfriends before, Nick. I told you about Josh." I press my hands down on the merch table and look at him as I lean forward so I don't have to shout it. "I told you *everything* about Josh."

Then, as I am feeling my most vulnerable, with the conversation about Josh hanging in the air between us, Nick comes out from behind the table. I think he's going to hug me or comfort me in some way, so I brace my body. Flinch a little. But he doesn't try to comfort me at all.

He walks away.

I prepare myself to run as quickly as I can back to Grace and Lo and drag them out of this venue, out of this casino, out of this godforsaken city. Before I can do anything, though, Nick is back, pulling a floppy string bean of a kid behind him. "Mo," he says in a voice that leaves no room for conversation. "I need you to cover merch until Chang gets here." This no-nonsense voice of his surprises me; I've never heard it before.

Mo's thin mouth twists up in confusion. "But I don't know—"

"You'll figure it out. No one buys anything anyway." He turns to me. "I'm so sorry. I can't talk here. Like this. Can we go for a walk?"

The urge to run is still strong, but I want to hear what he has to say for himself, so I nod. He starts toward the makeshift exit indicated by the ropes we walked through earlier, and he leads me along, through the groups of people walking into the show, by placing his fingers gently on the small of my back. That light touch, only the second time we have touched ever, sends sparks of electricity up my back, and I hate how my body betrays me like that. *Stop that. He lied to us. We're mad at him.*

My body doesn't listen.

We pass back through the spot where Grace, Lo, and I walked in, and Nick gives a fist bump to Scary Bouncer. "Hey, man, we're going to be back in a sec. Is that cool?" Scary Bouncer looks me up and down and grins at Nick, giving him an affirmative nod.

Walking away from House of Blues doesn't mean it gets any quieter; we're still on the casino floor. Slot machines ring and clang. Drunk people stumble back and forth between the doors to the Strip, the gambling tables, the bars and restaurants, and their hotel rooms, yelling and cheering and having no idea my life is falling apart around me.

"Um. Can we sit?" He motions to the chair attached to a *Wheel of Fortune* slot machine.

I lower myself into it carefully, and he flops down into the one next to mine.

A tentative smile spreads over his face, and he leans closer to me. "I can't believe you're here."

I glare at him. "Well, honestly, I'm sort of regretting it right now."

His smile drops away. "I'm sorry." He does seem to look sorry, but I'm not as familiar with his looks. I need to hear the regret in his voice to be sure.

"You said that already."

He makes eye contact and holds it. "I know. I just . . . I swear, I never meant to lie to you."

I do hear it in his voice. He means it. But lying isn't something you do by accident. Why did he do it?

"You know me, Ghost. You have to know that."

Goose bumps break out all over my arms, and I turn my focus to the elaborate, colorful pattern of the carpet. I open my mouth to say something—I'm not sure what, I just know the silence is killing me—but he continues before I can figure it out.

"And Frankie. I don't know. I didn't know how to explain her." His voice sounds sad, or maybe I'm imagining things. Although I know his voice better than I know anything else about him. "And after . . . Well, I didn't think it would matter all that much to you." He kicks the carpeted platform of the slot machine as he twists back and forth in the chair.

My first instinct is to yell out, *Of course it matters, you idiot!* But I remember that phone call, and how I told him I never thought of him that way and I never would.

God, what did I do?

"She seems nice." It's all I can manage. My brain works overtime trying to process all these new discoveries about the person I thought was my very best friend. Every mental picture I have of Nick involves him being in this band. Just like anytime I mention him, it's followed by, "We tell each other everything." I need a minute to adjust to a life where these two unshakable facts aren't true.

He stops swiveling in the chair and pokes absently at the buttons on the slot machine. "She is, Ghost. I think you'll like her."

I don't want to like her. I want to punch her in the face. I want to make her disappear so I never have to look at her funky style and big ol' boobs ever again.

He opens his mouth to say something, but then he closes it and keeps poking at the slot machine instead. The weight of this awkwardness between us is suffocating.

Our silences have never been like this.

"Are you going to play that or poke it to death?" I can't talk about Frankie anymore. I don't know if I have the words.

He shrugs. "Nah, I'm just— . . ."

"You should play it," I say. Play a slot machine, join a poker tournament, anything to change the subject. "You know you're feeling lucky."

"Not that lucky. I gave Alex the last of my cash so he could get Taco Bell earlier."

"I know you won't ask me for money since you just met me, but here." I dig in my pocket, pull out a five-dollar bill, and hand it to him. "Slot it up."

"Thanks." He smooths the bill out on his jeans before sliding it in the machine. "And, just met you? Please. We've known each other since middle school."

He's probably trying to break through the Great Wall of Weirdness by bringing up our shared dorky eighth-grade past, but it doesn't work. Instead we both watch in silence as the slot machine lights up and plays music. He pushes the large button on the bottom, and the three wheels spin around. BAR, 7, and the space between a BAR and a 7. Nothing.

He continues poking at the slot machine, and I can feel it between us. The distance. We were good for that moment when he hugged me. When, for just a second, the rest of the world dropped away and we were just us. Normal. Like the usual Hannah and Nick, talking until the wee hours of the night. Best friends. But then Frankie and now the band and the lies and weirdness keep getting bigger and bigger. They have created this impossible distance neither of us can cross. I'm not sure what to do. Or what I want to do. Can I still be friends with him?

Do I still want to be?

He's laser-focused on the wheels spinning around inside the machine, and I'm so flooded with weirdo, conflicting emotions, I can't even sit still. I shift to one side of the chair as I imagine myself punching him in the face and kicking him in the balls for lying to me, and then elbowing Frankie in the gut for good measure. I shift back to the other side as I picture myself reaching over right now and smoothing down his messy hair. I scratch the back of my leg with the toe of my shoe as I plot a way to quietly sneak away and have some time alone to figure out how I'm feeling, but the slot machine dings. He has some matches, and the number of credits on the screen in front of him increases. "I wish coins actually fell out the bottom like on TV," he says absently, looking over at me with a smile that is small, but reaches all the way to his eyes under his black-framed glasses. "It seems so much more satisfying, don't you think?"

I don't mean to, I don't want to, but I completely melt at his little smile. One stupid smile and my stomach drops out from under me and I feel out of control, like I'm falling from a great height. God, I'm being so ridiculous. I've never lost control of my feelings over a guy like this before.

"So, are you mad at me, Ghost? If you are, it would kill me, but I understand. I'd be mad at me, too."

I cringe.

Grace gave me plenty of lessons about guys over the past few years, both directly and indirectly. She'd sit me down in her big-sisterly way and tell me, "Watch out for guys who don't want you to hang out with their friends," or "Never trust a guy who is more attractive than you are—you should be the hot one in the couple." And I'd sit back and watch how things slowly went wrong with her own relationships and try to figure out why. I know it's nerdy, but I had a list saved on my computer because I wanted to make sure I didn't make the same mistakes she did. I didn't get to see the slow breakdown of Grace's relationship with Gabe, because she was away at school, but I feel like their matchy-matchy G names were the first hint of impending disaster.

She had this boyfriend in high school, Sam, who was not only better looking than she was (he was better looking than pretty much everyone), but he was also a smooth talker. Mom and I always knew he was saying exactly what Grace wanted to hear, but what he was actually doing was manipulating her into doing what he wanted. Grace never saw it, though, and thought everything Sam did was The! Best! Ever!

What Nick says about being mad at him, it sounds exactly like something Smooth-Talking Sam would say, and I realize this night is only going to get worse from here. The real Nick is not the person I thought he was at all.

"Ghost?"

"Sorry, I . . . For real? That sounds like such a line." I look around for a sign hanging from the ceiling of the casino that will point my way out of this disaster. "Look, this was super fun and all, but I'm going to go."

"Wait! Please!" He reaches his hand out and rests it on my arm before I can get up. "I'm messing this all up." He takes off his glasses and rubs his eyes, and when he puts them back on and looks at me I see panic in them. "Why didn't you call? Why didn't you tell me you were coming?"

"Oh, so you could hide everything so I wouldn't find out? So you could figure out who to be for the next few days?" Blood pumping, adrenaline rushes through my veins. I stand up; fight or flight is kicking in, and I'm tired of fighting. "I'm glad I didn't call."

"This isn't who—Oh my God! Look!" His slot machine makes noise and flashes. "I get to spin the wheel!" He moves to smack the big round *Wheel of Fortune* button with his palm, but he stops at the last second. "You do it," he says. "It's your money."

Unbelievable. I can't even yell and make a dramatic exit without getting upstaged. Of course he would win at a slot machine now.

"Whatever." I lean over and punch the button with my knuckles, and the wheel on the top of the machine lights up and spins. People walking by us stop to watch the wheel go in circles, spinning around, whizzing past different numbers.

Arms crossed, I drum my fingers on my elbow and wait for the flashing to end so we can say everything we have to say to each other and I can get out of here.

"Nick," I say, not even waiting for the wheel to stop spinning anymore.

"Hold on, Ghost," he says. He's on his feet and clapping. "Come on, wheel!"

The wheel slows to a stop and lands on 1,000.

One thousand credits. On a one-dollar machine.

It takes a few seconds of processing before this registers. "Nick!" I hop up and down. "A thousand dollars!"

He hops up and down, too. Then, before I even realize it, he reaches over to me, grabs my arms, and pulls me into him. So close, his arms tightly around my waist. I'm surprised for a split-second by the closeness, but then I let myself press into him. He lifts me up off my feet and twirls me around halfway before he puts me down.

I don't know if it's just because of his hand placement, but his fingers tangle up a little in the ends of my hair when he puts me down. Then they trail slowly down and linger for a beat or two longer than I expect on the small of my back.

This feeling, it's like nothing I've ever experienced before. Electricity races up my spine. My body lights up like the slot machine.

I stare up at him, waiting for something. For him to move or apologize or tell another lie. But he doesn't. He stares down at me, eyes locked with mine, and he doesn't move his fingers from my back.

And I'm stuck somewhere between hating him so much, I never want to see him again and never, ever wanting him to let me go.

CHAPTER 12

"What happened?" Frankie's voice surprises me, and Nick and I both jump. It's not that I'm super shocked to find her here. I know we left her back inside House of Blues, and it was a matter of time before Automatic Friday's short opening set was over. No, I'm surprised because of her tone. I mean, had I come out to the casino to find my boyfriend wrapped around some chick I'd just met, I'd have been spitting fire. But not Frankie. She doesn't sound jealous or pissed at all. She's just curious.

But I feel like I'm doing something wrong anyway, and apparently, so does Nick. And, so it seems, do Lo and Grace, who are standing behind Frankie with the biggest *WTF* looks on their faces.

Before Nick or I have to fumble to explain the intense moment we were in the middle of to a surprisingly un-pissed Frankie, Grace notices the wheel and points at Nick. "Mini Cooper, did you win a thousand dollars?"

"Well, it was—"

"Shut! Up!" Frankie crosses the space between them remarkably quickly for someone so tiny, and she throws her arms around his neck. "Dude, my boyfriend is such a rock star." Then she kisses him.

I look away. It's too much. How can he kiss her in front of me like that after the moment we just had?

And he's *not* a rock star, I think as I stare at the patterned carpet.

"This is perfect," she says. Since she's talking, I assume they are done kissing, so I turn back around. She leans against him, where I was a second ago, and I wonder if it's possible to literally choke on jealously. "Now we can take these girls out and show them a fantastic time in Vegas."

Nick looks at us all nervously. "Well, Hannah gave me the money, so she's the rock star in this situation." Then he laughs and looks right at me, and it's almost like the rest of the group disappears. "You're always the rock star out of the two of us anyway. Remember our 'art contest'?" He uses his fingers to make air quotes for those last two words, and when he says them, his voice changes. It's slight, and I don't know that anyone else would notice it. But it sounds so much more like the Nick I talk to on the phone than the one I've been talking to for the last thirty minutes or so. "Here I am with my stick people, and you're freaking Rembrandt all of a sudden. 'I can't even draw, Nick. Don't judge me!' Such crap, Ghost. Such crap."

I let out a little half laugh that comes from the back of my throat. "Hey, you challenged me and offered a prize, and I'm going to bring all my skills to the table when a Starbucks gift card is on the line. You know I don't mess around when it comes to coffee."

"Always so competitive," he says, taking a step closer to me. "You know I let you win."

"Now who's full of crap? You told me you got a C-minus in Art your sophomore year. Who gets a C-minus in Art? Bruce Lee could walk over a sketchbook with paint on his paws and get a better grade than that."

He shakes his head. "You promised you would never mention that again. You were supposed to take that to the grave. You traitor. You want me to bring up what happened when you tried to skateboard? Because I know you haven't told Grace about that, and I'd be happy to fill her in."

Our eyes lock and we're laughing out loud at our inside jokes and for a second it feels like things are normal between us.

But then, Frankie.

"Come on, Nick. If it's Hannah's money, then give it to her already, and let's get this night going."

I notice a look crossing over his face. It's so strange that as much as I know every nuance of his voice, I'm not so familiar with these expressions. We video-chat sometimes, but both of us prefer the phone or texting or even chatting online, him because his home Wi-Fi is slow and me because video is a little too real, so his faces are still new territory. This one seems pretty irritated. Probably about being forced by Frankie to give me the money. I bet he wants to use it to take her out or something a perfect boyfriend would do.

He takes her arm and pulls her close, leaning down and whispering in her ear. She shakes her head and says, "That's ridiculous." She's smiling, so I guess he isn't too upset.

I'm about to tell them both they can have the freaking money, they don't have to worry about the three of us, and they can go off and have their romantic dinner or whatever Nick wants to do with the winnings. I'd pay ten thousand dollars to get away from this barf-inducing little couple session. But before I say anything, Lo leans forward and whispers, "Don't you have to be twenty-one to gamble? Are you going to be able to cash that in?"

I look up at Nick, and he has the panic on his face that probably matches my own. He started playing with the slot machine to distract himself from the uncomfortable turn our conversation was taking. It didn't occur to either of us we would win any money.

"Never fear, minors. I'm twenty-one." Grace leans over the chair to the slot machine and pushes the blinking CASH OUT button, then grabs the ticket that slides out of a slot toward the top. "Stay here," she says. "I'll go hit up the cashier."

Grace wanders off into the depths of the casino, leaving Nick, Frankie, Lo, and me standing around, looking at one another. There's still some apparent tension between Nick and Frankie. Well, apparent to me, anyway, because I'm watching Nick's every move like a hawk. He's staring at the *Wheel of Fortune* slot machine like it's trying to tell him a secret, avoiding eye contact with both me and his girlfriend.

The awkwardness . . . it burns.

Frankie, in what I'm realizing must be her typical Frankie fashion, doesn't seem to notice the weirdness at all. She's pulled out her phone and is texting like a maniac. "Nick, I'm going to text the guys, okay? They're going to be pissed at you for not helping pack up the equipment, by the way. They can make Drew take it all home, though, since it goes in his garage anyway, and I know Oscar'll kill us if we go out without him. And didn't Grace say she knew your brother? Make sure you text him. This is going to be so fun."

"Ahhh, the mysterious Alex." I feel like I know him so well from Nick's stories. On one hand, he's the guy responsible for us becoming friends, so I'd like to meet him. On the other hand, all Nick ever does is complain about him, and I know they aren't exactly best of friends. How could Frankie not know that? And I don't know how Grace will feel about hanging out with him, since she pretty much never called him again after they got me and Nick talking, but whatever. It's Grace's fault I'm in this mess; I'll enjoy watching her squirm.

"Fine." Irritation is thick in Nick's voice, but he pulls out his phone and starts texting.

"Aww, look how cute the two of you are on your phones," Lo says.

That's all it takes for the jealousy flood to rush back over me. I glare at Lo, and she shrugs and mouths *"Sorry."*

Frankie doesn't look up from her phone, but she laughs. "I know, right? Nick texts like it's his job."

Nick's eyes meet mine, and he points at me and mouths, *"Texting you."* I smile, and Frankie, not noticing our exchange, just rambles on.

"And I have a blog, which I pretty much run from my phone and my tablet." Her tablet and her camera peek out of a black Moxie Patrol tote bag slung over her tiny shoulder.

"Oh yeah?" Lo asks. "What kind of blog?"

The opportunity to talk about her blog seems to pry Frankie's attention from her phone. "Oh, it's no big deal," she says in a tone that indicates the exact opposite. "It's a Vegas scene blog for teenagers. Like, all-ages shows, flash mobs, arcades, street fashion, fun things to do here when you're underage, stuff like that."

"She's practically a local celebrity," Nick says, quiet pride in his voice.

"Ah. Is that why you went for her, Nick? Trying to tap in on that fame?" Lo asks it in a joking way, but I want to kiss her for asking how they got together. That's why she's my bestie.

"Yeah, right!" Frankie starts laughing and has a hard time stopping. "Nick hates my blog. Hates. It."

"What? Why?" I'm surprised to hear this about Nick. As far as I know, he doesn't hate much of anything except yellow mustard, spiders, and eating food directly off a bone. And hatred definitely contradicts that pride I just heard.

"Why are you bringing this up now?" he says to Frankie, poking her playfully in the side.

"They asked," she says, throwing her hands up in surrender.

"She's putting words in my mouth. Her blog is awesome. She gets recognized everywhere we go." He shakes his head, smiling. "Don't let her act like this is some little thing, either. It's a full-time job. She makes more money from this blog than Alex makes bartending, and she has hundreds of thousands of followers. It's insane."

"No way," says Lo. "So you really are a celebrity. That's amazing. How can you hate on that?"

"Stop, you guys." Nick, looking ganged up on, adjusts his glasses. "I swear. I. Don't. Hate. It. I think it's fantastic. Truly. She's unbelievable."

She smacks his arm lightly, then leans into him. "Don't lie. You hate it." She breaks into a singsongy voice. "You don't like to sha-are me-ee."

This new information about Frankie annoys me even more. Not

only is she adorable and all punk rock, but she's also successful and ambitious and mildly Vegas-famous and let's not forget how freaking nice and welcoming she is. Gah. I'm trying to hate her over here, and the fact that she's thwarting my hate at every turn is making me want to hate her even more.

"There's a guy in L.A. with a blog like that," Lo says. "He does videos, too, and Grace says she sees him sometimes at—"

Frankie's face drops faster than the lever on the slot machine, and she holds up her hand as if she can physically stop this conversation. "OMG, don't even talk to me about Jay Bankar. That guy is the worst. He's—" She's interrupted by her phone making a noise, and the lightness pops back on her face as fast as it went away. She says, "Oooh, hold on, it's the sister of one of the roadies from the Killers," to us, and walks a few feet away to answer it.

"I can't believe she's Internet famous," Lo says.

Nick smiles, but there's something insincere about it. Before I can ask him for more information, though, Grace returns from the cashier with a handful of cash at the same time my phone vibrates in my pocket.

"We're in the money," she sings.

"*We* aren't," I correct her. "Nick is. That's his money."

"No," he says. "You gave me the five dollars and you spun the wheel. It's your money."

I know I should want my share, but I'm so annoyed with this entire night. If Nick and I aren't going to have a chance to talk this out, then all I want to do is go back to the hotel room, crawl under the covers, and try to forget about this debacle until it's time to drive home.

"Well, according to the State of Nevada, it's my money." Grace winks, but she divides the stack in half and hands it to each of us. "And Frankie's right. We should do something super fun with it. You won money in Vegas. It's a sign. What do you guys want to do?"

I remember my text alert and pull out my phone. It's from

Grace, who must have sent it when she was walking back from the cashier.

> I KNOW THAT LOOK ON YOUR FACE. I'M NOT LETTING YOU GO BACK TO THE ROOM.

Oh, how I hate my sister sometimes.

"The guys are on their way," Nick says, "and then, um, I guess we can figure out a game plan for the night."

"I bet she knows all the fun things to do, huh?" I give a friendly nod in Frankie's direction. I should get a freaking gold medal for the effort I'm making.

"Oh yeah," Nick says with a humorless laugh. "We can count on her to have an itinerary for us within the next ten minutes."

We decide to walk over to the diner and get a table there while we wait for everyone else to show up. In the end, everyone else turns out to be just Oscar and Alex.

Alex saunters into the restaurant, still in his trucker hat, looking so much like an older, dirtier version of Nick. Grace's face lights up when she sees him, and I don't even think she realizes that the first thing she does is tuck her Tiffany key necklace into her shirt. "Still hitting on girls at shows, Cooper?" she says in this flirtatious voice I've never heard her use. From the look on her face, I know there will be none of the squirmy awkwardness or "sorry I forgot to text you for the last four years" between the two of them I'd been hoping for. He sits down at the table, and she practically jumps into his lap.

Trailing behind Alex is Oscar, who yells, "You guys are paying for this dinner, right, moneybags?" He put on a hat—thank God he covered up that hair—and he slaps hands with Alex and Nick. Then he looks right past me and Grace and zeroes in on Lo, who is drooling over him like he's a walking, talking T-bone steak.

Now there are seven of us. Nick and Frankie, who is recognized by our server and given a free cheesecake. Alex and Grace, who haven't spoken in four years, and even then only knew each other for, like, three hours, but now look like they are about to tear each other's clothes off within minutes of being reunited. And Oscar and Lo, who attaches herself to him the instant he sits down at our table whether he likes it or not.

And me.

The cheese stands alone.

This is going to be such a suck-tastic night.

CHAPTER 13

The first thing everyone in the group can agree to do tonight is the roller coaster at New York–New York. Well, not the whole group. I don't want to go, obviously, but no one listens to the lonely single person when apparently Alex has been, like, dying to ride this dumb thing his whole life but has never actually come over here to do it and Frankie wants to write about it on the blog. Nick tries to stick up for me when I give a pretty enthusiastic, "Oh *hell* no!" but we're quickly outnumbered. So, we're headed for the stupid roller coaster, but I'm still planning my sneaky exit. There's no way I'm getting on that thing, and I'm out of here as soon as I find my opportunity.

New York–New York is not far from where we are, so we catch two cabs at the front of Mandalay Bay and have them take us up the Strip. "We should get a limo for the whole night," Oscar suggests as I slide in the cab with him and Lo. I was going to try to squeeze in with Nick and Frankie, but I figure being in a separate cab might give me a chance to get myself together and come up with an escape route from this nightmare. With how far off the deep end this trip has gone, I need a Plan G.

"We didn't win *that* much money," I say, even though I have no idea how much limos cost to rent for a night. Oscar already guilted us into paying for all the food at the diner; I wonder what other plans he has for what's left of our winnings.

"Nick doesn't care about the money," Oscar says. He and Lo moved to the back row of the van cab, leaving me alone in the middle seat. It looks like he isn't minding that attention from her one bit. Go, Lo. "And besides, Frankie's loaded. I bet she even knows some limo company that'll hook us up with a free ride if she mentions them on her blog. I'm gonna text her right now and suggest that."

Oooh, an opportunity to pump him for information about Frankie. I'm going for it.

"So, her blog is that big a deal?"

"Oh yeah. Did she tell you about it? She's pretty famous in Vegas. She writes about things and then they blow up. That's how our band got into the Battle of the Bands thing that got us this gig with Moxie Patrol at House of Blues. She saw us play at a party a few months ago and loved the band. She wrote a review on the blog and—*bam!*—we get an invite to this competition and our stuff is selling on iTunes and Moxie Patrol is talking about taking us along on tour this summer."

"All because of Frankie's review? Wow." Lo's fake voice, about an octave higher than her normal one, is in full force, the one she uses when talking to guys she's into. I call it her *look at me* voice. I'm glad she can't see me rolling my eyes.

"So is that when she hooked up with Nick? At that party?" His mention of a party a few months ago sends chills all over my body, and now I'm rubbing my arms even though it's warm in this cab. "Was this Jeff's party?"

The party he called me from? The party where he drunk-dialed me and kinda sorta hinted he might have feelings for me? The party where I shot him down and pretty much told him to forget it and never say that again and—oh my God, I totally drove him into her arms.

This is all my fault. Frankie and Nick is all my fault.

My heart beats triple-time as I replay that night in my head.

This wouldn't have happened if I'd just been honest with him. Or even said I would talk to him about it in the morning. Or said literally anything else.

"Yeah, and they hooked up right after that." Oscar says, "She goes to a different school, but we'd seen her around, and, of course, we knew who she was because everyone in Vegas knows who she is. Man, she had her sights set on Nick like you wouldn't believe." He laughs. "And that chick always gets what she wants."

"I noticed." I slump down in the taxi van seat, and I watch the bright, flashing lights of the casinos and the crowds of people on the street out my window. I was supposed to be coming up with a plan of action for the evening, but now I'm thrown off by the news that the casual lie I tossed out three months ago exploded into stupid drama this evening. But I'm reminded of my need to do something, anything, as we pull up at the entrance to New York–New York. The other group is waiting for us right outside the door, and we all walk in, couple, couple, couple, single.

New York–New York is designed to look like Manhattan, and even though I've never been farther east than, well, Las Vegas, I immediately feel like I'm in the Big Apple. I'm so caught up in gawking at the NYC-themed decor as we push through the crowds of people on the casino floor that I almost forget what we're doing there.

"Here we go," Alex says, pointing at an escalator. "Roller coaster is this way."

Ugh. The roller coaster.

I'm never one to make a scene in a group, so I try to figure out how to explain that a thousand Chippendales dancers couldn't drag me on this thing. I decide to wave Lo aside. "I'm not doing this," I whisper as we step onto the escalator. "I'm leaving." But she pays absolutely no attention to my protests. Instead she grabs me by the arm, pulling me up the steps of the escalator behind her to catch up with everyone else. "Lo . . . ," I say, but I don't follow that up with much of anything, since she doesn't seem to be listening.

I don't know why she's ignoring me. She's supposed to be here for me. I need her.

We catch up with the group inside an arcade, where the line for the roller coaster hides in the back. Lo is still pulling me by the arm, but eventually I shake free of her grip and slow down. I need a minute to collect myself. As we pass a row of claw games, I let her go even farther ahead of me. Folding forward, I grip my knees with my hands and suck in deep gulps of air. There's no way I'm getting on this death trap. I'll wait here on blessedly solid ground until they're done. They won't even notice I'm not there, and I can use this opportunity to cab it back to Planet Hollywood and crawl into bed, covering myself with hotel sheets and denial.

"What's wrong? You okay?"

I don't have to look up to know it's Nick, so I don't. I focus on the wild design on the floor; a cartoon decal of people having the time of their lives on a roller coaster car like a bunch of masochists. I stare and I breathe and I do not look at Nick, who is standing mere feet away from me.

Somehow the sounds of the noisy arcade become overwhelmed by the silence between us. I realize he's waiting for an answer and for me to get my shit together.

So am I, Nick. So am I.

Smoothing my hair back, I straighten up and put some sort of smile-ish arrangement on my face. "I'm good," I say. "Let's go." I don't know why I say that. I was seconds away from going back to the hotel. I have no earthly intention of getting on this roller coaster. Why do things I don't even mean constantly come out of my mouth?

Nick takes a step closer. Now it's like he's mere inches from me instead of mere feet. Oh, holy hell. "Don't lie to me, Ghost." He searches my face. "I know you better than that."

I open my mouth to throw back something snarky, like maybe *You're one to talk,* or even *Where's Frankie?* But he cuts me off before I can say anything, almost like he knows I'm about to downshift into passive-aggressive gear and wants to save me from myself.

"I know you hate roller coasters. You couldn't even get on the Dumbo ride at Disneyland." He laughs a little and shakes his head, like, *Oh, Hannah, you silly little girl who is scared of even the kid-die rides—how cute.* And he's closer. How did he get closer?

"That was freshman year." I take a step back. I can't handle his nearness. "Seriously, I'm fine. I can do this." What the hell am I saying?

He narrows his eyes at me, and the side of his mouth curls up in a smile. "Well, I can't." He waves back at the roller coaster line, which has absorbed our group. "I'm going to sit this one out. Come with me?"

I blink at him. "What?"

"I'm not feeling so hot. I think it's that burger I got at the diner. Not sitting well. I'm sure you don't want me puking on your sister, right? That would make a terrible first impression." He jerks his head in the direction of the escalator we just rode to get up here. "Let's stay on solid ground."

All the tension flows from my shoulders, and my clenched stomach unclenches. I'm not sure what's more of a relief, that he's getting me out of this or that I am going to remain panic-attack-free for the time being.

We walk back through the arcade, weaving around other groups who seem excited to get on this death trap. He swerves around an attached-at-the-hand couple, and his arm brushes mine, sending a path of hairs on my arm standing straight up. I'm struck with the urge to reach across the inch or two that separates us and grab his hand, his fingers, his wrist, something—but I know I can't.

The cab conversation with Oscar pops back into my head. Nick met Frankie that night, the night of that party, when I told him I would never have any feelings for him. I want to ask him about that. And we need to finish our conversation from earlier, when he was playing the slot machine. I'm still mad at him for lying, and I need an explanation. As much as I want to hide in the hotel, we have so much to say to each other. "Can we finish talking now?"

I figure we'll find a bench or sit at some slots right by the escalator up to the arcade and the roller coaster. Instead he says, "Follow me," and walks deeper into the casino.

"Where are we going?" He's walking quickly, his legs so much longer than mine, and I'm practically trotting to keep up with him.

"Let's get a coffee," he says. He knows coffee is my weakness. After a few minutes, we're in a food court area that, according to the sign, is supposed to look like Greenwich Village. We wander until we find a walk-up coffee shop, and he motions me into line. "Caffeine first," Nick says. "Then we'll talk."

He's behind me in the line, and there's no one after him. But he's standing close to me—so close, I can sense him against every part of me. Too close. The only part of him touching me is his leather jacket grazing my bare arms, but he might as well be pressed right up against my back.

I hold my breath. I can't help it.

When we're next in line, I scan the choices. But before I can say anything, Nick looks down at me and says, "Skinny hazelnut latte, right?" He's smiling, proud of himself for remembering my favorite. I'm so overcome with . . . something. With the feelings for Nick I've kept locked up in a box in my head. I thought I'd be able to take them out tonight, but I had to seal them back up. Now they're trying to escape again, and they are at odds with the part of me that's still so hurt.

All I can do is nod at him. He knows my favorite coffee. *It's just a little thing,* I tell myself. *Don't make a big deal out of it.*

We take our coffees to one of the little tables across from the shop. Even though I know we're in the middle of a casino and everyone we're with is still close by, on the roller coaster, I also feel like I do when we are on the phone. Like it's just me and Nick and no one else, and we're in this secret, private world occupied by only the two of us.

We sip in silence, but I know this time I can't sit around and wait for him to explain. I tried to let him go at his own pace back at the slots, and look where that led us.

"So," I say.

"I owe you an explanation."

"And there are no slot machines here to distract you."

He scratches the back of his head and looks down at the table.

"You have to admit, winning a thousand bucks was a pretty worthwhile distraction."

"I'm not complaining."

"Good." He looks up and smiles at me, and it's even better than in his pictures because the real thing comes with eye contact. I hold on to that like it's keeping me from flying out of my chair. Like it's gravity itself.

"I like this," he says, still looking right in my eyes. Still smiling.

"What?"

"You. In real life."

"I'm not a ghost anymore," I say. But as soon as it's out of my mouth, I regret it. I don't want my nickname to go away.

He shakes his head. "You'll always be Ghost." He lets a sigh escape as he pulls the lid off his coffee, then snaps it back on. "So, the band. I know you told me to stop saying it, but I am so sorry. I was never in the band, not exactly. But I was trying to be. Because I hated lying to you." He looks up from his coffee, right at me. Having his face in front of me while we speak is still so strange. "I know it sounds dumb, but some part of me thought if I told you this thing, it would force me to try to make this thing happen. Like, have you heard of *The Secret*?"

I couldn't help my surprised laugh. "Are you serious? My mom totally went through a *Secret* phase when she read that book, like, ten years ago."

"Don't mock me!" He's trying to sound offended, but he can't keep himself from laughing. "So, it's based on something called the 'law of attraction.' My government teacher is super into it. Like, if you imagine something being yours long enough, it eventually becomes yours because you attract it to you with positive thoughts. So I just thought, well, if Ghost thinks I'm in this band, then I'll think I'm in this band, and eventually I'll be in this band." I must be giving him the side-eye, because he says, "Okay, I realize it sounds completely ridiculous when I say it out loud."

"During all this visualization, were you ever actually practicing the guitar? Because that seems like it would be more useful than just thinking about it."

"Yes, smart-ass." He laughs again. "And I am part of the band in a way, even though I don't play anything. But I've been trying to be official, you know? I wanted to surprise you."

"So, you're part of the band because you sell the merch?" My heart beats a little faster, and I can feel my mouth curl up in confusion. "That's the surprise?"

"No, that's not it." His face clouds over and he looks off into the distance. "I can't do it now."

I don't really get what he means, but what I want even more is to get to the heart of this Frankie situation. I want to ask about her, but that'll involve bringing up Jeff's party and what he said to me that night. I don't think I can do that, so I focus on my coffee lid, trying to figure out how to bring up this subject.

Right when I decide to go for it and I open my mouth, he beats me to it. "So, Grace's internship, huh? That's why you guys came out here?"

I look up at him. *No. It's because I realized I'm in love with you,* I think. *But it's too late, and it turns out you're a bit of a liar, anyway.* Instead I say, "Yup. That's it. And Lo and I had no spring break plans other than Netflix."

We both look anywhere but at each other. I shift on my chair and he sips his coffee and I wonder if he's wondering why this is so difficult, like I am. Why our connection is so easy on the phone, but when you add eye contact and nearness and realness and lies, feeling normal becomes impossible.

"I'm sorry," he mumbles.

"What?"

"I'm sorry I'm so weird. When you got here. You . . . you took me by surprise. I wasn't expecting you, and I'm so bad at stuff like this. I had these plans for when we met for real. . . ."

He trails off, and I can't help but think about how this scenario went in my head the whole way out here—him twirling me around, kissing me. I wonder if his "plans" were anything like mine.

"Ghost," he says, and his voice sounds strained. It cracks a little. Then he reaches across the table for my hand and gently covers it with his, sending all the hairs on my arm straight up, lighting my skin on fire. "Ghost, I need to—"

But suddenly I don't want to talk to him about this. It's weird, because I had wanted answers. But the answers I'm getting from him aren't the ones I want to hear. He is different in person. He told me so, but I wasn't completely prepared for it. And I don't want to hear the story of how or why he started dating Frankie, I don't want to hear how he was planning on surprising me with some more Automatic Friday T-shirts or whatever, and I certainly don't want to revisit the night of the party and how I ruined everything. I can't handle any of this, and I want it all to go away.

"We should go." I pick up my coffee cup and stand. "They'll be waiting for us. And I . . . um, I think I'm going to leave, anyway."

"Wait. Ghost." He grabs my wrist. Not hard or anything; he doesn't yank me or pull me. But I wrench my arm away anyway because he took me by surprise, and I see his face fall. "I thought you wanted to talk."

I shrug. "Isn't that what we just did?" And I walk back toward the roller coaster and the group, leaving this real version of Nick, and my chance at any sort of explanation, behind me.

CHAPTER 14

We meet the group back at the exit to the roller coaster, and they're all talking about what a blast the ride was. "I can't believe the guy working the ticket counter recognized you, Frankie," Grace says, and Frankie waves it off with her hand like it happens every day that ends in a *Y*. Did they for real get on the roller coaster free, too? They weren't joking about Frankie being a local celebrity.

"That drop, oh my God," Lo says, clinging to Oscar's arm. I roll my eyes at her, and she winks in return.

I notice Alex reach over and grab Grace's pinky finger, and I feel a stab of jealousy. That should have been me and Nick, not her and Alex. I'm glad to see my sister having fun; she wanted to use this little getaway as a chance to forget about Gabe for a couple of days, and it looks like she's doing just that. I know I should be happy for her, happy she's forgetting her heartbreak and flirting with a hot guy, but I find myself narrowing my eyes in her direction without even realizing I'm doing it. *She's having my trip.*

Frankie bounds up to us from the back of the group. "Why don't you like roller coasters, Hannah?" She slips her arm through my elbow and leads me through the arcade.

Her friendliness takes me by surprise. I was so convinced she'd be irritated that Nick ditched her on the coaster to hang out with me instead, I can't think of anything to say for several seconds. "I . . . uh . . . they . . ."

"She hates the feeling of being out of control," Nick says, coming up on the other side of Frankie. He looks at me as he says it, like he's talking to me and not her. And again, I have to struggle to keep myself in check. How am I supposed to stand here with all these emotions in me like this? I have too many feelings to function properly.

"She can speak for herself. Jeez," Frankie says, playfully jabbing him in the ribs with her tiny elbow.

Nick shakes his head. "God, I know. I was just saying—"

Frankie doesn't give him a chance to finish. She circles her free arm through Nick's elbow, and the three of us leave everyone behind, walking through the arcade like we're just three best friends who pal around all the time. "Well, Boyfriend, that was very nice of you to sit out with her. Even though it did mean I had to ride the roller coaster all by my lonesome."

"But I bet you got to pull the bar all the way down around your waist. You're so tiny, you'd have flown out of the car if you sat with me."

This is the first time I see Nick being sweet and playful with Frankie, the way he always is with me on the phone, and their intimacy stings.

But why? I can almost imagine Grace asking me this. *He lied to you. He pretended to be something he wasn't. He kept things from you. Why would you want to be with a guy like that?*

How could I explain to her that despite everything that happened tonight, he is still my best friend? That I can't just turn off four years of friendship like a light switch.

I remember what Nick said a long time ago, how he is "bad at real life." I never really understood what he'd meant, and thought it was just a thing he said to people. I mean, he dresses the part of this smooth guy, with his messy hair and leather jacket-hoodie combo and skinny jeans. But being here with him in person, I think his "look" is all part of a costume. Like he's wearing a mask, hiding behind the band and his brother. The real him is private and awkward and bad at expressing himself, just like he told me he was.

So, which Nick is my Nick?

Frankie snaps me out of my thoughts. "It looks like we lost Grace and Alex." They've slipped into a photo booth, only their legs visible from under the bottom of the curtain. Grace appears to be sitting on his lap, and she giggles each time the flash goes off. I'm glad this isn't one of those booths that shows the photos on the outside, because the last thing I need to see immortalized on camera is Alex's tongue down my sister's throat.

"Let's take some pictures next!" Lo drags Oscar to the booth, and Frankie does her little jumpy clap.

"We can take pictures on our phones," I say. "We don't need to pay money to take them in a booth."

"But this is more fun, Hannah!" Frankie is trying so hard to be nice and get me to like her.

I almost feel bad when I scowl at the back of her head.

If we're all taking couple pictures, I'll be left out again. This is getting really freaking old, and I'm sick of complaining about it, but I'm also sick of it happening. Sick of being left out. Sick of following the rules and getting nothing for my trouble. Sick of being the only solo act here in a crowd of duets. I thought this trip would finally be my turn to get something to go right for me, but it looks like I'm more empty and alone than ever.

Grace and Alex step out of the booth, and their pictures pop out after a few seconds. Their heads come together over the strips and they smile, but then they both slip the strips into their back pockets, not sharing with us. Frankie pulls Nick into the empty booth after that, and I make a point to watch their legs. She's not sitting on his lap the way Grace was sitting on Alex's. But she does wrap one of her Chuck Taylors around his ankle. I try not to imagine what's going on in there, but I can't help it. My mind takes more pictures than the photo booth itself does, each image worse than the one before. Frankie kissing Nick. Nick kissing Frankie back. Of course they kiss. They've been together for three months. They've kissed a lot, I'm sure. And done other stuff.

No. No. No.

I grab Lo and yank her away from Oscar. "Do you think Nick and Frankie have had sex?" The one and only time I talked about the subject with him, he told me he was a virgin. There's no way he'd keep a huge status change like that from me. He *couldn't.*

But if he could keep Frankie from me, if he could lie to me about the band all this time, if he could keep these two parts of his life so separate, then how do I know what else he's capable of hiding?

Lo looks quickly at Oscar and jerks her head over to the side, and we scoot away from the group.

"Are you freaking out right now? Keep it together, Hannah." She wraps her hands around my arms and gives me a comforting squeeze.

"I'm trying, but I'm about to lose it. They've been together three months. Do you think they've done it?"

"Is that the kind of thing he'd tell you about?"

"He didn't even tell me he had a girlfriend in the first place!"

She gives me a light shake, and I glance over her shoulder and notice Oscar watching us.

She opens her mouth to reply, but I cut her off. "We'll talk later. They're coming out now."

Nick and Frankie emerge from the photo booth. Well, Nick emerges. Frankie explodes. I'm noticing she doesn't do things the way a normal person does. And she must feed off my discomfort like a parasite, because the more unsettled I feel, the more she's acting like this is the best night of her freaking life.

Oscar raises an eyebrow at Lo, and they take their turn in the photo booth. Nice to see she's having a good spring break.

Frankie takes her pictures from the slot when they pop out and hands one to Nick, who is standing near me but not too near, and is moving his weight from one leg to the other and back again. "Here're our pics, Boy-friend," she singsongs. "So cute, huh?"

I wince at Frankie's obnoxious—and totally uncreative—name for Nick as he scans the photo strip. I wince again as he smiles, then sticks it in his back pocket the way Alex and Grace, who are now tucked close together up against the back of the booth, whispering to each other, did with their pictures.

"Hello! Rude!" Frankie says, smacking his chest with her tiny hand. "Aren't you going to show Hannah?"

I'm about to tell her I'd rather ride the roller coaster naked than look at their photos when she shoves the strip in my face. Four coupley pictures of Nick and Frankie. Oh, boy. I take it from her hand, and while all I want to do is throw a polite glance at the strip and hand it back, I find myself studying it. I can't help myself. Nick looking so much like the Nick I know from our video chats and all the photos I've seen over the past few years. If I stare long enough at it, I can almost forget the Nick standing next to me, the one who kept secrets and has a girlfriend. Nick of the photos would never do that to me. Phone Nick would never lie.

Then there's Frankie. In one picture, Nick's eyes crinkle up as she kisses him on the cheek. In another picture, Frankie makes a crazy face at the camera while he laughs at her silliness. In the third one, they both have huge, over-the-top grins, eyes open as wide as possible. And in the last one, his forehead is leaned down to hers. Their heads touch and they're looking at each other seriously. It's an intimate picture. It makes me feel like an intruder.

I guess I am.

"Cute," I say, handing the strip back to Frankie. I want to turn to look at Nick, but after seeing that last photo, I can't handle it.

Frankie takes her phone out from her pocket and snaps a photo of the strip. "I'm posting this right now."

Nick groans. "Frankie, no. Please don't."

"Why? It's totally Insta-worthy. Look how perfect we look. And it's a great teaser for my recap of tonight!"

"Recap?" I ask.

Nick lets out a long, tortured breath. "Anytime we go out and do something, Frankie recaps it on her blog. Every single evening is written up and posted online in great detail. Complete with pictures."

"Even our dates!" Frankie says this like she thinks it's the best thing in the world, photographing and blogging every minute of their time together, everything she does. But one look at Nick makes it clear he doesn't share her excitement.

She's still captioning the photo on her phone when Lo and Oscar climb out of the photo booth. I wasn't even paying attention to their leg body language, but with the way Lo is blushing, I go ahead and assume there was some smooching happening in there. Great. Now I'm officially the only one not getting kissed on this trip.

Frankie doesn't even look up from her phone. "Boyfriend, you and Hannah should take some long-distance bestie pictures in the booth now!"

"Oh no, we don't need to," I say at the same time Nick says, "Uhhhhh."

She snaps her head up. "Come on, you guys. You have to." Then this tiny girl actually puts her palm on my back and pushes me toward the booth. "Go."

Nick and I shuffle over to the photo booth. "We don't have to do this," he mumbles. But he doesn't stop walking.

I cross my arms at my chest and stare at my shoes. "It's fine." I'm trying to come up with an excuse to get us out of it anyway, but then he clears his throat and I see he's already sitting there, waiting for me.

The inside of the booth is small, and the bench against the back wall doesn't leave much room for personal space. I can see why Grace was on Alex's lap. Nick scoots over and I wedge myself into the free space next to him, pressing my hip as close to the wall as it can go in an attempt to keep a little room between the two of us. I know how to diagram a sentence and solve differential equations and Photoshop an entire person into a club photo they were absent for, but I have no idea how to navigate being alone with Nick. Can I touch him? Should I be so close? Probably not, better scoot over more. Too bad I can't climb up the wall.

He leans forward and pushes three dollar bills through the money slot, and the directions pop up on the screen. There's a square our faces have to squeeze into so we can fit in the frame, and my deliberate space bubble means only half my head is going to show up.

"Scoot in," Nick says. "Pretend like you like me." I scoot toward him, and our legs smoosh up against each other from hip to knee, sending a lightning bolt through my body. Our arms smash awkwardly together, so he adjusts his shoulder, pushing his arm behind my body. I can feel him hesitate just slightly; then he moves his arm so it wraps around my shoulder and he pulls me even closer.

I die. Oh my God, I die.

"There," he says. "Much better, don't you think?" My heart beats like crazy, and I wonder if he can feel the vibration. I know this doesn't mean anything romantic, his arm around me like this. He's pulling me against him only so we both fit in the picture.

But knowing it doesn't mean anything; it doesn't change the way his body feels when it's so close to mine. Like pulsating energy and slow-burning fire.

He leans forward and hits the OK button, and the countdown to the first picture begins.

"What are we going to do?" I ask.

"Should have thought about that before I pressed the button, huh? The pressure is on!"

"Make a funny face, I guess." I put my hands on the sides of my face and push all the skin forward. Then I purse my lips. Nick squints, wrinkles his nose, and sticks out his tongue. But he pulls me closer again with his arm, and we both dissolve into giggles as the countdown ends, and I'm leaning my head on his shoulder when the flash goes off.

For picture two, I turn to him, hands raised in an attack position, and make a scary face. He puts his hands up to his cheeks and opens his mouth like he's screaming. Picture three, I snatch his glasses from his face and put them on, and we both put our hands under our chins and stare stone-faced at the camera.

"Last one," I say, handing his glasses back. Much of the weirdness we'd brought into the booth with us is gone now, and we're having fun, the way I'd always hoped we would when we met for real. "What now?"

I watch him in the screen as various poses run through my head. Finger guns, normal faces, peace signs. I wave my hands around in panic as the countdown gets smaller. He stares back at me via the screen, and the silliness of previous moments is gone. He looks serious now, which takes me by surprise.

Right when the countdown hits one, he curves his arm around my head gently, pushing on my ear so my head leans in close. The heat of his breath tickles my neck, and he softly whispers in my ear, "God, Ghost. You're even more beautiful in real life," right as the flash goes off and the booth snaps our final photo.

It's the only picture where I'm smiling.

CHAPTER 15

I don't want to leave the photo booth. The screen loops back to its welcome message, and I know it'll be less than a minute before our pictures pop out. We can't stay in here forever.

But I want to.

I had a glimpse of My Nick when I first said hi to him. When I hugged him and buried my face in his jacket. Then when we had coffee and he put his hand over mine. And I got it again just now, when he pulled my head into his and he whispered in my ear.

Tapping into that Nick is key. That Nick, who wouldn't get all weird; and that Nick, who would never lie to me; and that Nick, who would make me feel better about this incredibly bizarre situation we've found ourselves in.

But after he lets go of my head and leaves the photo booth, I realize that Nick has gone into hiding again.

I climb out of the booth and he's waiting by the slot for our strips to come out. When they do, he hands me mine, then takes a few seconds to stare at his.

"Our first picture together." He doesn't look at me, but he gives the strip a small smile. "I always wondered if we'd ever get one."

"Pretty fitting we look like weirdos in all of them, huh?" I try to joke because I'm still feeling the pressure of his hand on the side

of my face and the lightness of his whisper in my ear and the weirdness of this whole encounter.

He finally looks at me. "Not in the last one."

Of course, that's when Frankie bounds up to us. "Boyfriend!"
she calls again, making me recoil like I've been hit. Is she *trying*
to be that obnoxious, or does it come naturally for her? "Your brother
called Jordy and invited him along. He's going to meet us here in,
like, twenty. Want to Skee-Ball with me while we wait?" She notices the photo strip in his hand. "Look at this adorableness. You
two are the cutest pair of friends in the world." She smiles at me.
No, she beams at me. She's absolutely freaking thrilled that I am
Nick's friend and that I'm here. "What is he saying to you in this
last picture?"

"That I was glad she came out to surprise me." Nick's eyes lock
with mine, and he squints the tiniest bit behind his glasses. Is
that what he does when he's lying?

"Aww," Frankie says.

"Did Alex seriously invite Jordy?" The question feels completely
out of the blue, and the lightness in Nick's voice drops away. Before either Frankie or I have a chance to say anything, Nick yells
for his brother and stomps off, looking for him, leaving the two of us
alone.

"Those two. I swear. It's always something with them. I get it,
though. I have a twin brother, and he drives me bonkers." Frankie
crinkles up her nose at Nick's back as he walks away in search of
Alex. "Anyway. Wanna Skee-Ball with me, Hannah? We've hardly
had a chance to talk."

Spending quality time with Frankie is literally the last thing
I want to do right now, especially after what Nick said in the photo
booth. I want to find Lo and go back to the room and girl-talk out
this whole evening. It's bad enough we got dragged on this buddy-
buddy tour of Vegas without a chance to debrief, but she also had
to go pair up with Oscar and run off to who knows where in this
arcade, leaving me alone to get pounced on by Frankie. But I look
around and I don't even see Lo. Or Grace.

And there's some saying about keeping your enemies close or

something, so I should probably play nice with Frankie, even though I sort of want to drop-kick her across the arcade.

"Fine," I say. "Let's play." What else am I supposed to say?

Frankie has a pocket full of quarters, so she drops some into each of our Skee-Ball aisles, and the balls release along the side and slam down by my leg. I'm not big on these games, and I can't help wondering how many gross, sticky fingers have touched those balls. I wipe my hand on my shirt, like that'll help, and pick up the first ball.

I toss it up the ramp as I struggle to think of something to say. How do you start casual conversation with the secret girlfriend of the guy you think you're in love with? Luckily, silence doesn't last long with Frankie, and I don't have to come up with anything. "Well, the good thing about Jordy showing up is that it'll even up our numbers." She raises an eyebrow at me. "He's single, you know. Jordy."

"Oh, um." I'm at a loss for how to respond to this information. "I don't know if he's my type."

"Jordy is everyone's type. Trust me."

From the stories Nick's told me about Jordy's long list of girlfriends, I don't doubt that. "Yeah, the guy can sing," Nick told me once, "but he's only in the band to get chicks. And it works."

I pick up another ball, toss it up the ramp again, and it drops into *10*. I watch Frankie, and she lands the *100* without even trying.

"Nice shot," I say. "I think I'm pretty bad at this." I add Skee-Ball to my long mental list of things I plan on never doing again in my life.

Frankie laughs—at either my comment or my Skee-Ball score, I'm not sure. "Six years of softball," she says. "I have good hand–eye coordination. Comes in handy every now and then."

I figure getting her talking about her blog will be a good way to keep us from drifting into uncomfortable silence, so I open my mouth to ask her about it. But before I get a chance to say anything, I hear a squeal from behind us. "Oh my God! Frankie!"

We both turn around, and there's a couple standing there. They look to be about our age, and the girl jumps up and down while the guy looks bored and mildly annoyed. "I thought that was you!" the girl squeals again. "I told him, I said, 'Oh my God, I think that's Frankie over there, from *Underage Vegas*.' And he said it probably wasn't. But I knew it was." She turns to her boyfriend and pushes him playfully on the arm as he rolls his eyes. "I told you it was her!"

Frankie's face explodes with the biggest grin I've seen on her all night. "You read my blog?" she says in this "What? Me? Really?" voice. She told me she has thousands of followers and she's already been recognized twice in the couple of hours I've been with her. There's no way this is surprising to her every time it happens.

The girl, who introduces herself as Ashley, gushes to Frankie about her love for the blog, and how she was at the flash mob in the Barnes & Noble parking lot last month, while her boyfriend, Reese, a buff guy in a flannel, plays on his cell phone. Frankie beams some more, hugs Ashley, and then turns to me, holding out her phone.

"Hannah, would you mind taking a picture of me and Ashley? I want to put it on the blog."

I nod, and Ashley's eyes widen like she got dealt a royal flush. "You're going to put me on the blog? Are you serious? Did you hear that, Reese? I'm going to be on the blog!"

Reese shrugs and doesn't look up from his phone.

Frankie wraps her arm around Ashley's waist and smiles while I snap a picture; then she gives her fan a huge hug. I watch Ashley and Reese as they walk away, thinking about what a bizarre life Frankie leads, but she goes back to the Skee-Ball game like absolutely nothing happened.

She throws a ball, then turns to face me. "So, Hannah. Nick talks about you a lot, you know, so I'm glad we get to hang out. What's up with you?"

I find it odd she can transition so quickly back to normal conversation, but I go with it. "Well, what has Nick said?"

"Let's see. . . . You're his best friend. You live in Orange County. You have an older sister named Grace who once met Alex at a show, and that's how you and Nick met. You talk all the time. You're the smartest, funniest, and most driven person he knows. You're going to UCLA next year." She counts each fun fact off on her fingers. "Oh, and I've now learned you hate roller coasters and you're terrible at Skee-Ball."

It surprises me how much Nick has told her, like I'm an actual part of his life he wants people to know about. I share him with people in my world on a need-to-know basis only, and aside from my family and Lo, no one needs to know. It has never been much of a challenge to keep our friendship hidden from everyone else, and I like it better that way. I've justified the secrecy by saying he is too hard to explain to my friends, but the truth is, my friendship with Nick is different from the friendships I have at school. More real. And I think that's what I have trouble explaining, even to myself, so I don't share him

Ghost is his name for me, but it turns out he's more of a ghost in my life than I am in his. As much as I'm feeling like he's a different person on the phone, at least he considers me a part of his life.

"That about covers it. I'm not very exciting. No band or famous blog or anything." I look around the arcade for everyone else. Lo and Oscar are giggling over some claw game, and Grace plays pinball while Alex and Nick talk off to the side. Alex's arms are crossed over his chest while Nick's flap around like he's trying to fly.

I jerk my head over to them. "So, what do you think that's all about?"

Frankie shrugs. "Who knows what it is this time. Last week, they were playing basketball in their driveway and it got so heated, I thought it was going to turn into an MMA fight or something."

I'm about to abandon the Skee-Ball game—since it's not like I'm going to beat Frankie or get anything out of it at this point—and go sneak closer to Nick and Alex to see if I can hear what they're arguing about, when Frankie grabs my arm.

"Look, Hannah, I hope this doesn't sound weird, but I'm so glad to meet you. Don't laugh, but when I first started hanging out with Nick, I was a little threatened by you. It's never easy when your new boyfriend has this gorgeous best friend, you know? But he promised me there was nothing going on between you two, that you're, like, not even a girl to him. And I trust him. But it's so great to meet you and see how cool you are. It makes me feel like such a crazy weirdo for freaking out about it so much." She gives me the biggest grin in the world and then pulls me into a hug.

I try to hug her back, but her words are bouncing around in my head. *"You're, like, not even a girl to him. Nothing going on between you two."*

I can't believe I ruined things so much. I told him I didn't think about him like that and I never would. I told him he wasn't even like a guy to me. I waited too long, I ignored all the signs, and now he's stolen my line and he's moved on.

I came out here for someone who has absolutely no feelings for me anymore.

CHAPTER 16

We wait for Jordy outside the casino, on the bridge over the Strip that connects New York–New York with MGM Grand. It's sort of surreal, standing on a bridge with cars going under us, a replica of the entire Manhattan skyline on one side, and a ginormous golden lion on the other. But my entire time in Vegas so far has been surreal, so the scene is fitting.

Down the Strip, away from Mandalay Bay and the pyramid of the Luxor, I see the bridge in front of New York–New York on my left and the Eiffel Tower at Paris Las Vegas, a giant Coca-Cola bottle, and Planet Hollywood on my right. The rest of the casinos spread down the street, one bright blur of lights I can't separate from each other.

"Impressive, huh?" Nick joins me in looking out at the lights. "It's weird. It sorta seems like it goes on forever, but it also feels like they're close enough, you could walk there." He shakes his head. "But trust me. They aren't as close as they look."

I don't say anything. I focus on the lights, my fingers wrapped around the metal fencing that probably keeps people from jumping into the street after a huge gambling loss, and I try to figure out what to say to him, where I want this friendship of ours to go. He isn't the person I thought he was, and I don't know what I still want, especially with Frankie in the picture.

"Locals don't really come out to the Strip much," he says with a pained sigh. "But I've been here a lot lately."

"Frankie?" I ask. I turn around and lean my back against the railing, facing out toward Mandalay Bay.

"Yeah." He stares at his hand as he picks at his thumbnail. "She's always blogging stuff going on out here, and she drags me along."

Frankie stands a few feet from us, phone balancing between her ear and her shoulder, yapping away while she taps on her tablet. Then off the other way on the bridge, Grace and Alex and Lo and Oscar are doing their couple thing. I've hardly talked to my sister and my best friend since they paired off with dudes the minute we got here. I need them. I need them to help me figure this out, and they've ditched me for guys in my time of need.

"I'll be right back," I mumble to Nick.

"Wait," he says, his voice cracking. "Ghost, I need to—"

"I need to talk to Lo and Grace." He has a girlfriend. I don't care what he needs to do.

"Emergency meeting. Now." I take Lo and Grace each by an elbow and pull them away from their flirting.

"Hey," Grace says, "we were planning the rest of the night."

"Do it later," I say through clenched teeth. "I'm having a crisis and I would love a minute of my older sister's and best friend's time, if that's not too much to ask."

I guess my voice or my harried expression is desperate enough, because they both stop looking longingly at the guys and follow me to the other side of the bridge. We have to weave through aggressive club promoters and step over a guy with a guitar singing a terrible version of a Bruno Mars song to get far enough away.

"First of all," I say as soon as we are out of earshot of the rest of the group, "I am calling BS on the two of you right now. How dare you ditch me in my hour of need in favor of hot boys? You've broken every single girl code there is."

Lo looks down at her feet as Grace mumbles sorry, but I don't give them much of a chance to grovel. "I don't want to hear it. You two left me alone with the girlfriend of the guy who I think I may be in love with. Like it's no big deal. You left me there to talk to her. What the hell, you guys?"

Grace shrugs. "You seemed like you were getting along. We wanted to give you some time to talk to Nick—"

"Yes, we're getting along because she is the nicest person on the face of the freaking planet. I need someone to help me hate her. You guys need to step it up with the smack talking."

They both lean in and wrap me in a group hug. "Sorry, girl," Lo says. "We were blinded by the shiny. We'll be by your side. I promise."

"Well, Lo will, anyway," Grace says, looking at her boots. "Ummm . . . don't be mad, but I think Alex and I are taking off."

"What?" Lo and I say it at the same time, as if we planned it or something.

"Look, I'll stay if you need me to. But we're in Vegas, and Alex and I are both over twenty-one. No offense, but we don't want to hang out at arcades all night."

"We have fake IDs," Lo says.

"I know, but . . ." She pulls off her beanie and runs her fingers through her hair, then shoves it back on again. "Look, you girls'll be good on your own, right?"

I stare at my sister with my mouth hanging open. After all I did to help her shake off her Gabe funk, I can't believe she's going to ditch me.

"Don't look at me like that," she says, absently playing with her necklace. "You know I need some time to have some fun. And, look, I'll get the scoop on this chick from Alex for you, okay? And Nick will chill out if I get Alex out of his hair."

Lo reaches over and grabs my hand, giving my fingers a firm squeeze. *Let her go,* she mouths.

"Fine," I say. "But if you two take off together, you better get some intel."

"I will. I promise."

"Before you go"—I reach out for her arm—"can you let me know if I'm doing the right thing here? Please?"

I fill them in on everything that happened, but Grace ends up being no help at all. Mainly because she disagrees with me. She is convinced I need more of a plan than "Go back to the hotel and deal with it later," and since she has the "older and wiser" thing going for her, I hear her out.

"You need to go after him," she says. "Make it clear how you feel. Throw your hat in the ring."

"But—Frankie," I say, my voice quiet. "And—"

Grace doesn't wait to hear the rest of what I have to say, though, because Alex calls for her and she motions for us to follow as she trots back over to him.

"I just want to leave," I whisper to Lo as we make our way back to the group. "I don't want to do this anymore."

Lo stops and grabs my shoulders, squaring me toward her. "Is that really what you want to do? Because if you want to ditch everyone here, I'm totally cool with that."

"Are you serious?" I'm so happy to hear this that I reach over and hug her. "All I want is to go back to the hotel and order some room service or something." I'm exhausted from pretending I don't care about all this, and from trying to figure Nick out. It's too much. "Grace can come back when she's done with Alex. Or not. I don't even care at this point."

"No problem," she says, patting my back. "Let's go."

I pull out of our hug. "What about Oscar?"

She shakes her head. "He's cute and all, but he's just a dude. No big deal when my best friend is in crisis."

"I'm totally failing you on this Girls Gone Wild thing."

"We can go wild at the pool tomorrow. That bikini top of yours is coming off, my friend."

"Only after I pour an entire bottle of vodka down your throat." We walk back to the group, and I immediately feel lighter. I can go back to the hotel room with Lo and deal with all of this tomorrow. Or never. It's not like Nick will even notice.

We're almost back to the group, who have all joined in a sing-along with the guitar guy, when Frankie comes up behind me and grabs my arm.

"Hannah. Can you do me a huge favor?"

It's easy to be nice to her, since I don't need to deal with her and Nick for much longer. "What's up?"

"I have to sneak off for a minute to talk to a guy over at MGM for the blog."

"What? Now? It's like ten P.M."

She tilts her head and replies to me in this way that makes me feel like a redneck from BFE. "Oh, honey, this is Vegas. He's just getting to work."

"Okay," I say. "Whatever. What do you need me for?"

"Nick's going to be totally pissed at me for leaving. He gets kinda weird when I just spring things on him, and it was my idea to show you guys around and now I'm taking off. I'll be back, though! Soon!"

I narrow my eyes at her. "Okaaaay."

"He's so super happy you're here and all. So if you could tell him for me? That I'm going to be gone for, like, an hour? He'll be so stoked to be able to hang out with you for a while, just the two of you. And then, you know, keep him company until I get back."

"Oh, Frankie, I don't know—"

"Sure she will, Frankie," Lo jumps in.

I shoot her a death look. What the hell? I continue to glare at her, but she's smiling at Frankie like Lo and I didn't just make a date for some room service and hotel movies.

"Awesome. Thanks, Hannah." She squeezes my arm and gives me this super-warm, genuine smile I want to smack right off her face. "I know you're the only person who can keep Nick from getting all annoyed with me right now. I owe you one."

I mumble, "You don't have to owe me," but she's already gone, walking across the bridge to the MGM Grand faster than it seems her little legs should be able to take her.

"Dude," I say to Lo as soon as Frankie is gone, "what was that?"

Her hands are already up in surrender. "Hear me out, okay?"

"I'm listening."

"I know you want to go back to the room, and I respect that. But I also think Grace is right. And this is a perfect situation: You have the chance to be alone with Nick and talk without Frankie interrupting you. Grace is going off with Alex, and I can get Oscar to do something else. You said Nick's more like the guy you're used to when it's just the two of you, right? Here you go—gift-wrapped alone time. With a sparkly bow on top."

When she puts it that way, it doesn't sound like such a bad idea. "I guess this will work." Frankie-free alone time with Nick? It probably beats pouting in the hotel room.

And Grace *is* right—I do need to tell him how I feel. I can't handle this uncertainty, this arm around my shoulder one minute and joking with Frankie the next. It will mean admitting I lied to him, but I have to do it regardless. I need to let him know.

I shake my head at her, then reach around and smack her butt. "This is why I love you."

"I know," she says. "I'm the best."

We finish our walk back to the group, who are all reluctantly posing for pictures Grace is taking with her phone, probably to prove to her editor she was here talking to an actual Vegas band. "Okay, everyone," Lo says. "It looks like we have a little change of plans."

"Where's Frankie?" Alex asks.

I rub my hands down the front of my jeans. "Well, she, uh, had to run and do something for the blog really quick." Nick makes a face I can't quite figure out, and I try my best to give him a comforting smile. "But she'll be back in a bit."

"So, Hannah was telling me"—Lo turns to me and gives me a look that clearly says I told her nothing at all like what she's about to say, but I better play along anyway—"that she has been dying to go to the top of the Eiffel Tower."

Yuck. Of all the things she could pick. I don't hate heights the way I hate the idea of roller coasters, but I wouldn't say I *love* teetering so far above solid ground. I smile anyway. She evidently has a plan here.

"Dude. No." Oscar shakes his head violently, and I suddenly get what Lo is doing, that brilliant friend of mine. "I'm, uh, not going to go up there. There's no way."

I decide to play along. "Please, you guys? It's on my Vegas bucket list."

Grace catches on. "Alex and I are about to take off. But, Hannah, you were talking the whole way here about how much you wanted to go up there. You shouldn't miss it."

"Oh. Well," Nick says, shifting his weight from one foot to the other and back again, "why don't I go with Hannah to the Eiffel Tower? Grace and Alex, you two go get drunk or whatever, and Lo and Oscar, you guys go, um, hang out somewhere that's not hundreds of feet above the ground, and we'll call you when we're done. How does that sound?"

I'm so relieved Nick is going along with it and how well everything is finally working out. Sweet. Time alone to talk, just the two of us.

Then I hear a voice from behind us. "But what about me?"

Ugh. I totally forgot about Jordy. It looks like our night is about to take a turn for the douche.

CHAPTER 17

Jordy slaps hands with all the guys, including Nick, and apologizes for being late. Something about helping Drew get the equipment home and some hot girls at House of Blues or something. I'm not listening, because I'm trying to figure out how his arrival is going to affect my plan. There's only a small window of alone time with Nick before Frankie gets back, and I want to use it.

I know enough about Jordy to know I don't care about knowing more. Sure, he's the lead singer and songwriter for Automatic Friday and he's hot, but he also knows how hot he is, which makes him way less attractive overall. I know Nick hardly talks about him, so I assume they aren't on BFF-necklace level. And Nick got visibly annoyed tonight when Alex invited Jordy out.

Jordy's changed clothes since the show earlier. Now he's in almost the same uniform as the other guys—jeans, a black T-shirt, and a hoodie—but he wears it differently. Clothes look different on people who walk the other side of the line between confidence and cockiness.

"Hey, girls," he says in this way that seems to imply our night up until now had just been killing time until he could join us.

Nick jumps in with this bizarre forced and too-formal voice before I can introduce myself. "Jordy, this is Hannah." He rests his hand on my shoulder as he says it, and my shoulder lights on fire.

It feels like he's claiming me—and, I'm not gonna lie, I might be forced to turn in my feminism card with this admission, but I kinda love it. "Hannah is, uh, my best friend. From California."

"Hannah, huh?" Jordy moves closer in toward me and stretches out his hand. "Well, it's nice to meet you, Hannah. I can't believe Nick's never mentioned such a beautiful friend before."

"Maybe there's a reason for that," Nick mumbles, and I don't know if I should be flattered or annoyed or if I was even supposed to hear that.

"Hi." I shake Jordy's hand because he stuck it out to me like he's someone's dad or something. It feels like a washed-up piece of seaweed, limp and soggy.

"And this is her sister, Grace, and her friend Lo." Nick finishes off the introductions in his stiff voice and then shifts around on his feet again.

I look at him and we make eye contact, and then something weird happens: He raises his eyebrows at me, and I know exactly what this look of his means. He's annoyed with Jordy and the group and he wants to get away. I get it. Unlike his mystery look when Frankie left earlier, this time I can totally read his face.

I give a little nod back. "Well, I'm glad we got to meet you before we ran over to the Eiffel Tower. I, uh, have to pick up something from my hotel and I need Nick's help, so we're going to go, but we're going to call you all in a bit when we're done and meet up. Okay? We'll call you. Okay, bye!" I whip around before anyone has a chance to say anything and so does Nick and then we're walking full speed across the bridge. I'm giddy with relief that we managed to get away and so is he, it seems, and we are off on our own, just me and Nick, leaving the group and the weirdness behind us.

Nick was right. The Paris hotel didn't look all that far away from where we'd stood on the bridge, but now that we're faced with walking all the way there, the distance seems a little daunting. "Those are not walking shoes," Nick says, looking down at my wedges. "Let's go through MGM and get a cab."

MGM Grand is one of the largest hotels on the Strip, and for someone who claims he doesn't come out to this part of Vegas all that often, Nick sure seems to know a lot about it. "I heard there are so many rooms here," he tells me as he navigates the casino floor, weaving us in and out of blackjack, roulette, and craps tables, "that if you stayed in a different room every night, it would take you over five years to stay in all of them. Can you believe that?"

"Wow." This is the fourth casino I've been in so far, and they all look so different and so overwhelming. MGM doesn't seem to have a theme aside from "huge," but it's beautiful inside, with gold accents on the wall and lion details everywhere. We pass expensive restaurant after expensive restaurant, and we linger by the menus, pointing out the dishes we would order if we had that kind of money before moving on to the next one.

According to the signs, we're almost to the front lobby when a loud *whoop* stops us in our tracks. The *whoop*s continue, fast and loud and full of excitement, until they are right on top of us.

It's a couple doing the *whoop*ing. She's wearing a skintight white sequined strapless dress that's so short, it looks more like a top, a hot pink feather boa, and the highest platform stilettos I've ever seen a real person manage to walk in. Her black hair is twisted into an updo and topped with a birdcage veil. The guy has on dark skinny jeans, a tuxedo T-shirt, and a top hat. JUST MARRIED is scribbled in Sharpie up his right forearm, and a beer bottle dangles from his fingers. The *whoop*ing is because he keeps smacking her on the butt with his free hand, and she seems to enjoy it immensely.

"Aww, look," I say, elbowing Nick in the ribs. "A Vegas wedding."

"Congratulations!" Nick shouts at them as they *whoop* by.

The groom stops and turns around, his hazy eyes searching the casino crowd until he lands on Nick and then on me. He walks back toward us and clasps his hand, the one that had previously been on his new wife's backside, on Nick's shoulder. "Thanks, man! It's awesome." He jerks his head toward me. "You gonna marry this one? You should. Being married is the best."

"You've been married for forty-five minutes, babe," the bride calls from a few feet away. "You have no idea."

"Uh," Nick looks at his feet, his cheeks turning the color of the bride's boa. "We're . . . um . . ."

"Oh no," I say, probably way too quickly. "We're not together. We're just friends."

"Best friends," Nick adds, also way too quickly.

The groom reaches his arm around Nick's shoulder and pulls him into a bro hug. "Mai and I were best friends in high school," he says. "I dated her sister, actually. But we don't talk about that anymore. She gets mad." He adds the last part in a stage whisper and sends an overexaggerated wink in her direction.

"Jason! Are you seriously telling this story to strangers? On our wedding night?" The bride, Mai, rolls her eyes and shakes her head, but her exasperation isn't all that convincing when paired with her enormous smile. "Come on. We need to get back to the reception."

The groom stares at us for a second, smiles, and says, "You two want some cake? Come eat cake with us." Still in the bro hug, he pulls Nick lightly in the direction of his wife. "We just lost some wedding gift money at the roulette table, so we need some more cake to take the edge off."

I'm tempted to blurt out a quick no, pull Nick away from Jason, and get the heck away from these drunk strangers. But I notice the light tug from Jason made Nick's glasses slide down his face a bit, where they wobble all askew on the end of his nose, which is probably the most adorable thing I've ever seen. Even more adorable? Nick's wide-eyed expression full of *WTF is happening?* mixed with *This is the best ever!* He's enjoying everything about this bizarre encounter.

"Are you inviting randoms to our reception?" Mai says it in a way that implies Jason does this sort of thing often and that's exactly one of the things she loves about him.

"Look at them!" Jason waves his hand up and down in front of a laughing Nick, whose glasses continue to slide down his face. "They're a mini us! I have to invite them! It's like having our past selves at our own wedding! Wedding-ception!"

And it's true. Jason is a brown-haired white guy in black-framed glasses, like Nick, and Mai, while not Korean, is tiny and

Asian. They do sort of look like the two of us, even though I could never pull off those shoes and that dress in public. Where did she get those boobs?

Jason takes a swig of his beer. "So, you guys coming?"

Nick and I look at each other. "You want to?" he asks, raising an eyebrow. His face is alive with excitement and adventure in a way I've only ever heard in his voice. *Get crazy with me,* he seems to be saying. *Let's be crazy together.*

I raise both my eyebrows back, because I've never been able to master that one-eyebrow thing he can do, even after the hour-long tutorial he gave me in tenth grade. My instinct is to say no and get the heck out of here, and I know he knows it.

And if you asked me yesterday, I would have said I would never in a million years wander off into a Las Vegas casino with drunk strangers. But something in me changed when I got in the car and drove out here. This trip isn't just about meeting Nick; it's about breaking the rules, too. Trying new things. Sure, I didn't go on the roller coaster, but I can eat some freaking cake. Dessert isn't going to send me plummeting to my bloody death.

And something else in me changed when Nick and I ran off alone together. Making these decisions, doing these things that are so against my good-girl DNA, opened up a secret part of me. Now my desire to be involved in one of Nick's stories—like the time he and Oscar snuck into an empty pool to skateboard or the time they started a bonfire hot dog party in an empty lot—is strong. I want to gain membership into that side of his life.

And maybe this will be the place for me to tell him how I feel. What better setting than a romantic Vegas wedding?

I nod and shrug and smile at him all at the same time. "When in Vegas."

CHAPTER 18

We all follow Mai's lead through the casino, and Nick shakes loose from Jason's bro hug, finally fixes his glasses, and walks close to me again.

"A Vegas wedding," I say as we trail behind the couple. "I feel like we're in a movie or something."

Nick shoves his hands into the pockets of his jacket. "Do you think Elvis performed the ceremony?"

"If it wasn't Elvis or a drag queen, they're doing this Vegas wedding thing all wrong. According to those movies, anyway."

"According to those movies, though, they should have just met two hours ago, not back in high school."

We're quiet, both of us watching Mai and Jason ahead of us, who are now holding hands and skipping through the casino back to their reception. Well, skipping as best they can, given Mai's footwear.

"You sure you're okay with this, Ghost?" Nick bumps my shoulder with his, and I bump back without thinking about it. As soon as I realize what I've done, a shiver of panic runs through me. Was that too flirty? Too familiar? Should I have done that? But then the panic ebbs a bit when I tell myself he bumped me first.

I bump him again.

"You promise they aren't going to drug us and take us out to the desert for some kind of occult sacrifice ritual?"

Nick laughs so suddenly that he snorts. "I can't promise that. But I can promise that if they try, I will gallantly come to your rescue and drag you to safety if I have to."

"How can you drag me if you are drugged, too?"

"I will battle through the bleary haze of the drugs to save you, Ghost. That's what real friends do."

A loud *whoop* sounds through the casino, and I see that, once again, Jason has smacked Mai on the butt. Dang, he can't keep his hands off her. This time, though, as he pulls his hand away, she snatches it back and places it firmly on her backside.

Their easy banter, their natural chemistry, and the undeniable love that passes between them make me feel warm inside. As we walk, I look at Nick and he's smiling. But he's not looking at them; he's looking at me. "They remind me of us," he whispers to me, his mouth as close as it's ever been to my skin.

We follow them through the casino to a hallway full of rooms I assume are used for conventions, conferences, and weddings like Jason and Mai's. Their reception is in full swing when we walk in one of the doors. Lights string the walls, flowers decorate the tables, and guests pack the dance floor, as I would expect at any wedding. But I should have known by Jason and Mai's unconventional wedding attire that this wouldn't be a typical reception.

Instead of wearing fancy dresses and suits, their guests are all in costumes.

Loud, uncensored hip-hop blasts from the speakers, played by a DJ in a clown costume. A group of sexy Disney princesses dances in a circle. Two Elvises—or is it Elvii?—knock shot glasses together in a cheers. A guy dressed in drag hands a slice of wedding cake to someone in a full gorilla suit and a bow tie.

And Nick and I, dressed as normal as can be, stand in the doorway, mouths agape.

Nick scratches the back of his head. "Did we take a wrong turn into Halloweentown?"

"Now, this is the Vegas I was hoping to see," I say.

"I have lived here my whole life, and I've never seen this Vegas."

"Clearly, you are hanging out in the wrong places."

"Here." It's Jason, and he shoves two small paper plates at us. "Teenage Jason and Mai, you two need to have some wedding cake. It's chocolate and it's delicious. I've had three slices already, and the night isn't over yet."

We take the cake, which seems to please him immensely. "Now, if you don't mind, I'm going to go grind on my hot wife. Stay out of trouble, you two."

I ate a piece of cake at the pizza place before Nick's show earlier, and I'm not usually a sweets person, so I'll be racking up more sugar on this trip than I've consumed in the past month. But I couldn't say no to Jason, his face glowing with love and excitement. And I followed the newlyweds here to eat some cake, after all. So I'm going to eat the dang cake.

I take one bite, and it's so sugary and oversweet that my mouth twists up as I swallow it. Taking one bite totally counts as having the cake, right?

"For you," I say, passing my cake plate to Nick.

"You are the biggest enabler of my sweet tooth ever." He has already swallowed his first piece, and he tosses that empty plate in the trash can behind him and greedily starts in on mine. "I can't believe I'm not morbidly obese from all the baked goods you always send me."

"I send them to you so I don't become morbidly obese."

As he's finishing his second piece of cake, I try to figure out what else to say to him. This isn't exactly the romantic setting I was hoping for when it came to getting honest about my feelings. I'm about to tell Nick that now that we've had the cake, we should just sneak out before Jason and Mai notice. Walking over here was crazy enough, we have a good story, and now we need to get back to our journey to Paris and the Eiffel Tower. Before the words can form in my mouth, though, Nick turns to me and says, "Wanna dance?"

I shake my head because the whole situation is so ridiculous;

I know he must be joking. It looks like a Halloween party is in full swing on the dance floor. One of the Elvii is doing some break-dance moves in the middle of a circle. A sexy Elsa from *Frozen* dances on top of a chair that has been dragged onto the dance floor. Mai is piggyback on Jason's shoulders—how did she manage in that tiny dress?—and he bounces her around the dance floor to the music. Her arms are wrapped around his neck and she looks at him like the sun rises and sets behind his black-framed glasses.

Then I look up at Nick, and for the second time in the past ten minutes, he's smiling at me. That open Nick smile from all his pictures, so uninhibited and full of joy. This one has a hint of mischief, though. I can tell the loud music and the randomness of this whole encounter have put the reality of our current situation out of his mind. It's like we walked through MGM Grand and into this parallel universe full of sexy Disney characters and free cake and Nick and Hannah as best friends, just like always, with absolutely no real-world complications.

Like we walked out of reality and into our computer-text-online-phone world, where it's just the two of us and anything can happen.

He looks happy to live in that parallel universe for a little bit— and honestly, I am, too. This is what I've been wanting all night. More than telling him the truth, I've wanted to be alone with Nick and have a chance to be normal with him.

And it's not like they're playing slow songs here or anything. This is fast dancing, not cuddling set to music. Nothing wrong with that.

I smile back.

"You want to dance with me?" I cover my mouth with my hand in mock shock. "Not with Sexy Elsa?"

"Eh. I'm sure she's a nice girl, but she comes off as a little cold."

"Wow," I groan. "That was—"

"Ghost, just let it go." He rests his hand on the small of my back and we walk to the dance floor.

The music pulses through the small reception room. The dance floor is crowded with costumed wedding guests, so Nick and I are standing close to each other. So close that I'm aware of every inch of him and how near he is to every inch of me. We aren't touching, but one bump from the guy in the gorilla costume behind me and we could be.

I start to move my hips to the completely wedding-inappropriate hip-hop.

"Now we really get to see who the worst dancer is," Nick says. "We never quite determined the biggest loser during the great eleventh-grade video dance off."

"That's because we didn't have an outside judge."

"Because Alex couldn't be bothered to put down his video game and watch us—"

"He would have voted against you no matter what, anyway."

"Fact."

"And Grace wasn't home. So the title of worst dancer is still up for grabs."

We start off by trying to out-bad-dance each other. I do the Sprinkler. He responds with the Washing Machine. I wave my hands in the air like I just don't care. He robots his arms and turns himself in circles. We both laugh until we double over, our heads knocking against each other, which brings even more laughter.

Then the music changes. It's still uncensored hip-hop, but this song is faster, sexier. There's a sudden shift in the atmosphere in the room, and I know I'm not the only one who feels it. Everyone moves in closer. Closer to the dance floor. Closer to each other. Alcohol and sweat and bodies close in around us, forcing me into Nick's space and Nick into mine. The music pounds and we're dancing, but not like before. Now we're moving with the music like we don't have a choice, like it has taken over. I could look around the dance floor to see if the song has had this effect on everyone, but I can't tear my eyes from Nick. His face is as close to mine as it's ever been and I didn't even realize his arm had wrapped around my back and pulled me in tighter.

Our hips touch and our eyes are locked and we are moving with this music and each other and I want to put my arms around his neck or his shoulders or his back and pull him in tighter. I want to tell him everything I've been thinking. I open my mouth and try to stretch myself up, but he's too tall and the music is too loud and the gorilla keeps bumping into my back, pitching me against Nick over and over.

Now isn't the time for talking; now is the time for dancing.

So we do. We dance, closer than we've ever been, and our eyes and bodies are locked together. I'm tuned in to so many things about him. His Adam's apple moving up and down his neck as he swallows. His mouth parted slightly, his fingers pressed firm and strong against my spine, the small beads of sweat building up on his forehead.

Slow dancing might be cuddling set to music, but somehow this ends up being more intense. More intimate.

I'm almost completely lost in the music and in Nick when the clown DJ gets on the mic, reminding me quickly where I am. "Okay, party people! It's time for the bouquet toss!"

Nick and I snap out of our dance trance. I blink at him as I'm brought back to reality and "Single Ladies" blasts over the speakers, two of the sexy princesses doing the dance from the video right next to us.

"Bachelorettes, get out on the floor!" DJ Clown insists.

Still in a daze, I tug lightly on Nick's sleeve. "I think this is our cue to leave."

"You don't want to go do the 'Single Ladies' dance?" He jerks his head toward the enthusiastic dancers next to us. "There is no doubt you won this dance-off, Ghost. You could handle it."

I hold back a laugh. "Tempting. But I'm going to pass."

"Should we say good-bye to Jason and Mai?"

I locate the couple on the dance floor. Mai shakes a small bouquet of hot pink and white flowers over her head while Jason snaps pictures of her with his phone.

As I look at them, I'm body-slammed with feelings. I don't say what I'm thinking to Nick, though. Because what I'm thinking is this actually could be us someday. Not the wedding, certainly. I haven't spent much time daydreaming about my future wedding, but I can guarantee it will be nothing like this drunken costume party.

But Jason and Mai. It's clear how in love they are, and even though this wedding reception is weird as hell, it's so obviously *them,* and they are so obviously together. So obviously perfect.

This could be Nick and me someday.

It could have been.

And maybe it still can be, if I get my freaking mouth to work and admit to him that I lied. But instead, I say, "Nah. Let's just go. I don't want to interrupt."

On our way out the door, Nick snags another slice of cake. He scribbles

Congratulations, Jason & Mai
Love, Teenage Jason & Mai

in their guestbook, which is an album of pictures of them with a fluffy white dog, and waves good-bye to the party, even though everyone is paying attention to the bouquet toss and not the random wedding crashers.

We don't talk about the wedding as we make our way back through MGM toward the lobby exit. We don't talk about our dance or our closeness or our intense eye contact. We let ourselves exit that alternate reality we entered, but we aren't all the way back in the real world quite yet—I can still feel the oasis Nick and I shared surrounding us, thick and present.

Close to the main door, which leads out to a taxi stand, Nick stops. "Ghost, look." It's the first thing he's said since we left the wedding, and he's pointing at a small machine. I walk up next to him and see it's a souvenir penny flattener that stamps the MGM lion. "Remember the penny I—?"

I don't even let him finish. I pull my clown penny from my pocket and hold my hand out to him. Showing him I have this penny with me—that not only do I remember when he sent it, but I also brought it along on this trip—feels like exposing a secret part of myself, like skipping through the casino in my thong.

He stares down at it like it's something strange and wonderful, and he reaches out. I lift my hand so he can pick it up, but he doesn't reach for the clown penny like I think he's going to. Instead, he brings his fingers to his neck and pulls a long ball chain out from under his T-shirt. Hanging from the loop of chain is the Disneyland penny I sent him years ago. The one with the hitchhiking ghosts.

"I had one of Alex's friends put a hole in it for me." His cheeks are pink, and he looks everywhere but at my face as he tucks the necklace back under his shirt. "I wear it every day."

I stare at him, speechless. He wears the penny I sent him every day, tucked under his shirt? He has it with him all the time?

Do it now, I tell myself. *Tell him how you feel.* He threw me a ball, and I just need to swing. But I open my mouth and nothing comes out. I just fish-mouth and look down at the penny still in my hand.

He apparently doesn't know what to make of my silence. He smooths out his shirt, looks down at his shoes for entirely too long, then says, "Well, let's go find that taxi line," and turns toward the front lobby.

And . . . strikeout. The opportunity is gone. Crap.

Still speechless, I slip the penny back in my pocket and follow him to a cab. As we drive to Paris, I stare out the window again, soaking up the lights and the people on the street as I try to make sense of what Nick just showed me combined with our dance at the wedding. I finally figure out how to use my words when I notice several guys lining the curb in neon T-shirts with signs on their backs, handing things out to people who pass. "What are they doing?"

"Oh," he says, "those cards are for escorts. Like, call this girl and she'll show you a good time tonight."

"Ew. Why did they try to give one to that woman?"

He shrugs. "Hey, some ladies want lady company. You never know. Don't judge."

"I have enough lady company with Grace and Lo," I joke. "I'm certainly not paying for more."

We both laugh, and he leans back in the seat, shoving his hands into the pockets of his jacket. "So, what's the big deal about the Eiffel Tower, anyway? Honestly, it sounds like exactly the kind of thing you would hate."

"Oh. You know. I want to see a killer view of Vegas." *And have more alone time with you so I can tell you all my feelings.* Although this alone time is going to be wasted if, when I can manage to speak, I use it to talk about prostitutes and Vegas trivia. On the phone, these random conversations have been a daily occurrence for four years, and I wouldn't think twice about them. Which Pokémon is the best. Our favorite types of socks. Pizza toppings in order of deliciousness. We talk and text for hours about anything. Nothing. But now that Nick is next to me, I can feel the reality of our lies and things not said and real-life feelings between us, and it's hard to bridge them. Especially given Frankie. And my inability to be honest about my feelings. And the fact that he wears something I sent him that has a picture of his nickname for me on a chain around his neck. He's so much closer, now that there's not a phone or screen between us, but somehow this small real space, and all the complications that come along with it, has become so much more difficult to cross.

We reach Paris Las Vegas and hop out of the cab, then wander a casino floor designed, obviously, to look like Paris, France, until we find the gift shop selling tickets for the "Eiffel Tower Experience." Nick pays for both of us with his portion of the slot machine winnings. I smoosh myself into the back corner of the elevator as we ride up because, honestly, long elevator rides freak me out almost as much as roller coasters do. I try not to be too conspicuous about the fact that I'm not loving every second of the Eiffel Tower Experience, since this was my genius idea, but Nick stands as close to me as he did when we were dancing and watches me from the corner of his eye.

I know because I'm watching him from the corner of my eye, too.

We get off at the observation deck, which is just a big fenced-in ledge. The lights of the Strip and the rest of the greater Las Vegas area stretch out ahead, but I can also see the street way below my feet through the openings in the deck's woven steel floor.

This was a freaking terrible idea. We could have gotten alone time riding a gondola at the Venetian or something. But Oscar probably isn't scared of water, so here we are. Gotta take what I can get tonight.

Nick immediately steps off the elevator and presses his face to the cage around the platform. "Check out this view, Ghost. It's unbelievable." He turns around and I'm still standing sort of stuck to the elevator door, even though it has closed and the car has gone back down to bring more people up here. He reaches out his hand to me. "I knew you weren't going to be into this," he says. "Like when you went on that school field trip to the Getty Center. Remember how much you hated being up there?"

A tingle spreads through my body when he mentions this old memory. I went on that field trip in ninth grade—so long ago, I hardly remember it myself. And here he is, pulling out the story like it's his own, like he's kept it close this whole time.

And just like that, the strange, unfamiliar real space between us is bridged. I take his hand, allowing him to lead me to the edge of the observation deck, and heat spreads up my arm from our touch. "How do you even remember that?"

We are next to each other, close, but we're both looking out over the lights of the Las Vegas Strip. The fountains at the Bellagio shoot high into the air, and he hasn't dropped my hand. I don't do anything to change that.

"I've told you a million times, Ghost. I'm an elephant. I never forget. Anything."

I'm so aware of him next to me, his fingers still wrapped around mine. Every cell in my body is on high alert, keeping close track of his nearness. The brush of his jacket against my bare arm sends an excited shiver all through me.

He drops my hand and turns to face me. "Oh, are you cold?" He moves to shrug off his jacket. "Do you want this? I don't need it."

I'm about to say, *No, I'm fine.* I'm not cold at all, and I'm certainly not going to say it was his accidental touch that made me shiver, and not the air temperature. But then I realize I don't want to say no to his jacket.

I sort of hate myself for letting him hold on to my hand and wanting to wear his jacket. He has a girlfriend, and as much as it pains me to admit it to myself, Frankie is actually pretty cool. I'd say she's someone I would be friends with, but the fact is, I doubt we'd even be friends because I'd be too intimidated by her. I like Frankie, and she's Nick's girlfriend.

And I did come up here to tell him how I feel about him. To tell him I lied about not ever wanting anything romantic to happen between us.

I take his jacket and slide it onto my shoulders. Hey, Frankie isn't here. And I always follow the rules and do the right thing—and, yeah, I usually end up with what I want, but that's because I work for it.

Maybe I need to work for this, too.

And maybe that work involves breaking a rule or two.

Because, damn it, Nick was mine first.

CHAPTER 19

We settle back into gazing out at the lights. I wish his hand were wrapped around my fingers again, but I have his jacket on me, and that's good enough. It's like a hug from him. I breathe in deep, realizing the smell on this jacket—cinnamon gum mixed with old, smoky leather—is Nick's scent. It's another missing piece to the real Nick, and another part of everything real about him I've always wanted.

I know I need to say something, that this is the time and the place for feelings to be shared, hearts to be exposed, but now that we've crossed another small divide, I'm even less sure how to start the conversation.

"Better?" he asks.

I nod.

"Good," he says. "I know you're cold-blooded."

"Better than coldhearted," I say, and we both laugh and then settle into silence.

Silence, but not the awkward kind. Comfortable silence. Not the type you can have with just anyone.

Last year, on the anniversary of his mom's death, Nick called me at night. "I don't feel like talking, Ghost," he'd said. "I just need someone to not talk to." So I stayed on the phone with him for twenty minutes, neither of us saying anything. I listened to his quiet breath and wondered how it must feel not to have a mom. I ripped a page out of my school notebook and wrote down things I wanted to say to him, questions I would have liked to ask. Finally, he'd said, "Thank you so much. That meant a lot to me." We hung up and never talked about it again. I haven't told Lo or Grace about that, because I can't imagine either of them not saying anything to someone for that long. I know they wouldn't get the silence.

But Nick and I do silence just as well as we do talking.

He clears his throat. "So, it's pretty crazy that Grace had to come out here of all places for her internship."

Oh yeah. I wish he would stop bringing up that lie. "Yeah, she's been pitching these story ideas. She wants to do something on the Vegas local scene or something. I don't even know. I didn't think interns got to do this kind of stuff, but apparently, she's some kind of prodigy."

"She should interview Frankie about her blog." I know I'm not imagining a hardening in his voice; I'm just not sure if it's because of Frankie or because of her blog. Or both.

"That's a good idea. I bet they'd love something like that. Teen blogger, local scene—sounds right up their alley." I turn around and lean my back against the cage. I've almost completely forgotten how scary it is up here. "Mind telling me why you sounded like you ate a bug right now when you brought it up?"

He turns so we are facing the same direction, our backs to the city. He seems to have gotten closer, and my body is back on high alert again.

"Don't get me wrong," he says. "You should see this thing. She's a total tech wizard, and her Web site looks like it belongs in a commercial. I knew about it before I ever knew Frankie, and I think it's ridiculously awesome what she's done with it. I'm proud of what she's done, so I don't want you to think I'm hating on her success. I'm not."

"So what *are* you hating on?"

He lets out a long sigh. "You know me, Ghost. I have my profile online only because you made it for me. If I didn't have you to talk to, I'd probably cancel it. You know how private I am. Having people all up in my business is the worst."

I do know him. I had to force him to add a profile picture that wasn't the House Stark logo from *Game of Thrones*. He had hardly any personal information on his page and added only a small handful of friends. He wasn't constantly updating his status like all my friends at school, who post duck-faced selfies and fill update after update with pictures of their boring lunches.

When I'd sent him the link and password after I set it up for him back in ninth grade, he'd chatted me right away, whining.

"Why do I even need this?" he'd said. "I already send you all my pictures." I joked that I wanted to be able to comment on them, so his friends could see how funny and witty I was, but he still hardly posted any, anyway. I'd acted all insulted, but a part of me has always liked how private he is. Nick's natural reserve makes me feel like I've really earned his friendship over the past few years.

That I have something with him no one else does.

"Frankie puts everything online. You should go look at her blog when you get a chance. You'll know her life story within five minutes." He lets out another long sigh. "But what bothers me most is that she talks about me on there. Posts my picture, says where I hang out. People knowing that stuff about me . . . ugh, it makes me so uncomfortable. And I tell her how I feel, but she won't stop doing it." He lowers his voice to a mumble. "It's the only thing we fight about, really. But we fight about it all the time."

He shoves his hands in the pockets of his jeans, which causes his elbow to land against my arm.

I lean into him ever so slightly, just an inch, and I watch out of the corner of my eye to see if he notices the contact. If he does, he doesn't move away, so I lean an inch more.

"Like, last week? I was out picking up dinner with Alex, and while we were waiting for our food, this weird-looking guy comes up to me. He seriously looks like a hobbit. And he says, 'Nick?' And

I'm trying to figure out how I know this guy. He's way too old to be from school. Some party I went to with Alex? Did I sell him a T-shirt at some show?" He stops and turns straight ahead, kicking his heel against the cage behind us. "Well, it turns out, he reads Frankie's blog. He knows we're together and he starts asking me about her, like he's my buddy and like I'm going to set him up on a date with my girlfriend or something."

"That's so scary," I say. "And dangerous for her, if people always know where she is all the time. People can be such weirdos, you know?" I think back to her fans in the arcade and wonder how that same encounter would have gone if Ashley hadn't been so nice.

"Exactly. I get all worried when she runs off by herself or some guy is talking to her or whatever. Who knows what freaks are reading that blog of hers. It *is* Vegas, you know."

I feel a pull inside at the tenderness in his voice when he talks about her. It makes me flash back to the night of that party, on the phone. He had that same tenderness in his voice then, but directed at me.

"Anyway," he said, "enough about that. It makes me mad, and I don't want to be mad when you're here."

I feel like I should give him some advice. That's what Hannah on the phone would do. But do I want to help him smooth things over with Frankie? I'm not sure, and I'm even less sure how I feel about this Evil Hannah who seems to be coming to light, so I change the subject.

I turn back around, scanning the Las Vegas skyline. "So, where is your house from here?"

"Well, I'm technically in Green Valley. So we'd have to go over there to see my house." He points to the other side of the platform, facing away from the Strip. "You think you can handle that journey?"

I've become comfortable in our little spot, and the idea of walking over to the other side doesn't sound at all appealing. "Er."

"Come on, Ghost," he says, and reaches out his hand again. "You can do this. I've got you."

My hand folds around his, and he leads me slowly to the other side of the platform. It's not as scary as it was when I first stepped out of the elevator, and with Nick's hand wrapped around mine and his jacket on my shoulders and his general closeness, I'm almost able to forget about the height and the general wobbliness of the Eiffel Tower Experience. It's a decent trade-off.

"That wasn't so bad, was it?" he says when we lean forward against the railing facing out to the rest of Nevada.

He hasn't let go of my hand.

It's not like we're holding hands like boyfriend–girlfriend. Our fingers aren't interlocked. His hand is folded around mine, which has caused my hand to fold back on his. It's totally innocent, I tell myself. He's comforting me. It's not like I'm making a move on him. It's not like he's making a move on me.

But it's not like I'd do this in front of Frankie, either.

"So, where is Casa de Cooper?"

The view from this side is different. Lights and buildings and cars stretch out on both sides of us when we are facing the Strip. There are still lights here, but the view is darker. Less dramatic. Normal. The Strip's frenetic energy isn't all Las Vegas has to offer. Las Vegas Boulevard isn't Nick's Vegas. This is.

He points off into the distance to a spattering of lights. "I'm right over there. Obviously, if it were daytime, you could see it all better."

I warm at the thought of seeing Nick's house, where he sits at his computer and chats with me while he works on his homework. Where he flops down on his bed and talks to me until all hours of the night. "I always picture your house in my head when you tell me stories. I'd love to see how the real thing compares."

He clears his throat. "Well, Alex is having some people over tomorrow for a barbecue. It's his friend's birthday," he says, his voice tentative. "You should come."

I turn from the view and back toward Nick to find him staring at me. His eyes wide behind his black-framed glasses, his cheeks flushed, his lips parted slightly. He's looking at me in this way that's so different from any way he has since I saw him for the first time. The expression reminds me of his voice soft on the phone late at night, whispered secrets, and inside jokes.

The air between us is charged and crackling, like neon lights on a casino sign. I want to smile at him, but I can't. I can only stare back.

He squeezes my hand in his, and I squeeze in return. He loosens his grip and I think he's going to pull his hand away, put it in his pocket, take it back. But instead he straightens out his fingers and finds mine, lacing our fingers together.

I pull his hand close to mine with my fingers. I can't even pretend this is innocent anymore.

What now?

What will happen if he leans closer? If he tries to kiss me?

What if he doesn't?

This is such a perfect time for a kiss. Alone, on top of Las Vegas, nights and lights and city stretching out ahead of us. Me wrapped in his jacket, him close enough it would take only the smallest movement to make full contact. Nick, the guy who has been in the background of everything important in my life for the past four years, the guy I can't stand to lose.

He lied to me, and I was hurt. But I lied, too. I lied to myself about my feelings, and I lied to him about them, too.

If I want him to give us a chance, I need to tell him the truth, and I need to do it now.

I move closer. It's just a millimeter, the tiniest scoot forward. But he notices, and his eyes move from mine and slowly travel up and down my body. He chews on his bottom lip.

Oh my God, he's thinking about it. He wants this, too. I know it.

If Nick were a normal guy, if he were Josh Ahmed, I would just lean forward, close the space, and put my lips gently on his. I wouldn't have to say any words to tell him how I feel about him.

But Nick isn't a normal guy. He's *the* guy.

But—Frankie.

Do I want to kiss a guy with a girlfriend? Do I want to break that rule? Be *that* girl? Do I want to turn Nick into *that* guy?

I bite my lip, and I move back that millimeter. We're too close, and we both want this too much.

Nick shakes his head almost imperceptibly and pulls me close using our intertwined hands, right up against him. He wraps his free arm behind the small of my back and eases me into him. But not for a kiss. He pulls me in and my head rests on his chest and his chin rests lightly on my head. He untangles our fingers and now his free hand is on my head, pressing it closer into him, stroking my hair.

"I never thought I would get this," he says quietly.

Now is my chance. "Nick, I—"

"Ghost, I need to tell you something." He blurts it out, like if he doesn't come out and say it, it will just wither up and die inside him.

"Me, too. Nick, here's the thing—"

"It's Frankie."

My heart sinks. It nose-dives off the side of the Eiffel Tower. I thought this moment was about me, us, but it's not. It's about her. It's been about her since I got here.

I can't say anything. I don't want to know where this is going. I grip the sweatshirt on his back tight in my fingers and squeeze my eyes shut, bracing for whatever he has to say.

"I started dating her because of Alex," he says after what seems like forever. "She was at this party and we had seen her around and Alex was totally into her, but she wasn't interested in him. At all. He's way too old for her, and she thinks he's a total douche. But she liked me, Ghost. She met us both and didn't like Alex and she liked me, and I was—" He cuts himself off, and I can feel his heart beating fast, so fast, under his shirt.

He pulls away from me. Not too much, and he doesn't let me go. Just backs up enough to look at me. "You've met her. Frankie is something special, you know? She's . . . she's amazing, Ghost. She's smart and funny and driven and she gets me. I've never had a girlfriend like her before, and part of the reason I didn't tell you about her ever was my own dumb fear I was going to ruin things with her." He moves one hand from my back and runs his fingers through my hair. His fingers skim the side of my face, and his thumb lingers by my cheek, moving slowly back and forth over my skin.

"And you . . ." He stares at me and I stare at him, frozen, with handfuls of his sweatshirt still in the tight grip of my fingers. I know what he almost says. *And you rejected me. And you told me it would never happen.*

"I know things have been weird tonight, and, God, I'm so sorry. That person on the phone, that's the real me. That's the me I am deep inside, that I can't always manage to be in real life. I have a hard time with people sometimes, but never with you. You're the only person who sees that version of me. The only one." He shakes his head, as if he can make the look of frustration and sadness fly right off it. "But lately I realized I need to try to share that side of me more. So, thanks. For helping me figure that out."

I let go of his sweatshirt with one of my hands and reach to his neck. I pull the loop of chain with my penny hanging from it out from under his shirt. I had put the clown penny in my pocket before we left the house because I knew I would be seeing Nick in person today, but he had no idea I'd show up here tonight. He really likes Frankie, but he wears my souvenir every day, just because. I rub my thumb over the three ghosts; then I let the charm fall against his chest so my fingers are free to reach up and skim the side of his face. His cheek is the slightest bit scruffy, with rough prickles along his jawline. I let my thumb trace small circles on his skin, and my entire insides are sloshing around, up and down, back and forth, out of control.

"Nick." He just made it a thousand times harder for me, but I need to tell him even so. Even though he has Frankie and even though he likes her and even though he's being the person with her he's only ever been with me, I need to tell him. And I want him to help me figure out why his hand is on my cheek and his other hand is on my back and why he's wearing my penny and why he's with Frankie and why he's looking at me like that and why he's not kissing me right now, when his phone buzzes and my phone buzzes at the same time.

We jump apart and pull our phones from our pockets on impulse and just like that the spell is broken.

CHAPTER 20

My text is from Lo: WHOLE GANG BACK 2GETHER, HEADING 2 PH. PROG-
RESS?

I assume Nick's text is from Frankie, but I'm sure it doesn't
say the same thing. I do imagine it has tons of exclamation points,
though.

"Well, it looks like everyone is going to the bar at Planet Hollywood," he says. He sounds as dazed as I feel.

"What? A club?" No. The girls promised no clubs.

"Frankie has this friend who bartends over there. And it's not
a club, don't worry. That wedding was more of a club than this is."
He slides his phone back in his pocket. "Wait. You don't have an
ID. We need IDs or they'll kick us out."

Maybe I'll tell him I don't have one, so we can stay up here at
the top of Vegas, or find something else to do, just the two of us. I
want to recapture that moment we were having a second ago, or
that moment on the dance floor. Moments that felt like our phone
calls, but better. There's no way to get those moments back and say
what we need to say at some loud bar with six other people.

And his girlfriend.

I don't have to tell him anything, though. His phone beeps with
another text. "Lo told Frankie you guys got fake IDs on the way

out here." He raises an eyebrow at me. "Seriously? Hannah Cho, straight-A student, got an illegal fake ID?"

I groan. I'm going to murder Lo for this. "It was Lo's idea. She took us to this shady parking lot in the middle of nowhere and bought us IDs from a guy in a pedo van. All in the name of adventure."

"Well," he says, a devious-looking half-smile spreading across his face. "Looks like we'll be breaking the law together, tonight. Partners in crime. Literally."

I don't want to go, I don't want to go, I don't want to go, I think, but I don't say that. Instead I say, "You have Alex's old ID, right?"

"Yup." He laughs a humorless laugh. "Aka his leftovers. As usual."

We're back in the elevator and this time I clutch his arm as we zoom down. I don't know why we're leaving. I guess we both know we're on dangerous ground, but I'm not sure how much I mind being there. I know I chickened out big-time on my chance to tell him the truth, but our moment has me feeling more confident now. I can do this. I grip his arm without realizing it, and I can feel him start to pull away, then change his mind and relax into me. While the ride up felt like a trip to the moon, the ride down is over in seconds. Too quickly, the door slides open, and I resist the impulse to send the elevator back up, and reluctantly let go of Nick's arm instead.

Planet Hollywood is right next to Paris, so we're there pretty quickly, no cab needed. The entire walk, I suppress my urge to reach over and grab his hand again, touch him more. Now that we're on solid ground, I don't have the height or the elevator or even the magic of the Eiffel Tower Experience as an excuse for physical contact. Plus, his hands are deep in his pants pockets.

I try to come up with a way to bring us back around to our earlier conversation, so I can finish what I started to say and just get it out there already. My mind races with everything said and unsaid between us, but I can't manage to get any of those thoughts out of my mouth.

God, I'm just as bad at life as he is.

"Oh," I manage to spit out as we walk up the steps leading to PH. "Your jacket. I should give this back to you."

He pulls his hand out of his pocket and reaches it in my direction, then stuffs it back in again, and I swear I see everything that passed between us on the top of the Eiffel Tower reflected back at me in his face. "You don't want to keep it on?" His voice is quiet.

"Well, I do. . . ." I trail off. "I mean, it's warm. But I think it might look weird if I wear it in here. You know."

"Oh, yeah." He says it like he got temporary amnesia and forgot his perfect girlfriend existed.

I shrug out of the jacket and hand it back to him. I don't want to. I'd rather stay in Nick's jacket even if it's a million degrees inside this bar. And knowing Frankie, she'd probably go on and on about how nice her boyfriend is for giving his jacket to me when I'm cold. Yup, he's a real saint.

We walk through the sliding doors and into the casino. It's more crowded now that it's late at night, full of people dressed in their Vegas best, ready to party. I spot our group right as we walk in, including Grace and Alex, who must have decided they weren't too cool to keep hanging out with us youngsters. They're right past the burger place, gathered around a long, waist-high table on our left-hand side that is covered in glasses.

"Is this the bar?" It's a dumb question. There is definitely a counter with two guys behind it pouring drinks, and our friends are clearly drinking. But I haven't seen this part of the casino yet, and I guess when he said "bar," I was picturing something different, like a bar on TV with wood paneling and beer signs and pool tables. Not this open area in the middle of the casino floor that doesn't even have walls.

"Yeah." He points to the small stage area where a drum kit and a guitar are sitting alone. "They have a cover band play here sometimes."

"I was expecting something more . . . like a bar," I admit.

"They have another one over in the middle that kinda has walls, if that's more up to your standards, Miss Bar Expert. Maybe we can go over there in a bit."

"I'm not looking for anything, smart-ass." I give him a playful shove on the arm, and then pull my hand back quickly when I realize what I've done. "You sure know a lot about this place for someone who doesn't come to the Strip much."

He shrugs. "Frankie."

"Hey, you guys!" Lo yells as soon as she sees us. She leaves the table and runs up, throwing her arms around my neck. "We're hanging out at a bar! In Las Vegas! For spring break! With a band! And a girl with tons of hookups! I feel like I'm in the best movie ever!"

I untangle myself from her arms. "Someone's been hitting the bottle."

"Frankie's bartender friend bought us all shots! Can you believe that? I took a shot, Hannah!" Lo drinks at the parties we go to at home, but it's always warm keg beer, a wine cooler, or some sort of mixed concoction. I go immediately into Mom mode, which is my normal role with Lo in social situations. "What did you take a shot of?" Like I know the difference between alcohols. "Did you have one right now? What else are you drinking?"

"Take it easy, control freak." She pulls me toward the group by the hem of my shirt. Nick is there already, greeting everyone. "I want to hear what happened at the top of the Eiffel Tower, you sneaky girl. And I need to tell you what happened while you were gone."

I lean into her ear to share some part of our moment from the top of Las Vegas with her. But when I lean forward, I focus on Nick. Frankie jumps up and down when she sees him, and she stands on her tiptoes, throws her arms tightly around his neck, and kisses him.

"Ew," Lo says.

I turn around before I have to see any more. "I can't," I spit out. "I can't do this. Come with me."

I wave to everyone crowded around the table, but I notice Frankie is still wrapped around Nick's waist. "Lo and I are going to run upstairs to the room to get my hoodie. Grace, do you need anything from the room?"

The look on Grace's face tells me the only thing she needs is Alex's tongue down her throat, so I grab Lo's arm and pull her through the casino toward the elevators, as far away from Nick and Frankie as my legs will take me.

CHAPTER 21

"So, what happened?" Lo asks as soon as the elevator doors slide shut. "Did you guys make out or what?"

"He has a girlfriend. That fact didn't change in the hour we were gone."

"Did he tell you why he lied about her?"

"Kinda. But we didn't get a chance to talk about—"

"Were you too busy drooling all over each other?"

"Do you want me to tell you this story, or do you want to make the whole thing up yourself?" I don't mean to snap at her. I know she's been drinking, and she rarely makes sense after half a cup of whatever her beverage of choice may be. "I'm sorry, I'm just annoyed by this whole situation."

We arrive on our floor and head to our room, where I fill her in on what happened between me and Nick: wedding crashing, jacket wearing, hand holding, hugging, touching, and all. I dig my hoodie out of my bag and brush my teeth since we're here and I could use some freshening up.

"Wow," she says. She's bracing herself on the side of the bed like she might slide off, so I pour some water into one of the glasses in the bathroom and bring it to her.

"Drink," I say.

She chugs the water, but only half the glass makes it into her mouth. The rest dribbles down her chin and pools on the front of her shirt. "It sounds like you guys had a moment."

"We did. But then you guys texted and we had to leave and meet up with you. I didn't want to. But he didn't seem to care, since he had no problem letting Frankie surgically attach herself to him downstairs." I sit down next to her, and then collapse flat back onto the bed. "I don't know what to think, Lo. I had so many chances to tell him how I felt and I just couldn't. I'm such a freaking coward." I let out a dramatic sigh. "He's been my best friend for four years. We talk every day. But it's not the same here. It's like he's the same person, but totally different."

Lo collapses next to me on the bed. "I know it sucks, and I wish I knew what to tell you. I think he's embarrassed. And confused. We showed up out of the blue, you know? It's a shock. And he seems to be pretty awkward in general."

"I know." I curl myself up in a ball. "I want to go back in time so this never happened. Our friendship is never going to be the same after this."

"Maybe that's a good thing." Lo starts rubbing my back, which is ironic because *she's* the drunk one. "I know I said you needed to tell him how you feel, but maybe you needed to come here to end this friendship, not take it to the next level. I know you'd never be happy if you were always wondering what-if about Nick. You don't have to wonder what-if anymore. Now you know. He lied to you and he has a girlfriend. You know what-if. Now you can move on."

Lo's words hurt like blunt force trauma to the head. So much so that I scoot myself away from her hand on my back, but I let what she said turn over in my mind as I lie there.

"Okay," she says, hopping off the bed. "Put on your hoodie. Let's go."

"Mnph," I mumble into the pillow. "Staying here. Giving up on this sucky night."

"Oh no, you're not." She pulls at my leg. "Get up right now."

"What's the point? Nick has a girlfriend."

"So you're just going to let Frankie win? Just like that? Because she has a huge rack and knows some loser roadies from the Killers and gets free cheesecake? Please. Get off your ass right now and do something about this, or I'm going to go down there and do it for you."

I roll over. "What am I supposed to do?"

This gets her going. She dances around the room. "Jordy!"

"What about Jordy?"

"Jordy was totally asking about you. Like, a million questions." She pulls me up to a sitting position. "Of course, I couldn't say you were crazy about Nick or anything. Because of Frankie, you know. I said you were Nick's longtime friend. And you should have heard Frankie singing your praises. She offered you up to him with a cherry on top."

"Nice." I don't know what is stranger about this story, Player Jordy showing interest in plain old me, or Frankie, girlfriend of the guy I'm in love with, trying to help me hook up. It's like I came down from the fake Eiffel Tower into Opposite Day.

"She feels bad you're the odd girl out. She wants to get you a man. I think it's sweet."

I narrow my eyes at her in a *Whose side are you on, anyway?* look, but she ignores it.

"So what I'm saying is, get over your emo and do something about this crappy situation. You have guaranteed booty from Jordy tonight. He's totally hot and I think you should go for it."

"I don't want Nick to think—" I'm about to say I don't want Nick to think I like Jordy, but does that matter? Nick had no problem letting Frankie kiss him right in front of me after that moment we'd had. Nick had no problem telling me how crazy he is about her. I'd love to give him a taste of how much that sucks.

If he even notices at all.

But, Jordy? "Jordy is nasty," I say. "Nick told me he hooks up with everyone."

"I know he has a reputation, but you don't have to do anything with him, Hannah. Just get down there and get your flirt on. He's hot. Have fun. Forget about Nick and remember you're a high school senior on spring break. You have a fake ID and a bartender pour-

ing you drinks and a gorgeous guy who's the lead singer in a band
you love flirting with you. You're making another hot guy jealous.
Do you know how many girls would kill for this? Get up and enjoy
yourself before I beat some fun into you."

I chew on the inside of my cheek. I did promise her and Grace
I'd step out of my comfort zone. If I keep the flirtation innocent,
what will it hurt? And there's the bonus of making Nick a little jealous while I'm at it, or at least giving him a taste of his own medi-
cine. I can't deny that the thought of turning the tables on Nick a
bit gives me a thrill.

I pull my clown penny out from my pocket, stare at it, then
place it on the cabinet next to the TV. "Fine," I say. "I'll talk to
Jordy. But that's it."

We rejoin the group at the bar, where more glasses have ac-
cumulated at the table. Frankie runs up as soon as she sees me
and gives me another one of those hugs of hers. "Thanks for smoothing things over with Nick for me when I left earlier." She's so
small, she has to get on her toes to whisper in my ear. I don't think
that has ever happened to me before.

"Oh, no worries," I say with a shrug. I'd forgotten about that
completely, to be honest, but I don't tell her. "He wasn't even pissed,
really."

"Hm." She crinkles up her forehead. "Well, I owe you a drink,
anyway." She links elbows with me and walks me back to the group.
"What do you want? My treat."

Aside from the drink of Grace's I sucked down earlier, I've
never had alcohol before. Someone usually needs to be the DD, and
it's certainly never going to be Lo, so I have no idea what people
even drink at a bar. Beer? A mixed drink? A cocktail? Are those even
different things?

I look at the glasses scattered on the bar table. "Uh, what are
you having?"

"Luis, he's the bartender here, he turned me on to orange-
flavored vodka with Sprite. It's so good. You want to try mine?"

I nod, and she slides her drink across the table. I take a quick
sip from the skinny straw and cough as it trickles down my throat.

The alcohol taste is harsh in my mouth, but the lemon-lime of the Sprite cuts it a little bit.

I shudder. "That's . . . good."

She walks me over to the bar and flags down the bartender. "Luis, this is Hannah, she's another one of my friends from California."

Luis nods at me. "Nice to meet you, Hannah. How're you liking Vegas?"

"It's, uh, interesting."

"Sounds like there's a story there. What can I get you?"

"She'll have my regular," Frankie steps in. "And put it on my tab."

"ID?" Luis asks. For the second time, I fumble around in my wallet for my fake ID and I hand it to Luis. He checks it out and smiles, then hands it back to me. I realize as he gives it back that the ID says Kristy but Frankie introduced me as Hannah. I hope that smile doesn't mean he's pressing some button on the bottom of the bar, alerting the authorities that I'm illegally drinking. Getting arrested would be the cherry on this fan-freaking-tastic day.

Instead he makes the drink for me, complete with an orange slice balanced on the rim, and slides it across the bar with a wink.

I walk with Frankie back to our table. "Why does he do that? Let us drink when he knows we're underage?" What spell does Frankie have over people? I swear.

"Luis is an old friend. He takes care of me, and I take care of him."

"Er . . ." Does Nick know about this?

"Not like that, you dirty girl. I talk him up on the blog. I let my readers know when he's working. I tell them to come here and ask for him. He makes piles of cash in tips every time I give him a shout-out, so he hooks me up. It's a nice little arrangement."

"I thought your blog was for underage Vegas."

"It is. But why do you think it's so popular?" She winks at me. "I blog about all kinds of hookups."

Everyone at the table shifts around to make room for our return. "Hannah, over here," Lo says, jerking her head toward the open spot she made next to her. With Jordy on the other side of the opening. The little sneak.

I walk around the tall table and slip in, but my focus is on Nick. He's down the table a bit, and Frankie has snuggled in next to him. He's watching me closely, his face giving nothing away, and I look back at him. Right when there has been just enough eye contact between me and Nick, I turn back to Jordy, who leans over and rests his elbow on the table, then his head on his hand. Damn, Hannah. That was pretty smooth.

"I'm glad you're back, Hannah. I've hardly had a chance to talk to you tonight."

"Oh, well, you know." It looks like my smoothness is gone as quickly as it arrived. I'm not very adept at this talking thing. "I was out seeing the sights."

"Is it your first time?"

I'm trying to turn slightly to see if Nick is looking, but Jordy's question snaps me back to attention. "What?"

"In Vegas? Have you been here before?"

He launches into the typical getting-to-know-you chitchat, and I realize pretty quickly from his questions that, although Frankie and Alex and Oscar all know about me, Nick has never once mentioned my name to this guy.

I try my best to keep myself from turning around to see what Nick is doing by flirting and laughing and focusing on how unfairly attractive Jordy is. Messy blond hair, piercing blue eyes. I'm not usually one to pay attention to eye color, but he has eyes that force themselves to be noticed. He has a killer smile, too, and one dimple on his right cheek. The more he talks to me, the closer he leans, so his leg is practically wrapped around mine after ten minutes of conversation, and I don't mind one bit.

I wonder if Nick sees that.

The whole time we talk, I sip my drink. It gets easier to swallow with each gulp, and the more I have, the more I start to have fun. My insides get warm and this hot guy is here and obviously into me—me!—and not making out with his secret girlfriend right in my face like *other people* I know and all of that makes me feel pretty damn good. Maybe coming back down here was a brilliant idea after all. I have good ideas.

"Looks like you're done with that," Jordy says, poking playfully at my drink, then again at my arm.

I give him a flirty smile in return. At least, I think it's a flirty smile. Who knows. "Get me another one? Just tell him it's Frankie's regular."

Jordy trots off to the bar for another round, and I turn to Lo to update her on our conversation and how, surprisingly, I'm having fun talking to him, but she's deep in the zone with Oscar. I look for Grace, but she's off away from the table a bit, talking animatedly with Alex and Frankie. Loud music playing in the casino means I can't hear them very well, but I do hear the word *"Rocker"* as her arms flail around, so I assume she's pumping Frankie for story ideas. Dang, maybe my sister is kicking ass at this internship, after all.

That means Nick is at the table alone. I turn to my right and he *is* there, alone, stabbing his straw into a drink and glaring at me.

Awesome.

Welcome to my life, Nick. Now you know how it feels.

CHAPTER 22

"What?" I ask. "What are you looking at?"

"Nothing," he says, but I know every nuance of his voice. He's seen us. He's pissed.

Tee-hee.

Before I can ask more, Jordy comes back with our drinks and leans into me, so I turn around, my back to Nick again.

We keep talking and Jordy keeps leaning. Before I fully realize it, his arm is around my waist. It doesn't feel bad, his touch on me, the light pressure of his hand on my back. Not like Nick's electric touch from earlier, but it's not terrible, either. I ask Jordy about the band, about his life. I didn't realize he was several years older than me and Nick. He's nice. He bought me a drink and he's listening to me and answering my questions and he likes bad reality TV, too, and he doesn't have a girlfriend—and, man, that smile. It's pretty damn sexy.

"You're really beautiful, Hannah." He leans over and whispers this in my ear. Honestly, though, he doesn't have to lean far, because we have scooted so close together, I'm practically wearing him like a coat. "I can't believe Nick's been your friend for so long and never made a move on you. What an idiot."

"I know, right?" I snort. "He is an idiot." Even Jordy knows.

"Can I ask you something, Hannah?"

It's weird the way he keeps saying my name, but I smile anyway because I kind of like hearing my name over and over. Nick rarely calls me by my name. But he does call me Ghost, and no one else calls me that. "Sure."

"There's another bar in the middle of the casino. Would you want to go over there and maybe sit down? They have couches. We can get comfortable."

I've done an awful lot of walking in these wedges since we arrived in Vegas, and the thought of sitting down is glorious. I nod and he grabs my hand and leads me away from the table, through the casino, and into the dimly lit bar in the middle of Planet Hollywood. I'm glad he's leading, because my head is feeling a little cloudy from the one-and-a-half drinks I've sucked down.

I want so badly to turn around and see Nick's reaction to us walking off together, hand in hand, but I think it will look so much cooler if I just saunter off like I don't care, so I let Jordy lead me.

But I think, *Please be looking, please be looking.*

Now, this is more what I was picturing when I heard we were going to a bar. The room is dark and circular and the bar is in the center with plush chairs and couches surrounding it and go-go dancers on platforms on the side. It's crowded in here, but we manage to find an empty couch. I plop down on the end and Jordy sits right next to me, as close as he can get without sitting in my lap. He puts his arm around me and leans in.

"This is so much better," he says.

"It feels good to sit down," I say stupidly because I have nothing else to say. I've been brought to this dark bar with a hot older guy who is buying me drinks and leaning so close, I can smell his fruity gum. Crap, I should've told Lo or Grace where I was going instead of walking off with no word, but I'd been too concerned with making a dramatic exit. I pull my phone out of my pocket and send a quick text to Lo: WITH JORDY. IN THE MIDDLE. Hopefully she can decipher that.

Slipping my phone back in my pocket, I take a small breath and look back up at him. This could be completely amazing or really freaking awkward. I guess it all depends on his next move.

Jordy brushes my hair out of my face, even though my hair wasn't even in my face, and gives me a look. "You're really beautiful, Hannah," he says again. A wordsmith this guy is not. For someone who writes such meaningful songs, he has no clue how to work it when it matters. But when I'm about to tell him maybe he should try expanding his repertoire of Lines That Get in Girls' Pants, he leans over and kisses me.

I've kissed a guy or two in the past few years. I mean, not a lot or anything, but it's not like this is my first time with a guy's tongue in my mouth. Now, Josh, Micah, and Ian have all been my boyfriends. Randomly kissing dudes isn't my style. But Lo did tell me to give Jordy a try. I'm positive she would approve of this. I hope she walks by.

Sadly, Jordy isn't the best kisser. I don't want to throw up, which, you know, is a thing I want to do sometimes. But I'm not totally into it, either, which is a bummer because he's so dang hot, and surprisingly fun to talk to. Perhaps we should go back to talking again, because his mouth on mine is the kissing equivalent of his handshake. One of those dead fish, limp handshakes old church ladies give you, but with lips and a floppy tongue, and before I realize it, I'm actually listening in on some of the conversations going on in the bar around us instead of paying attention to Jordy. Some chick has to get three more things crossed off her bachelorette party scavenger hunt. The guy across the bar wants to buy the girl on the chair behind us a drink, but she's not sure if he's attractive or not. The cocktail waitress spilled something on someone's Chanel purse, oh crap.

I'm more curious about what's going to happen with the purse— man, that girl sounds *pissed*—than I am interested in this make out session, so I sort of scoot my body back on the couch so I can get closer to the action and hear the details. Unfortunately, I end up lying back on the couch when I do this, which Jordy takes as a sign that I want to get more horizontal. He makes a grunty noise of approval and leans forward, pressing himself down on me. Yikes! This is not at all what I wanted, and the situation has ventured into creepy town, for sure. Public make out is already out of my comfort zone. Horizontal public make out is some next-level nope.

But before I have a chance to push Jordy off me and straighten up, I hear a sound that freezes me. I can't explain the noise. It's not a gasp, it's not a choke, it's not a scream, but it's some gravelly combination of all three. It doesn't matter what the noise is.

All that matters is I know it's coming from Nick.

CHAPTER 23

I push Jordy off me—I must catch him off guard, because he almost falls right onto the floor—and Nick and I stare at each other. He looks stunned and hurt, as if I've slapped him, open palm right across the cheek. But then his face changes, a subtle shift, and the hurt morphs into anger that pumps through his veins and seeps from his pores. I feel indignation radiating off him.

Jordy rights himself, then turns around to see what I'm gaping at. "Oh—hey, bro. What's up?"

Nick doesn't acknowledge Jordy. In fact, he doesn't break eye contact with me at all until he shakes his head, like he's trying to get a bug off his ear, and storms out of the bar.

"Hold on, Jordy. I, uh . . ." I don't even bother coming up with an explanation as I climb over him on the couch to chase after Nick.

"Hey!" I catch up on the casino floor right outside the bar, and I reach out and graze the arm of his jacket with my fingertips.

"What was that?" He's practically spitting at me. I thought I'd heard every tone of Nick's voice before, but I've never heard this: Fury. Hurt.

I've seen Nick mad before. He's frustrated with his brother almost every day for the endless string of thoughtless things Alex says and does to him. He's angry at his dad for not shaking himself out of his fog and living life again after Nick's mom died. He gets mad about bad grades in math or UNLV basketball losing or his phone battery dying.

I've never seen anger like this, though—deep and raw and painful.

And directed at me.

I guess we do have some parts we've never shown each other, secret sides of us we've kept hidden. We've stuffed these ugly sides, the sides full of jealousy and rage, deep in the dark corners of ourselves.

"What are you talking about?" I know damn well what he's talking about.

"You and Jordy. What the hell, Hannah?"

There are so many things I want to say in response, but my brain can't even process all of them. I wanted to get his attention, to make him feel what I've been feeling, but I wasn't prepared for *this*.

"Jordy is disgusting."

"He's your friend."

"Which is why I know how gross he is. I know how he is with girls." He takes a step back from me, like he wants to put as much distance between us as possible. There's an empty blackjack table behind him, though, and he backs up into it.

"Why does it matter who I kiss?" I should be able to make out with the entire cast of *Thunder from Down Under,* and he shouldn't have a word to say about it. "You kissed Frankie. I had to stand there and watch you—"

"That's different. Frankie is my girlfriend."

"I *know,* okay? That has been made very clear to me since the second I arrived. Frankie is your girlfriend. Frankie is kind of a big deal in Vegas. Frankie knows everyone. Frankie and her fans. Frankie and her tiny body and enormous boobs. Frankie and her phone. Frankie and her blog. Frankie is so goddamn nice that I can't even be pissed off at her for any of this." I search around for a desperate second, looking for something to throw because it seems like a perfect time to hurl a large object through the air, but there's nothing within reach except for the chairs tucked into the blackjack table. I figure the people behind the ceiling cameras would probably frown on that kind of scene, so I lamely flap my arms up and down.

Nick stares at me, his mouth slightly open. I shouldn't be reacting like this. I shouldn't be saying all these things about Frankie. It's not that I don't like her. I do. And that's the problem.

You're supposed to hate the girl who is with the love of your life, and I can't bring myself to do that.

"Pissed off at her for any of *what*?" Nick asks. He steps closer to me, just barely, and I can feel that some of the anger that was pulsing through his veins earlier has started to dissipate, and something familiar I can't place is creeping in. "Exactly what are you upset about?"

Jordy clearly realized I'm not coming back to him, and he chooses right now to wander out of the bar, eyes darting around the casino floor until he spots us. He shuffles over, rubbing his hand up and down the back of his head.

Honestly, I had already forgotten about him.

"Hey, beautiful. There you are."

"Oh, sorry," I say in the least convincing voice ever, waving my hand to indicate Nick standing next to me.

Jordy shakes his head and laughs. "Couldn't this wait, Cooper? Hannah and I were kind of in the middle of something."

When neither Nick nor I reply, Jordy stops laughing and his eyes dart back and forth between the two of us. I wonder what he notices. Our body language—both of us with arms crossed tightly over our chests. Our faces—Nick's still full of hurt and betrayal and a flicker of that something else, me clenching down on my teeth to keep tears from springing up.

"Oh, shit," Jordy says. He's obviously noticed it all. "Dude, you didn't tell me you guys had history. I thought you were just friends." He stuffs his hands in the pockets of his hoodie and stares at me for a second or two, then takes a step closer to Nick, lowering his voice to a whisper and jerking his head in my direction. "Is she—?"

"Yes," Nick says, cutting him off. He doesn't meet Jordy's eyes;

instead, he focuses on the carpet, where he's kicking his shoe into the ground over and over.

With the way Nick introduced us back at New York–New York and the questions Jordy asked earlier, I'd assumed Jordy didn't know anything about me. But it appears I was wrong; he definitely knows something. Jordy gives Nick a fist bump and says good-bye; then he turns and head nods in my direction. "It's been real, Hannah."

I watch Jordy walk away for only a second, and then I turn back to Nick. His face has desperation on it, and it's searching mine, as if I have an answer I don't realize I'm holding.

"Am I what?" I ask. "What was Jordy talking about?"

That familiar something flashes on Nick's face.

"He just knows that . . . He knows . . ." His voice is quiet now, almost every trace of that anger gone.

Stomach flip-flopping, I stare at him, waiting for him to finish. I step closer.

"He knows I've had feelings for someone for a long time, but I would never tell him anything about it." He sticks his hands into the back pockets of his jeans and looks directly at me. "He was wondering if that someone was you."

My mind is reeling. Lo told me she could tell from my stories that Nick had the same feelings for me as I had for him. And somewhere in the back of my head, all these years, I've always known he did.

And he tried to tell me. That night of the party. I know he did and I wouldn't let him and I told him I would never have those feelings for him and to just forget about it.

"You said yes."

He nods.

"Why didn't you tell me?"

For a fleeting second, I imagine us having a moment. Him crossing the distance between us, pulling me into his arms like he did at the top of the Eiffel Tower, confessing every feeling he's ever had. But instead—I don't know how or why—his anger returns. It's not loud now, but this quieter, controlled anger hits harder. "Oh, come on, Hannah. This isn't news. I've been in love with you for years. Years! And you always push me away, like I'm not real."

"I didn't know—"

"God, I tried to tell you and—"

"But you were drunk—"

"But I meant it, Hannah. And you had to know. All our conversations. You're the last person I talk to before bed and the first person I talk to when I wake up. Every day, for years. You know it's always been you."

He's right.

I know. I've always known.

"I try to meet you, you cancel. I give you hint after hint, and you just tell me about the guys you're dating. Of course I had to get drunk to tell you how I feel! There's only so much rejection I could take from you. And what else was I supposed to do? Sit around forever and wait for you to figure it out? And then you show up here out of the blue . . . Do you know how many times I've wished for this? How much I wanted to drive to you, or to look up and see you standing here?"

I can't even look at him. I hang my head and whisper, "No. I don't."

"All the time. I've dreamed about this so much. But when I don't drop everything for you, when I don't cheat on my girlfriend with you, you run off and make out with the grossest guy you can find. Were you trying to make me jealous? Because it worked. Congratulations."

"This is massively unfair. Don't you dare put this on me. You didn't even tell me about her," I say. "You lied to me."

"I did lie to you, okay? Is that what you want me to say? I didn't tell you about Frankie, because I kept holding out hope that one of these days you would feel the same way about me as I feel about you. And I didn't tell you about the band, because I was ashamed, and because I didn't know how to explain. . . . So, yes, I lied. And, believe me, I am so sorry. But I was so in love with you and I didn't know what to do about it and I didn't want to give you any reason not to fall in love with me back." He sighs and runs his hand through his hair, further messing it up. "But it obviously didn't matter. And then I met Frankie, and she's this cool girl who actually *wants* to be with me, so . . ."

My mind works overtime with all the things I can say to him right now: *I've been in love with you, too—I just didn't realize it until today. I completely understand why you lied, and I lied, too. I forgive you. Will you forgive me? Let's sit down and talk about this.*

But each declaration brings up a huge unknown. What will happen? And even more than that, does it even matter anymore?

I lost control of this situation so long ago, and this realization makes my stomach clench and my mind free-fall. I panic. Whatever I say right now will change everything.

But now he says he *was* in love with me. Past tense. It's pointless to tell him how I feel now.

I am done lying to myself, though, and to him, so I can't tell him I don't have any feelings.

Anything I might say is totally wrong and messy and will change too much.

Nick is still staring and still not talking. He wants a reply from me. A reaction. Something. But I don't know what to give him, and I can't stand there with this between us.

I take back control the only way I know how to.

I leave.

I turn and run. I run through the casino and dodge the tourists walking through and I run until I get to the elevator, where I jab the Up button and rest my arm on the wall, struggling and panting and trying to forget the hurt on Nick's face.

Running from him, from the truth, is probably the wrong thing to do. In fact, I know it is. But it's easier than telling him how I feel and having him reject me.

I'm going to leave Las Vegas a loser, but at least I didn't gamble my heart.

CHAPTER 24

I stumble into our empty hotel room and don't even bother turning on any of the lights. The small lamp between the beds was left on, and that's enough for me. I flop myself face-first on one of the beds and cover my head with a pillow, trying hard to forget the fight I just had with Nick. I didn't care about kissing Jordy, not at all. I kissed him in a moment of weakness. A moment of sadness and loneliness and jealousy and spite. Talk about all the wrong reasons. All I wanted was to make myself feel equal to Nick. If he's kissing someone who isn't me, I should be kissing someone who isn't him. It's only fair.

But then I got the chance to tell him how I felt, and I didn't. And I ran away.

I've ruined everything. Worse than losing the potential Nick as a boyfriend is losing the real Nick as my best friend.

I press the pillow harder over my head, trying to drown out the replay of our fight in my mind, but it doesn't work. So I try to replace it with our moment alone, arms around each other at the top of Las Vegas. But that seems so long ago now, like we were two different people.

After about five minutes or so, the lock on the door beeps and the door swings open. There's laughter, but it's muffled by my pillow, and I can tell it's Lo. And it sounds like she's with someone. Oscar, I'm sure, unless she found a new guy in the last hour and upgraded. With Lo, that wouldn't surprise me one bit.

Talking to them sounds like torture. Lo by herself, sure—I'll sit her down and tell her everything. But I can't deal with Oscar. And I don't want him knowing my business. Especially since he'll run and tell Nick all about it. No way.

Pulling the pillow down tighter, I try to sink down into the mattress. I pray they'll see me on the bed, think I'm sleeping, and go somewhere else to do whatever they came up here to do.

"Mmmm," Oscar says. "Come here." Lo laughs and I hear a rustle and a thump on the bed and some moving around and—oh my God, they are making out.

I have no idea what to do. They don't know I'm here, and here they are, kissing like the world is about to end in this room in the dark.

I've been in a room with Lo when she was kissing a guy before, but it had been more of a "seven minutes in heaven" kissing-game sort of situation. Not anything like this. Not with her thinking she was alone with a guy and not even knowing I was there.

I feel like I know everything about my bestie, but, sweet Lord, I don't want to know this much.

The pillow can't possibly be pulled down any tighter over my head, and it's not drowning out the sounds of Lo and Oscar kissing, no matter how hard I mentally recite the alphabet or sing the state capitals.

"Come on," I hear him say, and then she laughs again.

No, Lo, I think. *Don't do it.* But I don't say anything, because what can I say? *Hey, guys! I'm here and I'm not asleep—and, Oscar, please stop slobbering on my best friend.* I'm tired and too sad to come up with an appropriate response, so I just sit there on the bed with the pillow over my head.

Oh no. No no no no.

Then Oscar starts talking. "Seriously. Seriously. Oh my God, seriously, Lo. Seriously."

For the love of all that is good in this world, he can't *seriously* be narrating their make out session, right?

But Lo just giggles while Oscar makes slobbery noises and says, "Seriously. Seriously. Oh my God, seriously."

I can't. I can't lie here while my best friend makes out with this guy who keeps saying "seriously" over and over.

That's my line, Oscar, because I am wondering if this is seriously happening to me right now.

Ding ding ding.

That's my text notification. And it's such a habit, after spending the last four years texting Nick like it's my job at all hours of the day and night, for me to grab my phone without thinking about it. Instinctively, my arm reaches out to the table without remembering I'm supposed to be asleep.

My clamber for my phone stops them in their tracks. Lo squeals and fumbles around in the dark, and Oscar says, "Hannah?"

"Sorry," I mumble, like it ain't no thang, me lounging in the bed next to them while they're kissing like the *Titanic* is going down. "I got a text." If I act like it's perfectly normal that I've been here this whole time, maybe we can all get through this with no major incident.

"Hannah!" Lo screams. So much for staying incident-free.

"God, Hannah," Oscar says, sounding quite put out. "You were supposed to be asleep."

What? I shoot up in my bed. "You knew I was here? You knew I was here and you were hooking up next to me anyway?"

I'm so mad at Oscar because he doesn't know me, but I'm even more mad at Lo for not telling him, *Hey, maybe we should hold off on this until my BFF isn't feet away from us.* I mean, who does that? Has Vegas made her insane?

I glare at her, but she doesn't return my look.

"Fine." I shove my phone in my pocket and jump off the bed. "I guess I won't take a nap." My mind hadn't been able to calm itself enough even to attempt a nap, but they don't know that. And I'm pretty sure that sleeping at whatever time it is isn't a nap anyway, but actual sleep. "I'll leave you two alone."

I think I hear Oscar say "good" as I storm out the door of my own hotel room in the middle of the night, but I don't turn around to verify. I'll take this up with Lo tomorrow.

Once in the hallway, I lean my back against the wall and sink down to the ground.

I fought with Nick and ran away like a total coward after he told me he had feelings for me, and now I've been kicked out of my own hotel room so my best friend can stick her tongue down the throat of his best friend, some guy she met only a few hours ago.

My spring break really sucks.

Oh yeah, my text. The number isn't one I have saved in my phone, but as soon as I check the message, I see whose it is.

HEY HANNAH, IT'S FRANKIE. I'M DOWNSTAIRS AT YOUR HOTEL. CAN WE TALK?

To borrow a term from Oscar . . . Seriously? Could this night get any worse?

Well, I have nothing else to do. I have no hotel room to hide in. Nick will probably never talk to me again. Might as well go down and let Frankie yell at me or whatever she wants to do. Gotta end the trip on a high note, right? I answer,

BE RIGHT DOWN.

I get up, take a deep breath, and head back to the elevators.

I'm jabbing at the elevator button over and over with all the strength in my finger. There's a young couple in the elevator hallway with me, and they're watching my enthusiastic button pressing with horror. "I think it's going to come," the guy says to me after about my twentieth jab.

I'm so annoyed with Nick and with myself, but I'm also pissed at Lo for kicking me out of the room so she can hook up with Oscar, a guy she barely even knows. Especially when I have needed her all night. Giving her a piece of my mind takes priority over meeting up with Frankie.

"Sorry," I mumble to the couple. I give the DOWN button one last smack; then I whirl around and stomp back to the room. I pound on the door with the heel of my hand. I'm tempted to kick it and yell out her name, but it's pretty late and I'm already on enough shit lists as it is. I don't need to have everyone on this floor trying to sleep hating me, too. Although, if the crowd down in the casino is any indication, it doesn't matter what time it is in this city, no one is sleeping.

After what seems like an hour, the door opens a crack and Lo's head, hair all akimbo, pokes out.

"Did you forget your key?" she asks.

"No," I say. "I have it. I wanted to make sure you were decent." Truth is, I was more concerned about getting her attention in some dramatic fashion than I was about practicality. It didn't even occur to me to use my key. "Can we talk for a sec?"

"Right now? I'm a little busy."

"Don't care." I push the door open more and lean under her arm into the room. "Lo will be right back, Oscar. Hold on to that boner."

"Hannah!" Lo sounds all scandalized, but she also laughs, so I know she's not too mad at me. I take her arm and pull her outside into the hallway.

"Dude," I say as the door clicks shut behind us. "What the hell is all of this?"

"What? I'm having fun. That's what this trip is all about, right?"

"Right, but—" I jerk my head down the hallway to let her know we are going on a walk. I head out down the hall and she follows close behind. "You just met Oscar tonight."

"But he's Nick's friend. It's not like he's some random dude off the street."

"I know, but—"

"You were hooking up with Jordy."

"I know, but—"

"But what, Hannah?" Lo stops and looks at me, her face dead serious. "What are you getting at?"

"This isn't like you." I can't explain why I'm so annoyed.

Because I'm supposed to be the one going wild with Nick and I'm not? Because I've needed Lo and Grace and they both ditched me for guys at the first opportunity? Because this whole trip has been a nightmare since the second I left home?

Lo puts her hands on her hips. "Kissing some guy you just met in a bar when you came here for a different guy isn't like you, either."

"First of all, I was following your expert advice. Second, Nick has a girlfriend. And how did you know I was kissing Jordy?"

"We ran into Nick downstairs on the way up here. Oh man, he was pissed."

"I know he was," I say, kicking at the carpet. The shame from my public fight with him floods back to me. "He told me he loved me, but then I freaked out and ran away. I ruined everything."

"Oh shit, girl."

"What?" I snap my head up and narrow my eyes at her. "Now you're interested?"

Her head cocks to the side, and her eyebrows draw together. "What do you mean?"

"All night I've needed you and I've needed Grace. I've been going through hell here, and I thought I could count on you."

Lo's face twists up. "I know we came out here for you, Hannah, but this is my life, too. And Grace's. You're my best friend, but I'm not going to sit around and do nothing, life totally on hold, in case you need me. I'm in Vegas. I'm going to have a little fun."

"That's not what I'm saying." I shake my head, trying to clear the built-up frustration from the night. "I want you guys to have fun. But I needed you. I still need you. I don't know what's going on."

Lo stares at me, good and hard. I think her face is going to soften up and she'll pull me into a hug and tell me how to fix everything. But instead she narrows her eyes, sharpening all her features. "Look, I mean this in the nicest possible way, because you know I love you, but you act like a control freak and then take absolutely no control over the things that matter. You float around and wait for other people to make your decisions for you, but you don't actually do anything yourself. I think it's time for you to stop relying on me and Grace and everyone else, and solve this on your own."

"But, Lo—"

"I've had to listen to you talk about Nick for years, and, honestly, I'm getting sick of it. If you want him, go get him. Talk to him. Do something. If not, shut up about it and deal."

"I can't just—"

"This is tough love, baby," she says with a wry smile. "Go figure it out." Then she turns around and walks back to the room, and to Oscar, leaving me alone in the hallway.

I do want Nick, but I think it's too late to go get him.

And I'm going to have to go through Frankie first.

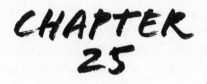

CHAPTER 25

It's not hard to find Frankie downstairs. At this hour, the casino is full of ridiculously drunk people stumbling back to their rooms and unbelievably trashy people powering through the night, gambling their last few dollars away.

Frankie is one of the few sober ones.

She's sitting at a table in front of a closed shop called Earl of Sandwich. I hesitate before she sees me, and I take a second to look at her. Her bright red hair is a little flat and dark circles have formed under her eyes, but besides that, she's as cute as she was when I saw her for the first time earlier tonight. Unbelievable, since I caught a glimpse of my reflection in the elevator on the way down and I look like I've been run over by a truck and then backed up over by it for good measure.

She's bent over and on her phone, of course. Texting some bouncer or club promoter, I'm sure, or maybe updating her blog with her recap of the night's exciting events. I can picture the tweet:

NICK'S PATHETIC FRIEND TRIED TO MOVE IN ON HIM #WTF.

I take a deep breath, gather everything I have inside me, and I walk up to her.

"Hey."

Her head snaps up and a smile is on her face immediately. "Thanks for coming down here, Hannah." She sounds so freaking happy to see me that I smile back in spite of myself.

"Sorry to keep you waiting." I stick my hands into my pockets and look at the ground. "Lo and I were having a fight."

"Oh no!" She jumps up from her chair and hugs me. Hard. "I'm so sorry, Hannah. Best-friend fights are the worst."

Tell me about it. I just had two in the span of an hour.

"I have an idea," she says as she pulls away from me, her eyes practically sparkling. "Let's go have some fun. Do you play blackjack?" She doesn't even wait for my answer; instead, she pulls me into the casino, weaving us through the maze of tables, about half of which are closed at this hour, and she slows down every time we pass one playing blackjack.

"There's blackjack." I point with my free arm.

"Ew. That's single deck."

I don't know what that means, or what any of these signs mean, so I let her lead me. She dismisses every table, though, mumbling things like "Spanish Twenty-one" and "Bah. High limits."

Finally she chooses a table that meets her standards. It's empty of players, in a pink area of tables called the Pleasure Pit. The dealer, a pretty dark-haired girl in a bustier with a necklace that says *Lourdes* in script, smiles at us as we approach. "This is perfect," Frankie says. "Sit down."

I sit.

"I don't know how to play blackjack," I say, adjusting myself on the tall chair.

"No big," Frankie says. "I'll tell you what to do. And so will Lourdes. Right, Lourdes?"

"Of course." Lourdes says it in this sexy, breathy voice, and I suddenly wonder if we are supposed to be sitting in this area called the Pleasure Pit.

"Are we okay to be here?" I whisper to Frankie. "This feels like the 'naked chicks on display' area. I feel a bit out of place."

Again, Lourdes smiles. "You're fine. Everyone is welcome in the Pleasure Pit." Behind her, a girl on a box is go-go dancing to the

Jay Z song playing throughout the casino, so I totally don't believe her, but no one is kicking us out yet. "But I do need to see your IDs."

Oh yeah. You have to be twenty-one to gamble. Luckily, I shoved my wallet in my back pocket when I stormed out of the hotel room earlier, so I have my fake with me. It's the third time I've used it tonight, but my hand still shakes as I pull it out of its sleeve in my wallet and hand it to Lourdes at the same time Frankie hands hers over.

I'm watching Lourdes's face as she examines our IDs. Her eyes flick back and forth from my picture to me, and then from Frankie's picture to Frankie's face.

"Drinks?" A cocktail waitress comes up behind us, and before I can wave her off, Frankie orders two Jack and Cokes for us.

"But—"

Frankie puts a hand up in my face. "We need to talk, and I'm going to need a drink to do it."

My stomach drops to the ground. What is she going to say that she needs me buzzed for? She was hugging me and smiling a minute ago. Was that all an act to get me comfortable so she can scream at me about her boyfriend?

"Fine," I say. "But can I have a water, too?"

The waitress nods and walks to the next table, and I turn around to find Lourdes has laid our IDs down on the table in front of us. Whew.

Lourdes stares at us like she's expecting something.

"So, what do we do now?" I whisper. "Make a bet or something?"

"I got this," Frankie says. "This is my treat, okay?"

I start to tell her I can use some of my slot machine money, but she stops me with her hand again. She reaches into her wallet and pulls out a one-hundred-dollar bill that she lays out on the table. Lourdes takes the bill, flattens it out in front of her, and calls something over her shoulder to the huge guy in a suit behind her.

"Oh my God," I whisper again. "What is she yelling? Are we in trouble? Where did you get that money? Is it stolen?"

"Settle down." Frankie pats my leg. "They do that with big bills, so the pit boss knows a big bill is getting changed into chips."

Lourdes pushes a stack of chips to us. Frankie divides up the chips between us and explains the rules to me as Lourdes deals.

I look at my two cards. An eight and a five. "I have thirteen. Hit, right?"

"Nope," Frankie says. "I know it seems like you should, but she has a sixteen." She waves her hands over the top of her queen and eight, and nods at me, like that's what I'm supposed to do, too. It goes against pretty much the only thing I know about blackjack, to stay on a thirteen, since I thought it was about trying to get to twenty-one, but I follow her lead. I don't know what it is about Frankie, but she has this way of making you do what she tells you even when it flies in the face of all logic and reason. I wonder if that Frankie Magic is how she got Nick to go out with her in the first place.

Now it's time for Lourdes to turn over her next card. It's a four. Lourdes gets a twenty. Frankie and I both lose.

"Sorry, ladies," Lourdes says as she leans over to collect our chips and our cards.

"That totally wasn't supposed to happen," Frankie says, shaking her head. "You should always stay on that hand. She's supposed to bust."

The waitress delivers our drinks, which are apparently free if you're sitting at a table, and Frankie continues giving me blackjack tips, all of which result in me losing every single hand.

"I hate blackjack," I say after losing a particularly painful hand where I put all kinds of extra bets down because Frankie told me to, and I lost them all.

Frankie runs her hand through her hair. "I don't know what's going on, Hannah. We are following all the rules exactly. Aren't we, Lourdes?"

"You sure are," Lourdes says. "I would have played all those hands exactly the same way."

"I guess I just have killer luck tonight," I mumble. Following the rules and having it get me nowhere has suddenly become a theme in my life. Rules I understand, rules I don't understand, they're all leading me down a dark path to nowhere.

I'm about to give up on blackjack for the night, since I've lost almost all Frankie's money and don't want to dip into my own. I'm realizing what a loser I am, and my patience for this stupid game is wearing thin. Lourdes's pile of cards is through, so she takes a quick break to shuffle everything up again, and I take a huge gulp of my drink.

"I hope this isn't weird," Frankie says, angling her chair to face me. "I need to talk to you about something. I know how close you and Nick are, and I don't know who else to go to."

What is this? I was worried she was going to get mad at me about something, but if she is trying to have some sort of sex talk with me about Nick, I think I might lose my ever-loving mind. There's no way I can sit here and listen to her talk about doing stuff with him. Sitting through Lo and Oscar's encounter upstairs was already more than my delicate imagination could handle. A play-by-play and color commentary about Nick and Frankie getting it on will likely break me into pieces.

"What's up?" I manage to squeak out.

"Well, I'm sure you've noticed we're having a few problems."

I had noticed a smidge of tension between them—but, honestly, I thought it was because of me. Is she going to confront me about it? Are the gambling tips a way to warm me up so she can sneak-attack me? I size her up. I'm not very big, but I'm definitely bigger than she is. If she tries to fight me, I have an advantage.

"I didn't notice," I say as I pull my hair back into a bun. I don't want her to have anything to grab on to if she does take a swing at me.

"Oh, that's good." She spreads her hands out on the felt table and stares at them. "We are, though. Having problems."

"Uh . . . why?" I don't want to get in the middle of it, but I have to know more.

"My blog. He doesn't like it. He hates that I have so much personal stuff online. He hates that everyone who reads my blog knows we're dating." Her phone beeps with a notification. She looks at it and puts it back in her pocket. "We just got in another fight about it, out of the blue. He blew up at me and stormed off. I don't know where he went, and he won't answer his phone."

"Oh." This isn't what I had been expecting at all. It's about Frankie's stupid blog this whole time. I take another huge swig of my drink. "Well, you know Nick's a private person."

"I know," she says. "I don't think he would ever leave his bedroom if he didn't have to. He told me the only reason he has a profile online is because of you. Is that true?"

I can't keep a smile off my face at the memory. "I started it for him and e-mailed him the password so he could keep it up. It was easier for us to keep in touch that way. The chat feature, you know?"

"He hardly ever updates the page."

"I know. He only has tagged photos up there. Or ones he texted me that I uploaded for him. I don't think he has any idea where the upload button even is."

She shakes her head. "We're so different that way, you know? I live my whole life online. My blog is who I am. It's not like I can not include him on it. That would feel like lying."

"But he hates it."

She nods and stabs her drink.

I try to figure out what to make of this odd situation, the girlfriend of the guy I'm desperately in love with—yes, even after everything—asking me for advice on how to work things out with him. She reaches over and grabs my hand, squeezing my fingers tightly. "I like Nick so much," she says. "You know. You know he's special."

As soon as she says that, I wonder how much she's aware of. How much do I wear my own feelings for Nick around on my face? Can Frankie tell? Or is she saying this only because she knows how deep our friendship is?

But she says she likes him. She doesn't say she loves him.

Has he told her he loves her?

I let her squeeze my hand, but I don't squeeze back. When she loosens her grip, I pull my hand back to my own lap. "Nick is special, Frankie." I choose my words carefully. I don't want to say the wrong thing here. "He's an amazing guy. He's sweet and thought-ful and funny and talented. He's . . ." I almost say he's honest, but I wince and keep it inside. He lied to me. Big-time. The sting is dying out quickly, though, because I can understand it. I get why he did it, and I did it, too. "Well, of course he's hot."

We both grin at that. "Yeah," she says. "He's gorgeous."

I clear my throat. "But there are other hot guys out there, you know? There's more to him than being hot." I can't believe I'm having this conversation with her. I must be a decent liar after all, and hid my feelings for Nick better than I thought. Or maybe Frankie, as sweet as she is, is completely clueless. Or smart enough to not see things she doesn't want to see. Like, what does she think about the fact that Nick wears a flattened Disneyland penny around his neck every day? Has she bothered to ask? Does she even care?

"I need you to tell me what to do, Hannah. I don't know how to do this. I just need to figure out if this is worth it, you know?"

This is the moment of truth. I probably could have it all right here. Frankie seems desperate, like she'll do whatever I say. If I tell her it doesn't seem like things will work out, Nick will never change, they aren't a good match, any of that, I can tell from the look on her face that she'll take me at my word and probably end things between them. That will get her out of the way.

That will leave Nick free for me.

But I look at Frankie and I see myself. I see someone who cares about Nick like I do, who wants to be with him.

She didn't overlook Nick, and she didn't run when things got too serious. She didn't leave behind chance after chance to tell him how she felt. She knew she wanted him, and she went after him.

I can't do this to her. Not after she's been so nice to me since the minute I met her. Not since I saw the two of them together, the way she looks at him.

But I can't tell her that being with him is the right thing to do, can I? I mean, if I do, that would mean cutting myself out of the picture. On purpose.

Giving up everything we had on the dance floor, at the top of the Eiffel Tower. For good.

I have no idea which set of rules to follow here.

"Here's the thing," I say. "It seems like you have to figure out what you want the most." I look right at Frankie. At her red, red hair and her perfectly fitted jeans and her perfectly distressed leather jacket. At her face, so worried and so desperate. "I've known Nick a long time. And in some ways, he's changed a lot. He's become more open. He's loosened up. But in some ways he hasn't changed, and I don't think those parts of Nick will ever change. He's always been stubborn. He's always been really private. He's never really liked to share."

I grin at a memory of Nick, when we were talking online and I told him I had a boyfriend the first time and he responded with frowny faces. He tried to act like he wasn't jealous, and he said he was just bummed because he knew we wouldn't be able to talk as often. He didn't want to share me. Of course I made sure nothing changed between us, and that first boyfriend lasted only two weeks.

I should have known right then.

"Yeah," Frankie says. "He won't even share his food with me when we go out. I always like to order one dish, and then have the person I'm with order something else and then we can both split our stuff to try more things. But Nick orders what he orders and doesn't want to split or share with me. Not even a bite."

I feel such a strong stab of jealousy that I flinch. I've known Nick for so much longer than Frankie, but I've never been out to eat with him. I'd never reach over to his plate and try to take some of his fries, because I don't like to share my food either. Other people touching the food on my plate? No way.

This whole time, I never knew we'd be perfect dinner companions.

"I don't think that's going to change about him," I tell her, dropping my voice. "If he doesn't want to share you with your blog readers, and if he doesn't feel comfortable being a public part of your blog, that's how it's going to be. And I think asking him to be okay with it would be like asking him to be something he's not."

Frankie lets out a sad sigh.

"I hate to tell you to change your blog, especially when it's so funny and good."

She beams. "It is funny, isn't it?"

"Oh yeah, it's the best." I chew the side of my mouth. I haven't even looked at her blog yet, but given everyone's reaction to it, I'm sure it's the best thing to hit the Internet since TMZ. Either that or everyone is easily impressed. "But I think what it comes down to is which Nick is more important to you? The Nick you write about online? Or the real Nick? The one who you can sit around and watch a movie with? Or that blog Nick from all your dates? Which Nick matters the most to you? That's what you need to ask yourself."

And I realize I'm not even asking Frankie. I'm asking myself. Which Nick is more important to me? This person who exists only on the phone and the computer screen? The one I so wanted to preserve a friendship with that I was willing to remain a ghost? Or the one who is real? The one who I've screwed things up with so royally, and he screwed things up right back, I wasn't sure if we would ever be the same?

Frankie's elbow leans on the padded edge of the blackjack table, and she's watching me intently, her mouth twisted up in concentration.

"I mean, isn't having an actual boyfriend more important than the Internet knowing you have a boyfriend?" My stomach flutters nervously as I say this to her, because I feel like I'm making a decision here. Crossing a line. "Wouldn't you rather have the real Nick all to yourself? That's why you're with him, right? And isn't he worth some sacrifices?"

"Cut the deck?" Lourdes asks, reminding me what we're doing there. She holds a green plastic card out to me, and the rest of the stack of cards is on the table in front of her. I'm sure my face gives away my confusion over what she's asking me to do. "Take this card," she says, waving it in front of me. "And stick it in here, wherever you think it will be a lucky cut."

"I'm the last one to know about luck today," I tell her, but I take the card from her anyway.

And as I lean over to stick the card in the stack, my elbow slides off the side of the table, hits my glass, and sends the half-full contents of my glass of Jack and Coke spilling all over the blackjack table, soaking the felt, drenching the cards, and dripping into a sticky pool collecting in the tray of multicolored chips right in front of Lourdes.

Based on the look of sheer hatred on her face, Lourdes no longer likes us.

Neither does Lourdes's pit boss, Bill, a large round man who frowns at us as Lourdes calls over to him to deal with the mess I caused.

"Oh my God, Frankie." I scramble to pick up my drink and the ice cubes that slide all over the felt table when I grab at them. My heart pounds so loudly, I swear Bill can hear it. I'm not supposed to be drinking. I'm not supposed to be gambling. I'm not supposed to be in Las Vegas at all. Bill probably looks at IDs for a living. His home is probably wallpapered with fake IDs of stupid underage girls from California. He'll know in one second mine isn't legit.

"He's going to take us to the back and break our legs," I whisper almost soundlessly through my teeth at Frankie. "We're going to get offed. He's going to off us."

"We should probably get out of here," she whispers back.

Bill glares. "What happened here?" He's studying us. Closely. Too closely. Adrenaline pumps through my body. I know I'm going into fight-or-flight mode, and I want to do nothing but GTFO.

I look at Frankie for help, but she's not giving me much. I hope that means her mind is working overtime to get us out of this situation.

Lourdes pulls out a towel from somewhere. "Well, these girls—" She jerks her head at us. "—spilled their drinks all over the table. And now I have to clean every—single—chip."

"So, ladies," Bill says, leaning over the table. He doesn't look kind. He looks at us like we're going to turn up dead in a ditch somewhere. Or at the very least suffer some broken kneecaps. So as he lectures us on proper casino behavior, I don't even think about it, I get up as fast as I can. I knock my chair over in the process of trying to make a hasty exit, which probably ticks ol' Bill off even more, but I don't even turn around.

I hear Frankie apologize and say, "She's had a little too much to drink. Twenty-first birthday party, you know. I'll take her upstairs," and I assume she collects our chips. I don't even know, I just walk as quickly as I can away from the table, leaving my mess behind for Lourdes and Bill to deal with.

I weave through the labyrinth of tables at full speed with no real destination. It takes Frankie until I get to the elevator hallway to catch up with me. I lean over onto my knees to catch my breath. "Is he following us?"

"If he is, it's only because you were making a scene. What *was* that?"

"I thought he was going to arrest me." As soon as the words are out of my mouth, I realize how ridiculous the idea is. My ID has been fine all night, and Lourdes checked it when we sat down. And I only knocked down a drink. Yeah, it was a klutzy move, but it wasn't like I was counting cards or stealing chips.

The adrenaline is still pumping through my system. I straighten up and smile at Frankie. "That was fun."

She shakes her head. "So, do you always do that?"

"What?"

"Run away? You took off like you were on fire."

She doesn't sound mad about me taking off and leaving her there, but when she says it, it dawns on me how much I do run from things. I ran from Nick just a few hours ago, when I didn't know what else to say to him. I ran from the roller coaster when everyone was going on it. I ran from Josh Ahmed when things got too weird.

I ran. I quit. I gave up. It's my first response whenever anything doesn't go my way.

I shrug. "I guess it's kinda my thing."

"You're a funny girl, Hannah. I'm glad I met you tonight." She pulls me into the ten millionth hug she's given me. "I'm going to hit up the cashier and get out of here." She pulls away, but her hands are vice-tight on my shoulders. "Thanks for the advice, by the way. You're so right about Nick."

"Sure," I say, shrugging. "Anytime."

She hugs me again, and this one is a tight one. "I'd love to stay friends."

"Well, yeah," I say as I stiffen up. I wish this hug would end already. "Of course we will." If Nick still wants to be my friend after this disaster of a visit, which I completely doubt.

She finally lets me go; then she turns and skips off to the cashier, leaving me to slowly lower myself down on the floor in the elevator hallway.

Well, there it goes. My chance with Nick. I practically wrapped the two of them up in a chain and locked the padlock myself. But I had to. I couldn't lie to Frankie. I couldn't pretend like Nick wasn't the best thing that was ever going to happen to her. As much as I wanted to tell her to run far and fast and leave Nick free for me, I couldn't do it. Because running is my move, apparently. And, the truth is, they are good together. I can see it, even through my jealousy and my sadness. I can see it, and I can't steer her away.

And even if they aren't perfect for each other, at least she's willing to fight for him, which is more than I can say for myself.

After a few minutes of self-pity, I get up and press the elevator button to head back to my room. I'm all alone, and I'm out of things to run from.

CHAPTER 26

SUNDAY

The best thing about sleeping in a hotel room is the blackout curtains. They block out every speck of light from the outside world, so you can doze until some ungodly hour and remain blissfully clueless to the fact that life is happening outside, until your hunger wakes you up at a time that's closer to evening than morning.

Of course, I don't get that on my one night sleeping at Planet Hollywood, because no one bothered to close the blackout curtains in the first place. I'm woken up at 6:45 A.M. by the sunrise reflecting off every shiny surface on the Las Vegas Strip and directly onto my eyes, only a few short hours after I stumbled up to the room, pounded on the door, and kicked Oscar out.

I drag myself out of bed and over to the window to shut the curtains. I pull them tight, grumbling that Lo doesn't seem to be disturbed by the light at all, the pillows from her bed covering every inch of her face. How does she breathe like that? I bump into her bed out of spite, but she doesn't even flinch. Ugh. There is nothing more annoying than someone sleeping peacefully when you couldn't be more awake. It's still early, though, and it's nice and dark now. Maybe it won't be too hard to fall back asleep.

Back under the covers, I stretch myself in every direction pos-

sible before I try to fall back asleep in the dark room. But as I
stretch my legs out, I realize something. I'm in this bed alone.
I spring up and look again over at Lo, covered in pillows. She's
alone in her bed, too. I was so relieved she was Oscar-free over
there, I didn't even realize she was also Grace-free.

How could I be so groggy that I didn't even notice my sister is
missing? I didn't think I drank that much last night.

I pull my phone off the charger and check it. Nothing. No texts
or calls from Grace at all. I call her, but her phone goes straight to
voice mail, so I type WHERE ARE YOU?!? as quickly as I can and stare
at the phone, willing her to reply. The sleepy haze of a few minutes ago is now replaced by adrenaline and paranoia. Is she dead
in a Vegas gutter somewhere? Did Alex sell her into a life of strip-
ping to buy a new guitar? Why hasn't she called me?

My head flops back down on the pillow, but my mind won't shut
off. Every horrible thing that could possibly happen to my sister,
alone on the streets of Las Vegas, is flashing through my mind.
I text her again. PLEASE CALL ASAP. I AM WORRIED ABOUT YOU.

A few minutes later, my phone vibrates. It's Grace. Thank God.
I'M DOWNSTAIRS. BE RIGHT UP.

Relief covers me like the hotel bed comforter. By the time my
sister's key slides into the lock and the door beeps her entrance,
I'm sitting upright on my bed, my leg shaking with worry.

"Where have you been?" I ask as soon as her face appears
through the door. "I just woke up and realized you weren't here.
I thought you were dead or something."

Grace's hair under her beanie is a tangled mess. I can smell
the booze coming off of her like she's wearing Eau de Liqueur per-
fume. Her makeup has completely worn off her face, and she looks
exhausted. Exhausted but happy.

"Why are you smiling? Do you know what you've put me
through?"

She sits on the bed next to me. "Calm down. I'm fine. Alex and
I were hanging out at some locals bar off the Strip. I didn't even
realize what time it was. There are no clocks anywhere, and you
can't see the outside, and—"

"Your phone has a clock on it, Grace. And you had to know it was late. You could have at least texted me."

I know I sound like our mom. In fact, I'm worse than Mom, who is never this panicked or naggy. Well, not with me, anyway, because I never do anything to cause her to freak out. But now I can see why Mom sometimes yells at Grace. I noticed she was gone only ten minutes ago, and it's been the worst ten minutes of my life.

"You knew I was with Alex. I was fine."

I stand up, all the frustration that built up over the course of the night coming to a head. "I did not know that, Grace." I've been trying to keep my voice low because Lo is sleeping, but now I don't even care anymore. This rant is for her, too. "I didn't know where you were going. I don't really know Alex, except that he's a total A-hole to his brother. I was worried, okay? Don't act like I have no reason to be upset because you took off and totally ditched me. That's not something I did wrong."

"Hannah, Lo's sleeping. Lower your voice."

"No. I won't. This is BS. We came here for me, so I could meet Nick. But things went to shit, and instead of helping me through this, you both ditched me for dudes at the first possible second. Lo kicked me out of the room so she could hook up with Oscar. I sat on the floor of the elevator hallway by myself in the middle of the night. And you, you left at the first available opportunity, didn't you? You said you were going to get intel for me. So, did you? What exactly did you find out for me?"

"Well," she says, looking down at her hands. "We didn't really get a chance to talk—"

"Oh, so you didn't do the one thing you promised me you would do? What a shocker!"

Lo, apparently awakened by my early morning freak-out, sits up in bed. "What's happening?" she mumbles. She's still in last night's clothes, and she didn't bother to wash off her makeup, which is now smeared all over her face and all the pillows she had been smothering herself with. If only Oscar could see her now.

"Hannah, I am exhausted," Grace says, rubbing her eyes. "So is Lo, obviously. We have a lot to talk about, but right now I think we all need to sleep, okay? Let's go to bed for now, and we can talk in a few hours."

I know arguing with my sister right now is pretty pointless. She gets downright unreasonable when she hasn't had enough sleep. Throwing my hands in the air, I say, "Whatever," and I crawl back into bed, rolling over so my back is to her.

I hear her wash her face in the bathroom, then change her clothes. I can't help but roll my eyes at the thought of her changing into her pajamas and getting into bed at 7:00 A.M., when there are people getting out of bed and changing out of their pajamas at this hour. Well, probably not in Vegas. But in other, normal places, that's totally what people are doing.

Eyes closed, I try to fall back to sleep, but I can't. The little bit of alcohol I'd had last night before I spilled it all over Lourdes and the blackjack table helped me pass out pretty quickly once I'd come up to the room. But now there is no booze in my system. The only thing running through me is my memory of last night and every single thing that has gone wrong:

My sister and my best friend ditched me.
I kissed Jordy.
I ruined things with Nick.
I pretty much gave up and handed him to Frankie.

I replay every scene over and over, from our arrival at House of Blues to Frankie's final hug. I mostly replay my moments with Nick—dancing at the wedding and together at the top of the Eiffel Tower. But those moments don't matter. I ran away. I ruined everything.

Trying to go back to sleep is useless, especially with Grace now snoring in my ear. I crawl out of bed, change and brush my teeth, and head downstairs to get some coffee and clear my head.

The casino is as packed first thing in the morning as it is late at night, but with a totally different crowd. Tourists and walk-of-shamers wander the casino floor, and I sit alone at the diner and sip my coffee, trying to figure out what I'm going to do, how I'm going to fix things with Nick. It's been years since I've been awake this long without some sort of contact from him, and I type and delete at least twenty different texts before giving up. After about ten coffee refills, I take my jitters out to the Strip, where I walk up Las Vegas Boulevard all the way to the Venetian and then back down again on the other side of the street. On some level, I'm aware I should be sightseeing and people watching. I mean, I've never been to Vegas before, and I just passed a line of people dressed up as dollar-store versions of popular cartoon characters. One sad wannabe Hello Kitty–esque person had her fake head off and balanced it in her lap while she smoked a cigarette. But I can't focus on anything other than all the mistakes I've made and the rules I've broken over the last twenty-four hours, and the long walk passes in a blur of sadness and regret.

Talk about a walk of shame. Nick and I are never going to be able to get past this. Four years of being each other's best friend, but neither one of us could be honest with each other.

Back at Planet Hollywood, I take the elevator up to the room. It's almost checkout time, and all I want to do is go home. Hands shaking from too much caffeine, I turn on the light and yell, "Wake up, girls, we're leaving!" at the top of my lungs.

"Turn off the light," Grace mumbles, rolling over and covering her head with the pillow.

"Nope," I say. "I gave you time to sleep. Now you need to get up so we can get out of here. It's almost noon. We need to check out, and I want to go home."

Lo sits up, rubbing her eyes. "I thought we were going to go to the pool or something today."

"That was the plan before I had the worst night of my life. Now the only thing I want to do is get back home. Can you please get out of bed and get dressed so we can go?"

"No," Grace mumbles.

I pull the comforter off her and throw it onto the floor. "You don't get to say no. You didn't have the night I had. I don't want to be in Vegas another second. If I could fly home right now, I honestly would, because the idea of spending four hours in a car with the two of you sounds absolutely freaking miserable. But if that's what it takes to get me out of this place, then it's what needs to be done. Now, get up now. Before I really get upset."

"Hannah—" Lo stands and wobbles toward me, but I hold my palm up, stopping her.

"I don't want to talk to you, either. Let's go."

I guess they're scared by my tone. That coffee did more than just get me going; apparently, it made me sound borderline insane, and they clearly don't want to see what else I'm going to rant about. So, no pool, no shopping, no Girls Gone Wild. Nothing but silently packing, showering, getting in the car, and heading back to California.

The drive home is nothing like our drive there. The radio is on some generic Vegas radio station no one bothers to change. Grace curses at every car that comes within ten feet of her, and Lo sits in the backseat, curled as much into the fetal position as her seat belt will allow, moaning about her headache.

I ignore both of them.

"I'm hungry," Lo mumbles from the back. "Need food. Need coffee. Need to chop off head."

"I'm not stopping anywhere besides this gas station until we are well into California," Grace says. "Run into the AMPM if you want something." Neither of us makes a move to leave, so she growls at us. "I'm not even kidding. You're the one who made me leave before I was ready. Pee, eat, whatever. Do it now, because I'm not stopping later."

I'm about to hop out of the car, leaving Lo to fend for herself, but I hear her moan from the backseat and I know she's struggling. Too much booze and Oscar, not enough water and sleep. I can only imagine the state of her head right now. I may be mad at her, but I'm not heartless.

"Do you want anything?"

"Coffee," she mumbles. "And carbs. Find me some carbs." She rolls over on the seat, and I head into the AMPM to get our food. I'm wandering through the aisles when my phone vibrates in my back pocket. A text.

My hands are full of coffee and snacks for Lo, and I grumble at my sister for texting me when she's right outside the door. But when I put everything down on the counter and pull out my phone, it's not Grace with a snack food wish list at all.

B4 U GO HOME U SHUD COME 2 BBQ @ OUR HOUSE. BAND PLAYIN @ 4.-ALEX

Followed by a Henderson address.
Nick's address.
I blink at my phone in disbelief with so many questions running through my head. Why would I want to go see the band play at a party? And why is Alex texting me this?
I consider ignoring it, but I don't want to be rude.

SORRY, ALREADY ON THE ROAD.

I want to ask him what this is all about—but honestly, I don't think I want to know. If Nick wanted me at this party, if he had something to say to me, he would've texted me. Not his brother.

TURN AROUND.

I pay for all the food and walk back to the car. "Sweet Jesus, thank you," Lo says as I hand her a coffee, a huge water, and a plastic bag of carbs ranging from cereal bars to chips to powdered doughnuts. "You are a god to me right now."
"Well, I don't want you puking all over Grace's car when we have a four-hour drive ahead of us. We'd all have to live with that." I leave a water bottle and a cereal bar in the center console for Grace. When she's done filling up the gas tank, she climbs into the driver's seat, opens the water and chugs it, then starts the car and heads out without even a word of thanks.
We're on the freeway in dead silence for about five minutes, and during that five minutes, I wonder if I should say anything to Grace about Alex's text. I don't want to go to this party; I want to see Las

Vegas in my rearview mirror and never think about it again. But I am curious if Alex gave her any clue about this party and why he thinks I should be there. And I think about what Frankie said to me last night. Am I running away again? Like Lo said, for someone who always wants to be in control, I don't seem to do anything to change my life. Maybe this is my chance. Maybe it's less about breaking rules and more about taking charge of the things I have control over. The prickly silence quickly becomes too much for me to take, and I can't come up with any answers on my own.

"Alex texted me," I say quietly.

"What? When?" Grace tries to keep her obvious interest and something else, maybe jealousy, out of her voice, but she fails miserably. I know her too well.

"Right now. He said the band was playing a party at his house this afternoon, and that I should stop by before we left Vegas." I clear my throat, trying to make sure I sound nonchalant. "Any idea why?"

Grace shakes her head. "He said they were playing at some afternoon birthday party today, but that's all I know. It didn't sound like it was a big deal." She stares ahead at the long stretch of freeway in front of us. "How did he get your number?"

I know what that means. It means, why did he text you and not me? I don't know how to answer that.

"Maybe he got it from Nick's phone? I don't know."

Now I stare at the freeway and try to use the bleak flatness of the desert landscape to clear my mind. None of us say anything for a long time, until Grace breaks the silence. "So, you don't want to go?"

"We're already on our way home," I say. "And I don't think Nick wants to see me anyway. Not after last night." If Nick had been the one to text me, then I would have been at that party as fast as Grace's car would take us. But what does Alex's invitation mean? I hardly spoke to the guy all night.

"What happened last night?" Grace asks.

Oh, yeah. Grace missed pretty much everything, since she was running around with Alex. I turn to the window with a long sigh.

I don't want to share anything with her, since I'm still mad. But my need to have someone else's opinion on this is outweighing my anger, so I fill her in on everything that happened between Nick and me, including the talk I had with Frankie over blackjack.

Grace doesn't say anything for a long time, and she keeps staring out the window. I want to bug her for a response, but I don't really want to know what she has to say, so I stare, too.

"Why did you do that?" Lo squeaks out from the backseat. "Why did you tell Frankie to keep Nick for herself?"

"Well," I snap, "last night, she was the only friend I had, so I couldn't exactly be awful to her. At least *she* wanted to spend time with me."

Lo ignores my dig at her. "I think you should go to the party."

"Why? So Nick can yell at me some more? So I can humiliate myself further? What would the point be?"

"Alex thinks there's a point," Grace says.

"Yeah, well, Alex and Nick don't even get along." I think about the moment I had with Nick, how he said his brother had been interested in Frankie originally. I don't mention that to my sister, but I think it's a pretty good reason to doubt Alex's intentions for getting me to this party.

"Well," Grace says, turning her head slightly to look at me. "I think you should go, too."

But we keep on driving on the freeway, putting more and more distance between our car and Vegas.

As soon as we leave the Greater Las Vegas area, the scenery is nothing but rocks and dirt. But ahead of us looms a small cluster of buildings, and I realize we're already approaching the California–Nevada state line.

And the three random casinos right there on the border.

I watch as the buildings get closer and closer and I can see it, the huge yellow track snaking its way around the Buffalo Bill's hotel and casino.

Hitting the state line means we're leaving Nevada, and I'm officially running away from Nick and ignoring Alex's invitation. I don't want to see Nick, because I think everything is ruined, but

I don't even know for sure. I'm letting myself get scared of something that could possibly be fixed because I'm afraid fixing it is going to be scary.

That's stupid, I tell myself. *I don't want to live like that.*

So I decide not to.

"Pull over," I say to Grace. "I'm going to ride the roller coaster."

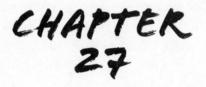

CHAPTER 27

We're sitting in the expansive parking lot of Buffalo Bill's Resort & Casino, and it is surprisingly quite full. I'd wondered who would bother coming to a casino on the state line when Vegas is a short forty-minute drive away, but apparently the answer is everyone. Dozens of tour buses line the far side of the parking lot, and we have to circle the lot a couple of times to find a spot to pull into.

Now we're parked, and the yellow roller coaster tracks are much closer and much scarier than they were all the way from the freeway. I don't know what I was thinking when I told Grace to pull over. I must've had a stroke or something.

"Never mind," I say. "I was only kidding. I don't want to do this."

Lo groans from the backseat and rolls over.

Grace shifts in her seat so she can face me. "Look," she says. "I know you're mad at me right now, and I get it. I do. But I need you to take a break from hating me and listen to some big-sisterly advice, okay?"

Listening to advice from Grace isn't what I want to do right now, but I guess the alternative would be getting on that roller coaster, so I let her talk.

"You don't have to wait until college for your life to start, you know? You can start it now."

I stare at her, silent.

"You've spent the past four years of your life not doing anything. You study, you get good grades, but you haven't been living. You've dated guys you didn't even like much so you would never feel anything real for them. You've been falling for Nick and not even admitting it to yourself. You always say you'll do this or that in college, but it's an excuse."

"It is not."

"Yes, it is. It's a lame excuse to stay safe and stay in control. What do you think is going to happen in college? You're still going to have to study and get good grades, you know? It's going to be harder, to be honest. You'll have to work, too. Will you still put living your life on hold? Will you keep making excuses?"

I let visions of life at UCLA next year float into my head. Even though Grace tells me about her papers and exams, I let college party movies dominate my imagination when it comes to the next four years. The truth is, as much as I like to imagine partying it up and YOLO-ing, I want to do well in college. I want to study and pass my classes and keep up a solid GPA.

If I'm doing all of that, when will I have time for a life? When I graduate? What about grad school? Or a job? Will I have time for fun then? Or will I put work first and everything else second?

If I keep waiting to have fun, running away from new things, until I have my life under control, will that ever happen?

"I'm never going to have fun, am I?"

"You don't have to choose, Hannah. It's not success or fun. It's not life or love. You don't have to just pick one door to walk through." She runs her hands through her hair and looks at me. Really looks at me. "You can have both. It's okay. You just have to go out and do something about it. Don't sit back and let life happen to you. Go grab what you want, whatever it is."

She fingers her key necklace as she talks, and it turns my mind to what she's been through with Gabe. What she gave up for that relationship, and how she's now left with nothing. But she doesn't have nothing. She has the other parts of herself. Gabe wasn't everything there was to Grace. She's UCLA and *Rocker* and my sister. She has all those things, and that's why losing her relation-ship broke her, but only temporarily. She has the rest of the things in her life to put her back together.

I rest my elbows on my knees and lean my head forward onto my hands. "I've been doing this all wrong." Letting good things pass me by because I don't know how to multitask. Because I'm too afraid to fail.

"You'll be okay," Grace says, reaching her arm around me and pulling me into her. My instinct is to pull away; after the past few hours we've had, I don't want her to comfort me. But instead I let myself sink into her hug, and she squeezes me tight.

"Fine," I say, straightening back up in my seat. "I'll do this. I'll go on the roller coaster. But let's hurry before I change my mind."

"I don't have to go on this thing with you, do I?" Lo moans.

I hop out of the car. "You sure do." I swing the backseat door open, reach in, and pull her up to a sitting position. "This is your penance for last night's shenanigans, you Mistress of the Night. You owe me a ride on this death trap."

"Hannah. I'm totally going to barf."

"Don't care. Get out."

Lo struggles to get out of the backseat, and the three of us walk into Buffalo Bill's in search of the entrance to the roller coaster.

There aren't enough words in the English language to describe how different Buffalo Bill's is from the casinos we visited in Vegas. While Planet Hollywood was all white and red and sparkly, Buf-falo Bill's is brown and dingy and decorated like the Old West. It smells like an ashtray, and we are far and away the youngest people in the joint. By many, many decades.

"This obviously isn't the place for us to find dudes," Grace whis-pers as we walk through the doors and into the dimly lit casino.

"This isn't the place for us to find anything except lung can-cer," I reply, trying not to inhale the scent of cigarette smoke and body odor. People smoked in the casinos in Vegas, but I guess the ventilation in there was better because I hardly noticed. Here the smoke seeps down into my bloodstream.

"Can we make this fast?" Lo's face looks even greener as we walk through Buffalo Bill's, and I didn't think that was humanly possible. "This place is not doing anything to lower my desire to puke."

"Boom!" Grace says, pointing to sign that says ROLLER COASTER. "This way."

"There are a lot of cowboy boots here," I say to Grace as she pulls us through the casino floor. She's in the lead, holding my wrist while I hang on to Lo's, a human chain of miserable girls.

"It's like the country music version of People of Walmart," Grace says.

Finding the ticket counter for the roller coaster is nowhere near as complicated as it was last night at New York–New York, mainly because good ol' Buffalo Bill's doesn't seem to have quite so much to offer. I'm holding on to my secret hope the coaster is closed, which isn't too ridiculous, given that we haven't ever seen it running. But we follow the roller coaster signs—it's called the Desperado—and we see someone sitting behind the ticket counter, a bored-looking guy in his midtwenties, one earbud in his ear and playing on his phone.

"Hey," Grace says as we walk up. "Is the roller coaster running?"

"It'll run if you guys wanna ride it," he says. "It'd give me something to do." His voice cracks like he hasn't spoken in hours.

"You'll run it for just the three of us?" I'm hoping he'll say we have to wait around for all the cars to fill up, and clearly that's not going to happen.

"Sure. I have nothing else going on right now." He rings us up for three tickets and points us down the way to the entrance to the coaster.

"Hannah should go in the front," Lo says. She looks like she's going to collapse right there on the ground, and she's using the bar that would form the roller coaster line, if there were anyone here, to hold her upright. I shouldn't delight so much in her misery, but I can't help it.

I'm delighted.

"Yeah," Grace says. "Hannah in front. We'll sit right behind you."

I stare at the car. It's a long roller coaster car, and we're the only ones who are going to ride it. This whole death trap all to ourselves.

Panic floods my system. My heart beats out of control, my stomach bottoms out, I'm sweating like I'm sitting in a sauna, and we haven't even made a move to get in the car yet.

I take a deep breath. Then I take another one.

"You guys," I say. But I don't even know if I can finish my thought. The sign says the Desperado is one of the tallest and fastest coasters in the country, and I suddenly regret not having this revelation about taking charge of my life back home when I could try one of the kiddie rides at Disneyland instead.

Grace grips my hand. "You can do this," she says. "Don't think of the out-of-control feeling, okay? Focus on the feeling of freedom. Like you're flying. It's not scary. It's liberating."

Lo straightens herself up. "Take a deep breath."

I do.

"Are you guys going on this, or what?" the guy asks. For someone who is bored out of his mind, he sure is rushing us along.

"It's not like you have anything better to do than wait for us," Grace snaps. I smile. My sister is getting back on my good side.

She looks at me, and I suck down yet another deep breath as I picture Nick's face last night. He bared it all to me, told me all his feelings. How would things have gone differently if, instead of running away, I'd taken control and done the same? I picture how his face would have looked different, how things would have been different, and I hold on to that image as hard as I can.

"Okay," I say. "Let's do this."

I lower myself into the car. I pull the bar down across my lap, and I turn around to see Lo and Grace doing the same thing behind me.

"You can do it." Grace reaches forward and ruffles my hair with her hand. "Remember. It's possible for life to be scary and fun at the same time. The scariness is the fun."

I turn around and keep my breathing going. In. Out. In. Out. I can lose control. It's not going to kill me. It's not going to make me puke.

The roller coaster makes a noise, and before I can panic more, it jerks forward and we are moving. We creep out of the casino through the wall and we're outside, on the yellow track we saw from the freeway. The car speeds up, and before I even know what's happening, we are at full speed, climbing up the huge hill of track in front of us.

"*You guys!*" I scream. I've taken AP Physics, so I know what going up this big track means. It means we're about to go down it.

The car clicks as we climb higher and higher and my stomach jerks and my palms sweat on the bar in front of me.

Grace yells, "You can do this!" while Lo groans sadly.

Then we're at the top of the track hill. I take a second and look around me. I see the freeway, cars zooming by. There's the parking lot and the other casinos and the outlet mall and miles and miles of desert ahead. It's desolate, but it's also pretty in a strange way. And before I have another second to think about what I'm looking at, we're falling.

I scream.

The coaster is fast. We drop into a dark tunnel, my hair blowing in my face and behind me, and I feel like my cheeks are going to pull right off my skull. My butt leaves the seat just slightly as we fall, and I hold on to the bar in front of me as tight as I can.

Behind me, Grace screams, too, but it's a scream of delight, not one of terror. And I realize, as the velocity from our fall brings us up another hill, that I'm not all that terrified myself.

I'm actually having fun.

"*Woooo!*" I scream.

"Put your hands in the air!" Grace yells at me, and as we go down the next drop, which twists into an insane spiral, I try it. I lift one hand off the bar and then the other, and as we fall, I look out at the vast expanse of desert and I feel like I'm flying. I feel like I'm free.

It's amazing.

Our ride on the roller coaster is much too short. Before I even realize it, the car pulls back into the casino, and the ride is over. I lift the bar off me and jump back on the platform. Lo crawls out of the car and runs over to the trash can in the corner, where she pukes.

"Well?" Grace asks.

I don't know how to explain it to her. The feeling of letting go. The feeling of falling and freedom and not worrying about the drop and letting it take me.

I try to figure out how to put all of it into words, but when nothing comes to me, I just say, "I want to do it again."

CHAPTER 28

We ride the Desperado three more times, putting the remainder of my slot machine winnings to excellent use. Well, Grace and I ride it. Lo heads off to the bathroom while we go back for more. I have more fun each time, screaming through the drops, hands up on the spiral. Laughing and shouting and almost crying, I'm having so much fun.

On our third ride, as we click our way up the track hill, Grace reaches behind her neck and unclasps her key necklace. She holds it in her hand as we pause at the highest point; then as the car tips down to rush down the track at full speed, she throws her arms up and uncurls her fingers, letting the necklace fly out into the air behind us.

After we climb out of the car, I lean over, my hands on my knees, catching my breath. "I can't believe you did that," I say. "That necklace was expensive, Grace."

Grace shrugs. "You didn't want to go on the roller coaster, but you did, and you loved it." She runs her hand through her hair. "So, I figured . . . I should have done it a long time ago."

I don't want to say something cheesy about how proud I am of her, so I pull her into a tight hug. Then I straighten up, look at her, and say, "I need to go to that party."

I'd be lying if I said Nick hadn't been on my mind every time we went on that roller coaster. I'm conquering my fears here, and as much as I feared losing control, I also fear losing Nick. So, he's with Frankie, and he's mad at me. That isn't enough to lose a four-year friendship over. I might not be able to be with him, but I can't leave Vegas without making things right. I can't run away. Sure, I don't know what is going to happen when I show up at this party, but it can't be any worse than the way I left things with him. If Grace can let go of Gabe, then I can face my feelings head-on. I need to fix this. Talk. Apologize. Get my best friend back.

Grace wraps her arm around my shoulder and squeezes. "Let's get Lo and get out of here."

Lo waits for us outside the entrance to the Desperado, sucking on a soda. She looks a little less green, and she gives us a wan smile as we approach. "Four times?" she asks.

I nod. "I'm in love. You can be the maid of honor when I marry the Desperado."

"You should do something super wild when we get home. I'll make a list of illicit activities you can try your hand at." She gets up from her chair and puts her arm around my other shoulder.

"Let's not go crazy now," I say, and we all laugh as we walk out to the car.

I look up the address to the party on Grace's GPS and we head back toward Vegas, in considerably better moods than we had been in only an hour earlier. My irritation with them has dissipated, and it's replaced with nervousness very similar to the butterflies I had when we drove this way yesterday. Will Nick be happy to see me? Will showing up at this party make things worse? I don't think Alex would have told me to come if Nick really didn't want me there, but who knows. Things have always been weird between them.

I'm empowered by my roller-coaster ride, but that doesn't turn off my mind, thinking about every possible thing that can go wrong.

"Are you going to tell him you're coming?" Grace asks.

"Nope. This time I'm embracing the element of surprise. Hopefully it will be on my side." I grab my purse from the floor by my feet and dig around on the bottom of it for my clown penny. I tossed it in there along with my wallet this morning while we were packing up, but now I want it on me again. Smiling, I rub my thumb over the bumps, and then I stuff it into the side pocket of my jeans.

I turn around to face Lo, who is sitting upright now and looking slightly less pukey. "So, you don't mind helping me out?"

She leans forward in her seat, as far as her seat belt will allow, and grabs my arm. "Girl, I'm sorry about last night. I don't know what happened to me."

Grace chuckles from the front seat. "Um, I think his name was Oscar."

Lo rolls her eyes. "You know how I get. You had Nick and I wanted to have fun with a cute boy, too. But I didn't mean to ruin your night."

"I wasn't having fun with a cute boy, though. I was having drama with a guy who has a girlfriend."

"I know this." She flops back to her seat. "But I've always been frustrated by the obvious sexual tension you have with this best friend of yours. I wanted you to do something about it, you know? I guess in my own weird way, I thought if I left you alone, you'd get this whole thing solved."

"You and Hannah are so the best friends for each other," Grace says, elbowing me from across the console. "She needs someone to drag her kicking and screaming out of her comfort zone every now and then. Try to get her to take some action."

I snort. "Not too much action, though. Can you imagine if we were both trying to hook up in the hotel room?"

"Instead of you sitting in the dark, watching us?" She leans forward again and winks at me. "Why were you lying there like a creeper, you creeper?"

"I was trying to wallow in my self-pity over this Nick situation! You interrupted my ennui!"

"We really are a pair, aren't we?"

I try to turn around in my seat to hug her, but since there's no way I'm taking my seat belt off in a moving vehicle, I end up patting her shoulder instead. "Are you going to talk to Oscar again?"

She shrugs and gives me a sly grin. "Maybe I will, if you can fix things with his best friend."

I turn back around, staring at the long stretch of freeway spilling out in front of us. "That's the plan."

CHAPTER 29

We exit the freeway in Henderson, and now we're only a few minutes from Nick and Alex's house, according to the GPS. I pull down the mirror on the sun visor and try desperately to fix my hair and makeup. We left the hotel in such a huff this morning that none of us are looking even close to our best. Even though I know there is no hope for Nick and me in any sort of romantic way, I still want his last memory of me in real life to be a good one. He's heard me on the phone at my worst, but he doesn't need to see me looking like ass. The last thing I want is my beat-down face distracting him from my apology.

"Here we are," Grace says, turning onto a street of older tract homes, each one a copy of the one next to it. I texted Alex to let him know we're on our way, but other than the fact that the guys in the band are going to be there, I have no idea what to expect. This unknown element would usually freak me out to the point of inaction, but it doesn't faze me right now. All that matters is fixing things with Nick.

We find the house, but we can't park too close, because there are cars in the driveway and parked all along the street. "Okay, girls," I say. "This is it."

"You got this," Lo says. Grace pats my leg reassuringly.

"I hope so." I smile at them. "Thanks."

We walk toward the house, where music pounds from the backyard. We're almost to the party when I hear my name, and Alex hops out from the bed of the truck parked at the edge of the driveway.

I wave to him, and I see a huge grin spread over Grace's face out of the corner of my eye.

The whole time we've been in Vegas, I haven't paid much attention to Alex. My focus was on Nick, and honestly, Nick has never painted a flattering picture of his brother. It was pretty natural for me to try to avoid him since we got here yesterday, and he made it easier by taking off with my sister at every opportunity. Now that I look at him, though, I can see why Grace picked him out in a concert crowd all those years ago. He's an older, more outgoing, more punk rock version of Nick, with colorful birds tattooed up his right arm and some mysterious saying peeking out of his V-neck. And when my sister smiles at him, he grins back, a carbon copy of Nick's adorable smile, but with a little more attitude.

"I'm glad you guys came by." He shoves his hands in the front pockets of his hoodie, and he looks back and forth between Grace and the crack in the driveway, never once glancing at me. "Hannah, can I talk to you alone for a minute?" he mumbles to the ground.

I catch my sister's face fall for a fleeting second, but she turns it into a small smile. "We'll be over here," she says, and she leads Lo on a walk down the sidewalk.

Alex sits back down in the bed of the truck, swinging his feet like a little boy at the playground, and he pats the empty spot next to him. I hop up.

"So, uh, thanks for coming," he says.

"Yeah, sure." I'm trying to keep it out of my voice, but this is Code Red awkward. He's focused intently on his shoes as his feet swing back and forth, and I figure I should say something because this situation is too weird for me to handle right now. "So, is this about Grace?" I ask. "Or is it Nick? I just want to know what to prepare myself for."

He lets out a nervous laugh. "Dude, I think your sister is unbelievable, but that's no secret. I don't need your help there."

I want to smile because, man, that's super cute, but it's impossible when my insides are dropping down to my shoes. It takes all my focus to try to sound nonchalant as I squeak out, "So it's Nick, then?" The Cooper brothers aren't close. Nick has told me many times that I know way more about him than his brother does, and Alex never seems to pass up an opportunity to torment Nick in some way. Why is he getting involved with our friendship now?

Alex stops swinging his feet and pulls one leg up under himself on the truck bed, angling himself so he is facing me. "Look, Hannah. I know I haven't always been the best brother to Nick, okay? It's just how we are. It's just the two of us here with our dad, you know? You have a sister. You know how it is."

I shrug. From what I know, my relationship with Grace is about as opposite from his relationship with Nick as Planet Hollywood was from Buffalo Bill's, but I don't think that's the point here.

"I'm sort of a dick to him sometimes. I get that. But—" He reaches up and adjusts his hat, scratching the back of his head. "—I know this about my brother. He's upset right now, but he'd regret it so much if he let you leave Vegas like this. He always gets in his own way, and I can't let him do that this time."

I twist my hair into a bun as I let this all turn over in my head. Then I remember Nick's admission last night at the top of the Eiffel Tower.

"Does this have anything to do with Frankie?"

He shakes his head as he laughs. "Nah, dude. She's a whole other story."

I narrow my eyes at him. "So, you told me to come here for no other reason than you wanted to help Nick out? Really?"

"I know you don't believe me, but—" He shakes his head again, like he can't even believe he is saying any of this. "—I feel like I owe him. He kept talking to you, but I never kept in touch with Grace after we met. I'd ask Nick about her and stuff, but I never did anything about it."

Well, this is surprising. "Why not?"

"Too cool, I guess." His laugh doesn't have a trace of humor in it. "I'm stupid. But then when you guys showed up last night, and

Grace was there, man, I felt like it was a sign from the universe or something. It was weird."

I open my mouth to respond, ready to tell him that even though Grace threw her necklace off the roller coaster, I'm pretty sure she has no intention of getting into another relationship anytime soon, but he holds up his hand, stopping me. "I don't know what happened between you and my brother last night. But it doesn't matter. You guys have history. You're important to him. And I know you think I'm an asshole, and maybe I am, but Nick's my brother, and, well, you know he sometimes has trouble saying the right thing. This whole 'dealing with people' thing has never been easy for him, and I do want him to be happy. I don't want to see him be an idiot like I am."

His admissions stun me into silence. I stare down at my knees, trying to process it all, then look back at him. I open my mouth, but nothing comes out.

"Anyway," he says, "will you come out back to the party? Nick doesn't know you're here, and I was thinking, well, maybe it could be a surprise. Like last night, but hopefully more successful."

"Sure," I say. "As long as you're not revealing any Cooper family secrets or anything. I've had about all the drama I can take." Here we go. I came here to talk to Nick and make things right. The fact that his brother wants to help me do it, well, it makes the whole thing easier, I guess.

Alex smiles and helps me out of the truck bed. I wave to the girls, who are sitting on the curb across the street, watching us. As soon as Grace reaches arm distance of Alex, he reaches his arm around her shoulder and pulls her in close, kissing her on the top of her head. "Glad I got to see you again, sexy."

"We're surprising Nick, I guess," I tell them, and shrug.

"Wheee!" Lo says. "I love a good surprise. And last night's was such an epic bust, we need a do-over."

Instead of walking us through the front door, Alex opens a gate on the side of the house and ushers us through. He holds a finger up to his mouth as we each pass him; then he carefully eases the gate shut. "Okay," he whispers. "Nick is back there, but I don't want him to see you guys yet."

"There's seriously no need to whisper," Lo says. "We could hear this music from the state line."

Alex rolls his eyes, but the three of us can't help but laugh. "Fine," he says in a normal voice. "The band is going to start playing in, like, five minutes. It would be best if Nick didn't know you were here just yet, so maybe you girls could just hang out here for a few. Cool?"

"So, that's it? You're just going to leave us back here?" I wave my hand around to indicate the three trash cans, storage shed, and lawn mower. "How is this surprise going to work?"

"Oh, you'll know. I promise. Just hang out here and keep an eye on things." He pulls down on the strings on the front of his hoodie. "Do you want a beer or something?"

Lo makes a gagging noise at the suggestion of more alcohol, but Grace nods enthusiastically. I flash back to last night and how my first time drinking led to kissing limp-tongue-Jordy and almost getting offed by a pit boss. "I'm good," I say, shuddering. "Thanks."

Alex returns a minute later with a red party cup full of beer for Grace, and I study the peeling paint on the wall of the house while he pulls her into a kiss. "Okay, Hannah," he says once his mouth is available again. "You ready for this?"

"Honestly, no. I have no idea what I'm doing." Giving this control over to Alex has my heart beating like it was at the top of the Desperado. But I try to hold on to how much fun that ended up being, the rush of the free fall, the thrill of the speed and the wind in my hair. I have to trust Alex here.

"Just wait for the signal."

"What's the signal?" I ask, but he walks off toward the clamor of the party, leaving me more confused than I was when I arrived.

"So, what now?" I look at the girls, hoping they'll have some answers for me. A pretty pointless hope, since this plan is all Alex's, and he's just wandered off to set up the band's equipment.

Grace takes a huge gulp of her beer and then shrugs. "I guess now we wait."

CHAPTER 30

Seven minutes, five spiders, and fifteen peeks around the corner of the house later, we're still lurking in the space between the Cooper home and the wood fence that separates it from the neighbor's lot. I'm rubbing my penny like a genie is about to emerge from it, while Grace has a solo dance party to the music blasting from the speakers in the yard. Lo, annoyed with all the excess energy, sticks her head into the storage shed, pulls out a couple of old towels for the two of us to sit on, and spreads them on the grass.

"I can't believe you're not freaking out about this more, Hannah," Grace says, twirling in a circle. She's right. I'm mildly annoyed at the lack of information from Alex, but aside from that, I'm surprisingly Zen even though I have literally no idea what we're waiting for.

"So, what are you going to do when you see Nick?" Lo turns around and leans into my propped-up knees, and I reach for a chunk of her hair and start braiding in an effort to keep my hands and mind occupied. "If we're really going to make this an epic surprise, I think you should run out to the band and steal the mic away from Jordy and sing him a song or something."

"No! Gross! Nick would absolutely hate that." I shudder at the thought. "Can you imagine? Everyone pulling out their cameras and Instagramming it? If anything, it would support his decision to never speak to me again."

"Well, luckily, you have Frankie as president of your fan club," Grace says. "And Nick adores you. You could shout from the top of the Stratosphere, and you know he'd forgive you."

Before we can come up with a real plan, one that doesn't involve public humiliation, the loud music turns off and it's replaced by the clatter of drums and the tuning strums of guitars. The band is getting ready to play.

"I think this is what we're waiting for," Grace says, extending a hand to Lo and then to me, helping us up.

I dust off the back of my jeans as I peek around the side of the house for the millionth time. The yard is full of people, so many more than it seems would be there, even though the street is packed with cars. The band's equipment is set up in the back right corner, opposite from where we are hiding behind the wall, and the guys are all warming up their instruments, getting ready to play.

"Do you see Nick?" Lo whispers. She grips my shoulders and leans over me. "Where is he?" We spotted him briefly when we first peeked, but since then, he pretty much disappeared. I don't know how this apology thing is supposed to work if I can't even keep a lock on his position.

But then it doesn't matter, because Jordy grabs the mic and taps a couple of times before speaking into it. "What's up, everyone? Thanks for coming out. We have some new stuff to play for you today."

A whoop goes up in the crowd, and the guys onstage all laugh. "I know you love our old stuff, but we've been working on some new songs, so you all, our dearest friends, get to be the first to hear these new jams."

Someone in the crowd cheers, and some chick yells, "I love you, Jordy!" She's clearly never kissed him.

"Well, if you love these new songs, be sure to let Nick know. Mr. Sensitive has been slaving over these ones." Jordy shakes his head. "This is one we wanted to debut last night at House of Blues, but Nick had a fit at the last minute and begged us not to play it, which totally makes sense to me now. Anyway, I think you'll be into it. It's called 'Haunted.'" Then Jordy says a quick "One, two, three" into the mic while Drew on the drums hits the beat out and Automatic Friday launches into a song I've never heard before.

I try to listen, but I'm stuck on what Jordy said before he started singing.

"What did he mean?" I ask the girls without turning away from the band and the crowd. I still haven't found Nick. "When he said to tell Nick if you love the songs. What did that mean?"

They don't answer me and I don't try to get a reply, because right then Nick walks out of the sliding glass door from the house. He doesn't step down on to the patio; he lingers there in the door-way, the sliding glass door framing him. He's wearing a plain gray T-shirt and jeans, and he has his glasses on and his hair is rumpled, not in a "I spent ten minutes trying to make my hair look like this" kind of way, but in a "I didn't get any sleep and then I brushed my hair with my shoe" kind of way.

He looks gorgeous.

He's holding a red plastic cup and he's watching Jordy intently. His mouth moves along with the lyrics of the song, like he's the one up there onstage, and for the first time since Jordy started singing, I listen to the words.

> *Some people have a love story*
> *But we have a ghost story*
> *You haunt my every space*
> *I see nothing but your face*

Jordy is singing the words, but Nick is mouthing along like they belong to him, and it all clicks in my head.

Why Nick is almost like a member of the band.

What he said he wanted to surprise me with.

Why Jordy was so bad at smooth talking.

Why Alex wanted me to see the band playing.

It's not Jordy who writes Automatic Friday's songs.

It's Nick.

This is the signal, I know it is, and I'm frozen. Absolutely frozen in place. I sense the girls behind me have come to the same realization I have, but I don't turn around to confirm, because I can't tear my eyes away from Nick, lightly tapping his foot on the ledge of the sliding glass door and singing along with Jordy. I watch him pull his phone from his back pocket. He looks at it, thumb hovering over the screen. He frowns and puts it back in his pocket, looking disappointed, then pulls on the ball chain around his neck, bringing the ghost penny to the outside of his T-shirt and tucking it back in.

Finally, I snap out of this daze and turn around, to see Grace and Lo staring at me, eyes about to pop out of their heads.

"Hannah," Lo says, her fingers digging into my arms. "What are you going to do?"

I pull out my phone and I type out a text to Nick.

THIS IS MY NEW FAVORITE SONG

I hit Send and peek back around the wall of the house. Yup, I'm being a total creeper, but it's worth it when I see him pull his phone out again. He blinks at the screen, smiles, then frantically scans the crowd. This is right when Jordy finishes up the song, so I mumble, "Wish me luck," to Grace and Lo, and I walk out to the party, across the yard packed with strangers, and right up to the sliding glass door.

There he is. My Nick. My best friend. His glasses a little askew, much like his hair. His fingers that have texted me thousands of times, now tapping nervously on his thigh. His mouth that laughs at my jokes and tells me secrets, pulled into a tight, serious line as he scans the crowd.

Looking for me.

For the first time since I ran downstairs and suggested this trip to Lo and Grace, I don't think. I don't worry about ruining our friendship or Frankie or breaking the rules. I light up from the inside when he sees me, and I cross the distance between us like he's a magnet, drawing me to him. And when I get there, I use both hands to pull his face down to mine and I kiss him.

CHAPTER 31

The instant my lips meet Nick's, my mind shuts off and four years of pent-up feelings—confusion, longing, and want—take over. This is it. This is happening.

Nick's hands grip my waist as soon as we make contact and he pulls me into his body. I move my hands from his face and wrap my arms around his neck, and I stand on my tiptoes, trying to get as close to him as possible. It seems there is no way to get close enough.

Just as soon as my brain turns back on and catches up to the fact that I am actually, really, truly kissing Nick Cooper, he pulls away. I'm stunned by the absence of his lips, and when I focus on his face, I see seriousness. Straight face. Concerned eyes. Not the expression of someone who finally kissed the girl he said he had feelings for.

"Ghost," he says. "Before we . . . we need to talk."

And the reality of our situation comes crashing down on me. I just kissed my best friend, who has a girlfriend, in front of all their friends. Shit.

"Oh God, Nick. I'm sorry. I—"

He smiles at me, though, and there's not a trace of anger on his face. "Not out here," he says. "Come with me."

Nick takes my hand, lacing our fingers together, and leads me through the sliding glass door. As soon as we walk in the empty house, I'm struck with an overwhelming sense of familiarity. I've never been in Nick's house, obviously, but I've seen it in the background of pictures, and the first time we video-chatted, he gave me a quick tour. We pass the couch where Nick had his first kiss (in seventh grade with Alex's girlfriend's sister while watching *Happy Feet*), and without needing him to show me the way, I know the hallway is on the left, and Nick's bedroom is the first door on the left with a scratch in the paint where Younger Alex threw a drumstick at Younger Nick, narrowly missing his face.

Nick opens the paint-chipped door, and I follow him into his room. He lets go of my hand and slowly closes the door while I wander his bedroom, feeling immediately at home in the space that is so familiar even though I've never been here before. His laptop closed on top of the hand-me-down desk, where he sat for the past four years, chatting with me. His mirrored closet door, where he posed for full-length selfies when he wanted me to green-light his ensemble before he left for the night. His rumpled bed, where he lay on his single pillow and talked to me, quietly curled up against the wall. I lower myself onto the edge of his bed and run my fingers across his plaid sheets, trying to imagine him here, talking to me. I turn my gaze to his nightstand, and I imagine his phone sitting there, buzzing with a text from me, and him picking it up as quickly as I pick up my phone when he texts me.

"I can't believe you're in my room," he says, sitting down next to me. Right next to me, so our legs touch from hip to knee.

"Nick, about outside, I didn't—"

"Stop it, Ghost." He rests his hand gently on my thigh and shifts on the bed so he's facing me. I miss the pressure of his leg as soon as he moves it, but the weight of his hand is a pretty wonderful replacement. "I want to show you something." He reaches across me to his nightstand, where books and notebooks sit in a haphazard pile. He slides a worn composition book out from the middle of the stack and hands it to me. "Open it."

I don't know what I'm expecting. I use these composition books to take notes at school, but I can't imagine why he would be showing me his English homework right now. It takes only one glance at the cover, though, for me to realize this isn't a school notebook at all.

In Nick's messy boy scrawl, *Songs About Ghosts* is written in the white space on the cover.

My heart races as I turn page after page after page and see lyrics. Automatic Friday lyrics. Lines written and crossed out and written again. Words with scribbles through them, titles at the top of pages in block letters, sloppy lists of rhymes, doodles of ghosts in the corners. I run my fingers over the paper and I can feel the places where the pen formed each word, thoughtfully and purposefully.

The lyrics to every song I've loved, every song I've listened to in the dark and wished for, every word I've imagined being just for me.

In Nick's handwriting.

"They're all about you. Every single one."

"Nick." It's everything I've ever wanted to hear him say, but my stomach clenches up in panic. "What does this mean?" The words stick in my throat as I say them, but I know I need to force them out. "What about Frankie? I can't do this to her. I shouldn't have kissed you. I'm not that girl who—"

"Oh, Ghost." He takes back the notebook and places it on the nightstand, then picks up my hand and brings it to his mouth, kissing each one of my fingers. My head screams at me to pull away, even though Nick's mouth brushes softly over my fingers and it somehow makes my motor skills completely shut down. I shake my hand loose from his grip and stand up to put distance between us. But I don't get too far before he grabs my hand again and pulls me back down to the bed.

"Frankie and I broke up. This morning."

The world stops. Screeches to a halt. "What?"

Words spill from his mouth, like he is so excited to tell me, he wants me to know as quickly as possible. "I broke up with her, Ghost. I mean, it was mutual, really. We both like each other a lot, but we weren't right together, and we both knew it. I always knew it, but when you showed up last night, it was so clear." He lets out a long sigh. "I called her this morning and we went to IHOP and broke up over pancakes. That she got for free."

I'm pretty sure my mouth is hanging open as I stare at him. Apparently, his lips on my fingers made me forget how to speak, too.

"She said you gave her some good advice last night." He tilts his head. "Did you really tell her the blog was more important than me?"

I pull my hand away. "What? No! That's not what I said at all! I told her she needed to figure out if the real Nick was more important than the Nick she blogged about." I let out a short laugh, and now I hold on to his hand, rubbing circles on his palm with my thumb. "I thought the choice was pretty obvious," I say in a whisper.

"I guess she did, too." He closes his fingers around my hand and squeezes. "And now you're here. And we can do this over. You know it's you, right. It's always been you."

He cups my face in his hands like I'm a fragile thing he wants to keep safe, and he softly kisses my lips. I'm pretty much melting into a Hannah-shaped puddle on his bed, because his lips are so soft and he's being so gentle and it feels like heaven. He gently parts my lips with his tongue, and I reach my hands up and run them through his hair, raking my fingers up and down the back of his head.

Something about my hands in his hair sets him off. This low moan releases from somewhere in the back of his throat, and he moves his mouth to my ear and down my neck and around to the other ear and back again, breathing hard and kissing my tingling skin and saying "Ghost" in my ear over and over. It's like being on the Desperado again; I'm free-falling in the most exhilarating way imaginable.

"What made you come here?" he breathes in my ear.

"Alex," is all I can manage. It's hard to think straight with his hands and lips and tongue all over me, and I've never felt better about not knowing what was going to happen next.

"Well, shit," he says. "Now I'm going to owe him." His breath tickles my ear, and I actually giggle. I don't know what has come over me.

Then I don't even know how it happens, but suddenly I'm on my back with his body balancing over mine. We're not kissing now; we're just staring at each other, breathing hard, trying not to blink. His hair is in complete disarray, thanks to my anxious fingers, and his face is flushed and my penny on a chain is hanging from his neck and grazing my chest and oh my God I can't believe this is happening. The songs are mine and Nick is kissing me. This is more than I even thought I could ask for.

"I was going to come to you," he says.

"What do you mean?"

"I was going to drive out to California tomorrow, Ghost. I'm so sorry I let you leave last night. I shouldn't have done that." He balances on one hand, using the other one to gently brush a stray piece of hair from my face, then trail his fingers lightly down my cheek. "I just needed some time alone to think. I had so many things I had to figure out, and there were too many people around and too many things going on."

I smile up at him, so full of relief. I open my mouth to fill him in on what happened on my end since the last time I saw him, but somehow, instead of talking, we're kissing again. That's fine—we can talk later. Kissing is better.

Deeper now, faster, and more confident of each other. He's still over me, but he lowers himself down, so he's resting on top of my body, pinning me down. His hand slides down to my hip, where he wraps his hand and pulls me closer. I move my hips up to him, arching my back, trying to get as close as possible while his mouth is still on mine, his tongue tracing around my lips. And I'm not thinking about anything but his lips and his body and how this is everything I never knew I was missing.

"I'm so sorry," I say in my first free opportunity, when his mouth moves from mine over to the space under my ear.

He stops and looks at me, confused. "About what?"

"About taking so long. To figure it out, I mean."

"Don't be sorry," he says. "It wasn't our time. This is our time."

He moves his arms and props his elbows up on the bed, framing my head. He looks down at me, drinking in every inch of my face.

"I just want to let you know—" I reach up to pull off his glasses and place them on the bedside table. "—that this is even better than the roller coaster."

"Ghost," he says. "That is the sexiest thing anyone has ever said to me." And he smiles down at me. His gorgeous, open Nick smile, and it's right here.

In real life.